D0592898

McIsaac, Meaghan

Bear House: Book 2:
Scales and stardust

# THE BEAR HOUSE
# SCALES AND STARDUST

# THE BEAR HOUSE
# SCALES
# AND
# STARDUST

### Meaghan McIsaac

HOLIDAY HOUSE • NEW YORK

HOLIDAY HOUSE is registered in the U.S. Patent and Trademark Office.
Printed and bound in August 2022 at Maple Press, York, PA, USA.
www.holidayhouse.com
First Edition
1 3 5 7 9 10 8 6 4 2

Library of Congress Cataloging-in-Publication Data is available.

ISBN: 978-0-8234-4661-2 (hardcover)

*For Mae, for Henry,*
*And for you, dearest reader—keep dreaming*
*and looking to the stars.*

THE KINGDOMS O

THE GOUGES

Celestial Sea

TAWNSHIRE
HEMOTH BEAR

LOURDES MANOR

KISHTOUL PASS

TAWNSHIRE
TOWN

SHIVER WOO

GREAT BEAR RIVER

WELLIN WOODS

DOWNSWIFT

HUNDFORD
HOUND

ROARQUE
LION

NORTH

W        E

S

TWIGATE
BLUE GIRAFFE

# THE BIRTH OF THE TERROR MAIDS

Far across the Celestial Sea, where the midnight-blue water runs as deep as the stars are high, and the sea is ice in winter, there was once an island.

A tiny mound of earth and rock, with a single pine, and a single house, with a single room, for a single family—sisters, of which there were three. Beautiful as the sun on the ocean's horizon—Faith, Hope, and Mercy—they lived alone, with no one to care for but each other. And this, for the girls, was enough.

For a time.

But time changes all things, from the mountainside to the human heart, and what had been enough became empty and hollow and dull.

The first sister, the oldest, Faith, wondered at the ships that passed on the horizon. Wondered at who might be on board.

Not long after she began to wonder, a fisherman appeared just off their shores. He toiled day and night, filling his nets until his hands were blistered and raw. And one night, when her sisters were asleep, Faith took their little boat and rowed out to the fisherman. He was young and handsome and his boat was well made and his catch was plentiful and he could sail her away from the island forever—if she could make him fall in love with her.

"Do you think you could love me?" she asked the young fisherman. "And take me as your own, away from my island to the land you call home?"

The young fisherman, seeing that Faith was as beautiful as the reefs, answered her honestly. "I could."

Pleased, Faith returned to her island to tell her sisters of her sudden engagement. The sisters, upon hearing of Faith's intention to leave them, wondered: What could lie beyond their shores, that anyone should want to leave? The second sister, Hope, wondered so much that that night, when her sisters were asleep, she rowed out to the young fisherman as he was pulling up his nets. "You would take away my sister," she accused him. "What better life than this can you give her?"

"I am a very talented fisherman," he told her. "My catch from your waters will bring me a great many riches. We will be wealthy beyond imagining, and I will give her a life of power and luxury."

Hope wondered at a life of fine things and influence. So much more exciting than the one she'd known on her island home with her sisters! And she wanted it for her own. "I am younger than my sister," Hope told the fisherman. "And more radiant besides. I am better at finding fish in these waters. I will go with you and make you richer, so you should make me your bride instead."

The young fisherman did not have to consider long before he agreed to take Hope instead of Faith. And after he agreed, Hope returned to her sisters to tell them the news.

Faith's heart was broken, her dreams of love and a life of her own dashed by her sister's deceit. And so she fell into a deep depression, leaving their little home to live in a cave on the other side of the island, where she cried until all of the things that made Faith so lovely and kind had leached out of her—and she became something else. A hollowed-out shadow.

Hope, for her part, was unmoved by her sister's sadness. After all, she had only followed Faith's example, offering herself to the fisherman just as her sister had. The fisherman did not have to accept Hope's offer. But he did, for he was a faithless man and callow.

The youngest of the three, Mercy, was devastated at the rift that had opened up between her older sisters. A chasm too great to cross that had been put there by a single man—an unimportant, unremarkable, mortal man, who did not care a whit that he had completely ruined Mercy's family, her life. He did not care that his actions had emptied Faith out into nothing. Did not care that his promises had consumed Hope's mind, so that there was nothing of her left, either. Did not care that what he took from their island could never, ever be restored.

And for that, Mercy decided, the fisherman would need to be punished. But how? Mercy was little more than a girl, and she had no experience with fishermen and the dangerous promises they make. If she was to punish him, she would need help. And so she looked to the moon.

"You brought him here," she accused the waning moon. "Your door is wide open. It was you who let him out of your prison so that he might come here to cause trouble for me and my sisters. You will take him back. Take him back and lock him behind your door forever."

The demons of the moon listened, their interest piqued by this young lady who spoke so forcefully to powers she did not understand. "We will take your fisherman," the Nightlocks promised. "But nothing is given for free in this world, and so we expect payment for our troubles."

"Anything," said Mercy.

"We shall have Faith's faith," said the Nightlocks. "We shall have Hope's hope." Mercy considered this. Faith, with her broken heart, had already lost her faith, so to Mercy this seemed a small price.

Hope had placed her hopes in the fisherman's hands, and soon he would be gone. This, too, was a small price, then. "I can grant you those," said Mercy.

"And finally," said the Nightlocks, "we ask for your mercy, Mercy." But anger in her heart had become so consuming that she wasn't sure she had that left to offer. So she said, "I have no mercy."

"Not anymore," the Nightlocks agreed, reaching down into her heart.

That night, as Hope packed her things and readied herself to leave with her fisherman, Mercy took their little boat and rowed out to meet the young man. When he saw her off his bow, he smiled, a handsome dimpled smile.

"Have you come to ask me to marry you instead of your sister?" the fisherman asked. Mercy did not answer. "You are younger than your sisters," the fisherman observed. "And more beautiful besides. Do you know where to find fish in these waters? If so, I may have you instead of Hope."

Mercy made no answer.

"Did you hear me, girl?" the fisherman said. "Can you fish?"

Mercy still did not answer.

It was then that the fisherman grew wary. The waters were still as glass, the black of night made darker with the moon just a sliver in the sky.

"You're a brave one, I'll grant you," said the fisherman, "on the sea alone with the door to death wide open tonight."

Now, for the first time since coming upon the fisherman, Mercy did speak. "I am not alone."

The fisherman noticed movement then, shadowed in the dim. Something pulsed, up and down, in the air above the little row-boat, as a hawk above a kill. But, the young fisherman realized with horror, the shadows were no hawks, but women, the very ones he had—in succession—promised to take as his brides.

"On-High take it!" the fisherman gasped, falling back with horror. Mercy stood in the little rowboat, and behind her the young fisherman watched wings unfurl, black and leathery as a Shadow Dragon's.

"The On-High," said Mercy, wings flapping powerfully enough to lift her into the air with her sisters, "cannot save you now."

Together, the sisters fell upon the fisherman, so fast and so terribly he had not even a moment to cry out. For Faith, they took his heart, his false love turning its color from vibrant red to a deceitful shade of black. For Hope, they took his tongue, his poison promises tainting the meat with a bitter flavor. For Mercy, they took his eyes, so that he might never again look upon her and her sisters. And when his body was destroyed, it was his soul the sisters claimed for the moon. They dragged it up into the sky, where the Nightlocks waited, moaning and hungry for what had been promised them.

And when the sisters arrived at the Moon Door, the open door to death, the Nightlocks took their prize. Faith, Hope, and Mercy were, with the soul of the fisherman, taken behind the Moon Door—their humanity twisted and broken. The Nightlocks transformed them into something new altogether.

When the sisters emerge on the nights when the moon has waned to nothing but a sliver in the sky, they emerge as the horrors they have become—the Terror Maids: Despair, Avarice, and Malice.

# PROLOGUE

THERE are ghosts in the Deadwood.

Quiet eyes, watching from the shadows. Eyes that watch anyone brave enough to enter the forest. They watch and they wait and they consider.

Consider who lives.

Consider who dies.

Everyone, be they king or peasant, man or child—the ghosts consider them. And this ghost—the high queen of them all—was at that moment considering Iris Goreman.

Iris was a child, but only just—and she knew her way around her knives and bows. The brook trout she was filleting filled the air with the scents of springwater and blood.

The ghost liked blood.

The ghost moved closer to Iris, silent as a shadow. Curious, that a girl of her age should be fishing at night. In the Deadwood, no less! But, the ghost knew, Iris was no ordinary girl.

Iris, like the ghost, was a queen. A new queen, but still a queen. Even if the whispering voices of the kingdom did not necessarily agree.

Bent over her trout, Queen Iris had no sense of the ghost at her back. Felt no chill from the ice-white eyes boring into her.

The ghost was behind Iris now, her heavy, fetid breath wafting over the girl's neck.

And Iris screamed.

In fact, she slid off the rock she'd been sitting on and toppled into the shallow brook with a splash. The ghost, for her part, claimed the filleted fish for her own.

"In the name of Tawn, Sileria!" Iris bellowed, her long dark hair and fine brocade tunic sopping. "Were you not a High Beast, I would strike you down for that!"

Nonsense, the ghost and Iris both knew. Sileria was the Great Lynx of Felisbrook, and the stars would not look kindly on such an end to her life. Besides, she and the girl were inseparable.

"Don't look at me like that," Iris snapped, trudging back onto the shore. "I mean it! I get enough looks like that at the palace—I don't need to see it from you."

Sileria only blinked, chewing what was left of the trout. She had looked at Iris in no special way. Only as a lynx does—consideringly. Sileria had had much time to consider young Iris. Indeed, she had watched the girl from the shadows of the trees for years. Iris had been fierce since her toddling days. Determined. And considering, just like a cat. Her eyes, in fact, were very lynxlike, which was what had first caught Sileria's attention all those years ago.

"I think you might have been wrong, stupid cat," said Iris, sitting back down on the edge of her rock. This name, Stupid Cat, was one Iris was fond of. Sileria didn't care for it. She was neither stupid…nor a mere cat. "Half the kingdom still thinks Pan Leander should be seated on my throne."

Sileria twitched an ear, irritated.

"I know," said Iris. "I know you don't believe I should care what they think. And I try not to! I just…" Iris's eyes, golden brown, dropped to her lap. She was quiet a moment. Then two. Searching for the right words. Iris was careful with her words. "And now this problem of the Keeper. What do I know about such things?"

Sileria moved closer to the girl, sitting so that her side pressed against Iris's arm. Words—man's words—were an extravagant thing. The young lynx often wished her Iris didn't always try so hard to reach for them. The slump of her shoulders, the flush of her cheeks, the wet of her eyes—these things were enough for Sileria to know what Iris was feeling.

Iris stroked the lynx's silver fur. Soft and thick, each hair so fine, with a brilliant sheen that glittered like the stars of the northern skies. "I just wish you hadn't done it—I wish you hadn't chosen me," Iris sniffed. "Stupid cat. I do love you, though."

Sileria had listened to Iris say this through tears many times since the lynx had chosen her as Queen of Felisbrook at the Northern Crowning. And she would listen many times more, she knew, letting the girl lean on her, stroke her fur, and feel the assurance of the only truth there was—that the stars had brought them together. No matter what the whispers of the kingdom said. No matter what Iris wished were different. The stars had willed it. And so it was. And would always be.

"You're right," Iris said through tears. And Sileria knew she was. Even in the months leading up to the Northern Crowning, when the High Lynx of Felisbrook stood watch over Iris's family home and the girl's father kept saying things like "young cat must be lost"—Sileria had known what she was doing. Known what the stars wanted for Felisbrook. And eventually, the Keepers came, telling Iris she must stand at the Northern Crowning—the Great Lynx had already made her choice.

If the girl said more, Sileria did not hear it. A flicker of movement had caught the lynx's sharp eye—across the river, a disturbance in the ferns.

Sileria got to her feet.

"I should get back," Iris said, rising too. "Before Leona sends the whole of the Fern Guard out for me."

A scent drifted on the wind. Burnt sugar. And sulfur.

Sileria moved up the bank of the brook, climbing onto a fallen log. The Deadwood was her home. Her domain. She knew every scent of every plant, every creature, every rock. This was not a scent she knew.

"What's wrong?" Iris asked, following.

Sileria watched the shadows of the trees, the flutter of the ferns. For all her vision's strength, she could not make out what moved in the dark. What creature could move outside the lynx's penetrating eyes?

And then a blaze—white and blinding and brilliant—lit up the northern sky.

The lynx and Iris Goreman watched it pass—a blistering light turning ghostly pale, plummeting, a tail of glittering dust billowing in its wake.

"Sileria," Iris said, placing a nervous hand on the lynx's back. "Is that—"

The thunder of an impact. Loud and fathoms deep, primordial, eternal, the earth itself groaning.

And then the ground beneath their feet—it swelled and pitched, tossing Iris, rattling Sileria's log. She clung to the spongy, worm-eaten wood with her claws, trying to keep from falling.

And then quiet.

"Sileria!" Iris called from somewhere near the brook. "Sileria! Where are you?"

The lynx leapt down from the log, searching for Iris. And at the edge of the bank, she saw it again—movement in the ferns, a fluttering of the reeds. There were creatures. They moved like wisps, shadows coiling through the bushes and tree trunks, rising like mist out of the undergrowth.

"Sileria!" Iris flung her arms around the lynx's neck, relieved to have found her in the dark, but the lynx took no notice. Her eyes were on the shadows.

Iris followed her gaze and gasped when the shadows began to glimmer as they rose, sparkling like diamond dust and drifting like glowing smoke—and shapes, figures, began to take shape.

"Dragons," whispered Iris.

They were indeed. Unlike any dragon Sileria had ever seen. More spirit than flesh. Waking ghosts.

And they were many.

In every direction, Sileria and Iris watched the glittering, ghostly dragons rise up out of the underbrush, into the night sky.

And drift together, like leaves on the brook, in the same direction.

They were chasing the light.

Sileria hissed, signaling Iris to follow, and bounded into the trees in the path of the dragons. The Deadwood was dark, but through the forest, the light burned, like white fire. And Sileria could feel it. It tickled the tip of each hair, her whole coat standing on end with the power of it, her bones humming in her skin. The lynx hurtled from root to rock, her heart aching from the pull of the light. It was calling her.

Until at last, Sileria came to the spot—a broken patch in the forest where the trees were nothing but ash and the earth melted like candle wax.

The ghostly dragons circled the glowing, burning light, dozens of them, coiling and winding like vines around a stone. Snakes on a sun-baked rock.

Iris appeared behind Sileria and gasped.

"Sileria," she breathed. "What's happened here?"

Had the lynx cared for man's extravagant words, she might have told Iris.

But yet again tonight, as in most things, the situation had no call for words.

What had happened was plain for anyone to see.

A star—an On-High—had fallen.

*Woe to the man who finds himself between the Hemoth and her cub, for there is no fiercer beast beneath the On-High's sky than the Mother Bear.*

—THE WRITINGS OF BERN,
On Hemoth Bears: The Age of Tawn, *Star Writ*

# ONE

THE Major Aster Lourdes was sulking. Again.

They'd been on the road from Tawnshire to Felisbrook for two days, and never had two days felt more like two thousand years to Dev. Trapped in the royal carriage beside Aster—and across from Aster's formidable mother, the Lady Lourdes, and sister, Ursula—Dev longed to be at the back of the royal convoy with Alcor the Hemoth Bear. The dirt and rock firmly beneath his feet, the smell of Alcor's musty coat, the sound of the bear's rumbling breath. That was his true place. Not here, in this gilded finery, with the Lourdes women, who, Dev had always been sure, would be the death of him.

When they had set out on the road from the Manor, Aster had begged him to join her and her family in the carriage, *to review important lessons of the Star Writ,* she said, to prepare her for their arrival in Felisbrook at the Shooting Star Parade. And, like a fool, he'd believed her. Dev looked down at the heavy tome in his hands—his copy of the *Star Writ*—feeling its comforting weight in his lap. He hadn't been asked to crack the cover once. Not once in two days.

"Really, Aster," Lady Lourdes scoffed. "The wrinkles you will set on your face with a scowl like that. And then who will have you?"

"Then stop making me scowl," said Aster darkly.

"You can be morose all you like, but the duty of marriage is as real for a Major as her duty to anything else. Isn't that right, Honorable High Keeper?"

Aster shot Dev a sideways look, and he knew she was warning him to be careful with his answer. He wanted to scream. But instead he cleared his throat and did his best to respond. "It is in the interest of the On-High, certainly. But the stars have never sought to rush—"

"There you have it!" interrupted Lady Lourdes triumphantly. "The High Keeper says so himself. This is not just coming from me."

They'd been doing this the entire journey. Bickering and arguing about everything from clothes to politics to food. And in everything, Aster—or her mother—looked to Dev to settle the argument. If he failed to support one or the other's argument, he could feel them logging it away to exact some petty revenge on him later. It was exhausting. But on this subject, the marriage subject, the tension between the Lourdes women was more intense than anything that had come before.

"You are fourteen, Aster," Lady Lourdes went on. "You cannot run from the topic forever."

"Ursula is eighteen!" Aster snapped, pointing an angry finger at her older sister, who sat wilted and exhausted beside their mother. "Focus your meddling on *her* love life and leave *me* in peace."

"Ursula is not in a fix for suitors, unlike you."

Aster laughed. "A *fix*?!"

"Yes, a *fix*. Who under Tawn's great sky will we find to match you, someone of suitable status?"

Aster sank lower in her seat, hands pulling at her hair. "Please, Mother!"

As much as Dev wanted to agree with Aster, he couldn't deny that her mother had a point. There was no one suitable to marry Aster. She was the Major. Tradition and etiquette outlined a very strict set of requirements for the spouse of the Major. And there was no one to fulfill it.

So, Dev just assumed, no one ever would.

And what was so wrong with that?

"Pity that Wyvern boy is King of Dracogart," Lady Lourdes said. "He's a gentle soul—and usually I would not recommend a gentle soul for a husband. Brute strength and mettle first, my mother always said. Goodness knows those were the admirable qualities I found in your father when we courted."

"Ursula," Aster begged. "Stop this!"

Ursula frowned—and really, what did Aster expect her to do? Once Luella Lourdes had set a cause in her mind, she was like a hound with a scent.

"But we can't have strength and mettle in a husband for you," Lady Lourdes went on. "Can't have some brute thinking he's got the best ideas and trying to order around our Major, can we? A gentle soul. That's what we need. But sadly, Quintin Wyvern is no option because he is a king himself."

Aster threw up her hands. "Perhaps there is no option at all. And would that be so terrible? High Keeper?"

All eyes turned to Dev.

Aster suddenly looked eager, gleeful. Like she was about to spring her trap. "What does the *Star Writ* say about Majors who don't marry?"

"Uh…" What sort of question was that? The *Star Writ* concerned itself with the glory of the Majors and their High Beasts, the will of the stars, and the history of the Highen. It didn't concern itself with matchmaking. "There is nothing in the *Star Writ* about these matters."

"Nothing in the *Star Writ*?" said Aster, feigning surprise. She looked pointedly at her mother, and suddenly Dev understood why she had insisted so forcefully that he ride in the carriage. "Well, I suppose if there is nothing in the *Star Writ* about who I must marry, then it doesn't matter at all and we can safely put the issue to rest!"

But Aster's trap was less successful than she'd hoped, because Lady Lourdes only shrugged, looking out the window as if Aster had said nothing at all. "The truth of it is, Lorcan Conri makes the most sense, doesn't he?"

Dev stiffened and turned to Aster, surprised. "Lorc?"

Aster was aghast. "We'd kill each other!"

Yes, that was true. And Dev was glad to hear she was wise enough to know it. But still, heat rushed into his cheeks.

Lady Lourdes waved an unconcerned hand. "You might try, now and then, but that's what Herman Guards are for. Perhaps it doesn't matter, what with his questionable reputation. Ursula at least is liable to marry the Hound king, what with the courtship they've been entertaining...."

Aster sat up. "Marry? Ursula and Arthur Conri?"

Ursula blushed. "You know we've become close, Aster."

"But *marry*?"

"He's not made any kind of proposal as yet."

"But he will," said Lady Lourdes with certainty. "And so that takes Lorc out of the running for Aster. Can't have you marrying your brother-in-law. Honestly, what are we? Härkädians?"

Lady Lourdes laughed, but Dev didn't see anything funny about it. He was, after all, Härkädian.

And that was something he'd been thinking about a lot these days—ever since finding his mother. It had been harder than he'd expected. Not finding her—that part was easy. Once Dev had learned to listen to the On-High, learned to receive their visions, they'd shown him where to find her. And he did. Found his mother, and a little brother called Stir. But knowing them. Being with them. That had been so hard. Conversation was awkward. They had nothing in common. And he'd been shy, unsure of what to say to this woman who'd haunted his dreams for so long. And the boy, his brother, mostly hid behind his mother's skirts, afraid to look Dev in the eye. So much time taken from them. A life together, lost the day Rizlan took Dev away to become a Keeper.

Dev thought of her then, the lines on her face, the sound of her laugh, the feel of her hand on his. Thought of Rizlan. The reason Dev was estranged from his mother, but also the closest thing to a father he'd ever known. This confusion, these memories—they plagued Dev's mind so much lately. And he lost himself in it all once again as Lady Lourdes droned on and on about eligible bachelors. Until, finally, Aster had had enough.

"Stop the carriage," she said, a tremor in her voice.

Ursula sat up, concerned. "Aster, are you all right?"

"I said *stop the carriage!*" She banged on the ceiling, and almost instantly the carriage ground to a halt. Aster slammed her shoulder into the door so hard that it flew open with a bang, and the young Major spilled out, stumbling onto the side of the muddy road to Felisbrook.

"Well, honestly," huffed Lady Lourdes. "Have you ever seen such a fuss over something as simple as marriage?"

"Enough, Mother," said Ursula, climbing out of the carriage.

Leaving Dev alone with Lady Lourdes.

Lady Lourdes pursed her lips and fussed with her sleeves, fluffing the ruffles and picking at the lace. Dev wanted to leap out the door, but he was too afraid to move, afraid to make her notice him. Suddenly, her inky dark eyes fixed on him.

He cleared his throat. "I'll just, uh—I'm going to go check on Aster."

Lady Lourdes raised a very dignified chin, considering his words. Dev was frozen. Did he need her permission? He was High Keeper now. Surely, if he wanted to leave the carriage, he could just leave the carriage. But Lady Lourdes' gaze had a way of putting him right back to his years as Dev the bear boy. Did he need her permission? He might.

Finally, after what felt like an excruciating eternity, Lady Lourdes said slowly, "Very well."

And Dev scrambled out the door, nearly falling into the mud.

The cool forest air engulfed him, a welcome relief from the stifling heat of the royal carriage. They were beyond the trees of Tawnshire now. A sweet and spicy scent perfumed the air—the towering spice cedars and thick bracken ferns that lined the road meant they had crossed into the realm of the Lynx.

At last.

The six dapple-gray horses that pulled the carriage were eating, grateful for the rest as their handlers fed them oats from gilded buckets. Over three score Hermans marched with the Major, most of them sitting on the side of the road, taking the unexpected stop as an opportunity to rub their blistered feet. The convoy that followed the Major was two tail-lengths long, bustling with horses and carriages, each one filled with goods for the Shooting Star Parade and servants and dignitaries to support the Major in her historic visit. There had not been a fallen star in the Highen in two hundred years.

Dev could just make out Alcor halfway down the convoy, rolling in the mud as Keepers and Hermans hurried about him in a panic. His fur would be filthy. If he didn't allow them to clean him, he'd look a mess for their arrival at the Felisbrook palace. And he wouldn't allow it, Dev knew. Lately, there was nothing Alcor enjoyed more than sending nervous Hermans running at a flash of his teeth. Dev would have to deal with Alcor himself.

But first, he had to deal with Aster.

She wasn't among her convoy, and Dev didn't expect her to be. If he knew Aster, she'd made her way well off the road. With a sigh, he crashed into the ferns, trudging deep under the cedars until he found her, striking at a crumbling old stone fence with a large stick.

"Aster!" he called to her.

Aster didn't turn around. She went on hitting, the fence taking the brunt of the battle in her mind.

"Aster," he growled, standing behind her. "What was all that for? Is that why you made me ride in the carriage with you? To put your mother off the marriage question?"

"Fat lot of good you were!" she cried. "You barely said anything at all!"

"What could I say? I'm a Keeper! I don't know anything about marriage!"

"Yes, it showed." The stick broke on the last strike and she sat on the edge of the fence, catching her breath. "Now thanks to you she'll probably have me married off to Quintin's second cousin by the end of the week."

"You're the Major," he reminded her. "You don't have to do anything she says."

"I know that." Aster shrugged. "It's not really Mother."

"Then what's wrong?"

She looked away, chewing on the thought. Dev waited. This was their way. She would always tell him what was wrong, eventually.

"Arthur Conri."

Dev nodded. He should have guessed as much.

"If my sister marries the Head of the House of Hounds," she said, "she'll leave us. She'll have to live in Hundford."

Dev nodded again. Yes. She would.

"And I'll be left alone."

"You won't be alone," Dev said. The Manor was as much his home as hers, and he wasn't going anywhere. Aster smiled, a small sad smile. Perhaps Dev would not be enough. "You'll have your mother."

At that, Aster threw back her head and laughed. "Always with the right wisdom, Honorable High Keeper."

They sat together, watching the Hermans mill about the

convoy through the screen of trees. The air was cold, but fresh with the scents of pine and cedar. It was nice to be on their own, away from all the other voices that forever seemed to interrupt their conversations. At the Manor, the only time they had to talk freely was in their official meetings every night as Major and High Keeper. Mostly, they just played Crowns & Stones and laughed about things Alcor or Ursula or Lady Lourdes had done. On the road to Felisbrook, their Crowns & Stones had had to be put aside.

Dev knew they couldn't hide forever. He could see Ursula coming after them, stepping off the road and picking her way through the ferns.

"We should get back," he said.

Aster nodded as Ursula waved at them to return. "I'll be glad to get back to Tawnshire. Back to our game."

Dev nodded, pleased they'd been thinking the same thing.

Ursula was waiting when they got back to the road, and she hooked her arm in Aster's. "She means well," Ursula said, clearly referring to their mother. "You know that, don't you?"

Aster said nothing.

Ursula sighed. "She's just nervous about returning to Felisbrook after so long."

At that, Aster exploded. "*She's* nervous? I'm the one who's nervous! Father never had to deal with a fallen star when he was Major."

Ursula laughed and pulled Aster closer. "Oh, little sister, believe me, in your reign you will do a great many things our father never did."

Dev watched the sisters climb back into the carriage, Aster's mood considerably improved. As the door closed, he realized that if Ursula left to marry the Head of the House of Hounds, the Manor would indeed be a lonelier place.

*When a thistle meets a rose, they are loath to remember that their mother was the same.*

—THE WRITINGS OF THUBAN,
On the Mysteries of the Natural World: The Star Majors, *Star Writ*

# TWO

IF water could choose a home for itself, it would, Aster suspected, choose Felisbrook. The air was crisp with the cool of fresh springs, and thick with moisture from many rivers, lakes, springs, and waterfalls, so that everything looked just a little bit blue. It was a beautiful place: ferns growing everywhere; trees blazing red with the change of the seasons; the granite High Gates Range to the west, pink and gray; the deep black obsidian of the Drakkan Range to the east—and all of it kissed with a faint watery haze. Best of all were the spice cedars, their coppery, shaggy trunks perfuming everything with the dreamy scent of mulled wine and hot cider.

They'd finally come to their destination—Thorn Manor, the seat of the House of the Lynx. It was an impressively tall, thick castle, set on a hill in the middle of Felisbrook Town, built of heavy pink-speckled stone from the High Gates mountains and adorned with more battlements than Aster thought a manor needed. They stood in the inner bailey, the door to the great hall before them carved with the image of the Great Lynx, the curtain wall behind and encircling them.

"Were there a great many battles in Felisbrook?" Aster asked her mother, who stood razor-straight, looking up at the high towers. "To need all this protection?"

"A great many disputes," her mother said delicately.

"Disputes with who?"

Her mother looked at Aster a moment. She gave no answer, but her eyes flicked to the gatehouse, then to the city streets beyond. There, Aster could see half her convoy, too large to fit within the castle's courtyard. The people of Felisbrook lined the narrow cobbled streets, cheering and clapping for their Major.

Aster looked back up at the battlements. *Disputes*, her mother said.

Ursula stood at Aster's right hand and took her sister's arm, patting it reassuringly. "It's beautiful," she agreed. "You never told us it was so beautiful, Mother."

Lady Lourdes said nothing, but Aster could see her mother's hand at her side, fidgeting anxiously with the fine lace of her sleeve. She wasn't comfortable being back at the place of her birth.

They stood together, the Lourdes women, awkwardly facing the Manor, not sure what to do next.

"Is there really no one to meet us?" Ursula said at last. "Surely they saw us coming ages ago."

Well, the people had met them, Aster thought, and that was something. The common folk of Felisbrook filled the streets, stuffing the narrow corridors framed by densely built wattle-and-daub houses. Among the splendid decorations for the Shooting Star Parade had hung banners with Alcor's name, strung with ribbons of red and amber, the colors of Tawnshire.

But the Manor remained closed and silent.

"Should we knock?" asked Aster, only half joking.

At that, there was a loud clang, and then the heavy oak doors were thrown open, revealing Felisbrook guards clad in livery of purple and silver and a stooped old man in a purple silk jacket. He walked with his hands clasped firmly behind his back, descending the stairs quickly and bowing before Aster.

"Major Aster Lourdes," he said stiffly, formally. "The Kingdom of Felisbrook welcomes you."

"Er... thank you," said Aster, "Sir..."

"Rion," Lady Lourdes said.

The old man smiled. "I am honored Your Majesty remembers me. I am the steward of Thorn Manor. I've been a proud servant of the Great Lynx's house for many long years. I even taught your mother and auntie how to read and write when they were young."

"It is good to see you, Sir Rion," her mother said, though her face did not show it.

"Where is your queen, Sir Rion?" asked Aster. "I would have expected her to meet us."

"She tends the great Sileria," a raspy voice answered.

At the top of the Manor steps stood a man and a woman. The man was young, thin and wiry and dressed in the white robes of a Keeper—the Keeper of the Lynx. And the woman—Aster gaped—could have been Aster's own mother, she looked so much like Lady Lourdes. But older. And more... severe. With the corners of her mouth drawn in what seemed a permanent frown, and heavy bags beneath her tired eyes.

Aster felt her sister take her hand, and the girls looked to their mother. Lady Lourdes had gone pale, and her eyes were wide—it was as if she were looking at a ghost.

"The queen is somewhere in the Deadwood," the woman said hoarsely, descending the steps. She had the voice of one who smoked too much Celeste root—just like Lady Lourdes. "Our Iris is more at home among twisted oaks than walled in with all this finery."

"Leona," Lady Lourdes said tightly as the woman came to stand before her.

Aster held her breath. Aunt Leona. Their mother's older sister, passed over by the Great Lynx at the Northern Crowning decades ago. The throne of Felisbrook had gone to Pan Leander, leaving their mother's family after a thousand years. It was a great shame—something Lady Lourdes never talked about, unless it was to warn Aster and Ursula to study harder, to caution them about the dangers of neglecting their *Star Writ* lessons, their sharps practice, or their political studies, lest they end up dispossessed.

Leona bowed, a very low and formal bow. And Aster's mother flinched.

The Lynx Keeper greeted Aster. "We are honored to welcome Alcor, the Great Hemoth, and his Major, Aster Lourdes."

Aster almost hadn't heard him, too preoccupied with all the unsaid things passing between her mother and aunt. It wasn't until Ursula kicked her shin that she focused on the Lynx Keeper. "The honor is mine, Keeper…?"

"Von, Major."

"Keeper Von," she repeated politely. Strange, she thought, to meet a Keeper without his High Beast. But then, what had Aunt Leona said? The lynx was in the Deadwood with the queen.

"I must confess it, Major Lourdes," said Keeper Von, rubbing his hands obsessively, one over the other like a squirrel hoping for a nut. A nervous fellow. "I had very much hoped to meet High Keeper Dev."

"Yes, of course!" Aster said, laughing. How exciting to hear Dev spoken of with such esteem! But he *was* High Keeper of the Highen now. It should have come as no surprise that the Lynx Keeper would want to meet him.

She turned and looked down the line of her Hermans to the massive, furry, heaving mass at the far end of the courtyard. Alcor was whining, clearly unhappy after a long journey. "There he is!" Aster said, pointing to where Dev was cradling Alcor's giant head. "Alcor's a bit cantankerous after being on the road for so long," she laughed. "Poor Dev will have his hands full till the big baby is fed."

Keeper Von looked suddenly aghast, and Ursula cleared her throat.

*Right*, Aster thought. Alcor was the Hemoth Bear. The Highest of High Beasts. People who didn't know him would not understand the way she spoke about him. She had to remember decorum.

"Er, High Keeper Dev is very attuned to Alcor's needs," she rephrased, trying to recover. "He must see that the Hemoth is fed."

"Yes, food!" interrupted Aunt Leona, taking Lady Lourdes' arm. "Come. The road from Tawnshire is long. You must all be hungry and tired. There is a meal prepared in the great hall."

Aster and Ursula followed Aunt Leona and Lady Lourdes up the steps, while Keeper Von fell in beside Aster, hands ever rubbing together. "Would—would the High Keeper be joining us?" he asked.

Aster stopped. She knew Dev. He would rather be with Alcor than sitting at an awkward, formal luncheon with people he didn't know. But Keeper Von was so excited to meet him, and she did not want to make poor first impressions in Felisbrook. "I'm sure nothing would delight him more," Aster lied, and nodded to a Herman to fetch Dev.

He'd be cross with her for this. There was nothing that made Dev sourer than when Aster sent a Herman with "orders from the Major." But she'd make it up to him later.

Thorn Manor was as foreboding and stern inside as it was outside. It was cold and dark, and the stone walls were a deep, bruised purple—Aster felt she was standing inside the artery of some great beast. Gloomy tapestries hung everywhere, the thread-eyed Lynxes of history looking down on the visitors with an uncomfortable scrutiny. The high ceilings were so dark with shadows that Aster suspected there were bats in the rafters. Or worse.

She hated it at once.

She couldn't imagine what it must have been like for her mother, growing up here. So unlike the sunny warmth of their manor in Tawnshire. Then again, their mother had always had a stark hardness to her, and her rooms in Lourdes Manor were decorated with a great many Felisbrook things. So maybe she had liked it.

"Is it as you remembered?" Aunt Leona was asking Lady Lourdes. "Or can you even remember after so long?"

"It seems just the same," said Lady Lourdes, her voice quiet. Aster had never known her mother to be so quiet.

Aunt Leona nodded. "I restored it to its former glory as best as I could. That vulgar Leander had hung *so many* absurd tapestries of himself in his time here. Can you imagine? And all of them in indecently bright colors!"

"I did not realize you had returned to Thorn Manor," Lady Lourdes said.

"Yes, shortly after the Northern Crowning," said Aunt Leona. "Fate, or the On-High, it would seem, were not done with me in this place just yet. It was Sir Rion who summoned me."

The old man, who'd been following at a polite distance, moved closer. "I did, yes. Our young queen is not of noble blood, so the demands of her station have required some tutelage. I could think of no better guide to life on the Felisbrook throne than Lady Leona."

Aster thought of the Lynx queen then—Iris Goreman. Aster had stood with her at the Northern Crowning. With Pan Leander in exhile and Felisbrook's leadership in tatters, she'd been put forward by the oracles of the Highen as the only worthy Felisbrook candidate, as told to them by the stars themselves. A bit older than Aster, with brown skin and black hair, very quiet. Her eyes kept on her feet, her curls forever in her face. Like she was always trying to hide. Like she hadn't wanted to be there at all. But the Great Lynx Sileria did not hesitate when the time came to choose the Head of the House of the Lynx.

Mostly, Aster remembered how miserable Iris had looked. Living in this wretched castle, she had to wonder if Iris would look any different now.

They were led to a long dining hall. A stained-glass window of purples, blues, and pinks formed the image of Kerrwick, the first sacred Lynx of Felisbrook, glowing at the head of the hall with the cool autumn light. The room was lined with five long wooden tables; there was also one in the middle, set with a fine-looking meal of pheasant and roasted root vegetables and decorated with still more of the purple ferns that grew everywhere in Felisbrook.

There were no seats, however.

Aster watched as her mother and Aunt Leona approached the head of the table and stood there, as if they did not know chairs were even expected. Aunt Leona poured two glasses of wine, one for Aster's mother and one for herself. As if signalled, Sir Rion and a flurry of servants suddenly moved about the table, pouring wine and handing glasses to Aster and Ursula and Keeper Von. Everyone stood at board.

Aunt Leona held her goblet aloft. "In honor of the fifty-fourth Major, Major Aster Lourdes, Felisbrook offers this humble meal. May Kerrwick, the Great Lynx, bless it. May the Great Lord Tawn be pleased. May the On-High shine their light upon us."

Keeper Von and Lady Lourdes lifted their glasses. "May the On-High shine their light upon us," they said in response. Aster and Ursula awkwardly raised their glasses and mumbled the line quietly, not quite sure of the customs here. From there, the gathered company grabbed plates and piled them with beautiful food, the girls following their mother's lead.

Ursula leaned down to Aster's ear. "Where are we supposed to sit?"

"There're no chairs anywhere!" Aster agreed, trying not to laugh. Her mother had never told them the people of Felisbrook didn't sit when they ate. She hadn't told them much about Felisbrook at all.

As Aster placed her unsipped goblet of wine on the table and took a bite of the crispy pheasant, Dev was brought into the hall. His narrowed eyes found hers immediately, his lips pursed in that sour expression of his.

Aster swallowed. So…yes, he was quite angry.

Keeper Von's gasp echoed through the great hall, and he put down his plate and hurried over to Dev, hands wringing in front of him.

"You'd better get over there," Ursula said. "You got Dev into this, the least you can do is help him through it."

With a sigh, Aster forced as much pheasant as she could into her mouth before leaving her plate on the table and following Keeper Von. He was shaking Dev's hand with more vigor than any handshake called for, and Dev looked completely helpless, not sure what to do with this reception.

"Honorable High Keeper," said Aster in her best Major voice. "I see you've met Keeper Von!"

"It is good to meet you, Keeper Von," Dev said, though his voice made it clear that it was decidedly not good.

"Oh, it is an honor, High Keeper," said Von. "A real honor. I have been waiting so long to meet you, and now that you are here in Felisbrook's time of great need, it is just so wonderful, the way the On-High align to bless us!"

"Time of great need?" asked Aster.

"Ah," said Von, suddenly looking afraid. "Yes, well. I ought not speak of it until our queen has arrived, of course. It is more her place than mine to discuss matters in Felisbrook. But I must say, meeting you, High Keeper, and you, Major Lourdes, is one of the greatest blessings the On-High have granted me in my lifetime."

"Keeper Von." Aunt Leona appeared behind him, her face stern in the same way Lady Lourdes' became when Aster had done something she knew was wrong. "Our guests have only just arrived. Please spare the Honorable High Keeper your fervor and let him and our Major enjoy their meal."

Keeper Von bowed, begrudgingly, and left to join the conversation at the table.

"Forgive Keeper Von," Aunt Leona said. "He worries excessively, but his constant fretting means our Sileria is well cared for."

"Is everything all right in Felisbrook?" Aster asked. "He spoke of 'a time of great need' here."

Aunt Leona laughed. "Oh, it is always a time of great need . . . to Keeper Von. Please, Major Lourdes, High Keeper. Enjoy the meal. You need to eat." At that, Aunt Leona left them, returning to the table to pour herself more wine.

"Aster," Dev hissed. "You sent a Herman to fetch me? Really?"

Aster noticed Von and Aunt Leona watching them, trying to appear as if they weren't. Mother and Ursula, Sir Rion, the servants. All eyes were on them, even if everyone was trying not to show it.

Aster laughed and grinned as wide as she could. "Quiet now," she said through her smiling teeth. "They're all watching." She hooked her arm through Dev's and walked with him toward the table. "I was put in an awkward position, Dev," she said, ever smiling. "I'm sorry. But they asked for you. You *are* High Keeper."

"In Tawn's name! You'd think Keeper Von, of all people, would know I'm needed with Alcor!"

"Smile, please," said Aster. "What do you make of what he said?"

"I haven't the faintest idea."

"He's an odd one, don't you think?"

Dev sighed. "I don't know, Aster. I don't think that's for you or me to say."

Aster wanted to roll her eyes, but she kept on smiling. "You *can* say, you just don't want to, because now you've got your Honorable Keeper boots on. But you don't even have to. *I* know you think the same thing. There's something going on here. The way Aunt Leona intervened like that?"

"I should really get back to Alcor."

"Has he eaten?"

"Yes, the Felisbrook guard brought him a wheelbarrow of fresh trout."

"Wonderful!" said Aster. "Then he's happy, and you can stay. Well done, Honorable High Keeper. Now make your Major happy: stuff your face with this wonderful pheasant and help me survive this awkward situation." She grabbed a plate and piled it with two cuts of pheasant, a bunch of vegetables, and a shining roll, then handed it to Dev.

"I'm still mad at you about the carriage," he hissed. "And now you do this to me? I should be with my charge."

"Stop acting like this is the worst situation I've ever put you in," she said, "or I'll throw you into Great Bear River again, and we'll see if you're so lucky this time."

Dev frowned, but relented, taking a bite of his pheasant. She watched as his eyes widened before he tore into the leg with more earnestness. The meat was very good. She nodded triumphantly and recovered her own plate from the table. Dev, she knew, couldn't be unhappy with good food in his belly. No one appreciated a good meal like Dev...except maybe Alcor.

Aster glanced back to where her mother was standing with Aunt Leona. Neither had touched their food, both sipping their wine and looking around the room uncomfortably. Aster couldn't begin to guess how many years had passed since the two sisters last spoke face-to-face—letters were one thing, but words...

A figure appeared beyond her mother and Aunt Leona, at the back of the great hall beneath the Kerrwick window just outside the light. No—two figures, their eyes reflecting the cold sunshine spilling through the glass.

Aster choked.

"You all right?" Dev asked through stuffed cheeks.

Aster coughed and sputtered, the pheasant caught in her throat, and motioned to the figures in the shadows. Everyone in the hall turned to look to where Aster was pointing.

Iris Goreman.

And the Great Lynx Sileria.

They were home.

*The shards of broken promises embed themselves in the heart—and fester.*

—FELISBROOK PROVERB

# THREE

"WHEN did they come in?" Dev whispered.

Aster pounded her chest, dislodging the pheasant. She had no idea where Iris and the lynx had come from. They hadn't used the great doors. They were like phantoms. Silent as ghosts in the dark.

The Queen of Felisbrook and the Great Lynx Sileria made their way to the table. Iris stood before Aster and curtsied—clumsily, as Sileria sat beside her, a bored look in her silver eyes. "Forgive my tardiness, Major," said Iris, her voice barely a whisper. "There is much activity in the Deadwood after a star has fallen. Sileria was worried for her forest."

Aster noted the word *worried*. Time of great need.... She glanced at Dev, who met her eye. He hadn't missed it either.

Aunt Leona was watching from the head of the table and raised her glass, inserting herself loudly into the conversation. "The great Sileria is admirably devoted to the forests of Felisbrook. It is her and Iris's stewardship of our trees that keeps Felisbrook lush and bountiful."

Aster frowned. Did Aunt Leona poke her nose into every conversation?

Aster returned to Iris and nodded politely. "I don't doubt there is much to tend to in Felisbrook at the moment. It's not every day one of the On-High falls to the realms of man."

"Yes, Major," said Iris.

An awkward silence opened up between them, and Iris Gore-man kept her eyes on the floor. Sileria, however, was happy to stare, studying Aster in a way Aster wasn't sure she cared much for.

Aunt Leona cleared her throat loudly, and Iris looked back as Aunt Leona nodded encouragingly.

"We, er, the p-people of Felisbrook and I," stammered Iris, "are so pleased you could join us for these blessed celebrations."

The Lynx queen didn't seem pleased at all. She seemed positively strangled by the niceties of ceremony.

"Thank you for your invitation," said Aster, as etiquette required. Her mother and Ursula were forever stressing the importance of proper manners in political settings. But truth be told, most of the time Aster felt the way Iris looked. Uncomfortable. Caged. She couldn't help but wonder how different their conversation might be out in the forest, with horses and dogs and their High Beasts.

"I should very much like to see what that disturbance in the woods you mention is about," Aster continued. She knew that her mother and Ursula were inwardly groaning at her forwardness.

Iris Goreman looked at Aunt Leona. She did that a lot. "C-certainly, M-Major Lourdes," she stammered. "It would be my honor to accompany you into the Deadwood—"

"Tomorrow," interrupted Aunt Leona. "Tonight, Queen Iris hosts a feast in your honor, and wishes for her guests to make themselves comfortable in their accommodations, so that they might be well rested."

Iris opened her mouth to say something, but seemed to reconsider, and simply nodded.

"I've rested plenty," said Aster dismissively. "I was stuck inside that stuffy carriage most of the entire way from Tawnshire. I'd much rather be out in the woods."

Iris Goreman blinked at her, clearly not sure what to do.

"Queen Iris," said Aunt Leona, "has not prepared properly for such a venture—"

"What's to prepare?" said Aster, looking to Iris Goreman, who kept her eyes on the floor. "Come now, all we'd need are horses."

Aunt Leona stepped forward. "But Queen Iris—"

"Queen Iris," snapped Aster, "can speak for herself, can't she? Why do you insist on putting all these words in her mouth?"

A tense silence took hold of the great hall. Dev shifted awkwardly beside Aster, and she could see Ursula wincing. She looked back at her mother, whose dark eyes flashed with anger. And Aster realized, with shame, that she had forgotten once again about the ever-important decorum.

"It would," Iris said quietly, carefully, "be a great honor to escort our Major into the Deadwood, to the place where the star has fallen. I only recommend tomorrow as the King of Dracogart—who I know is, for our Major, a dear friend—has yet to arrive. I thought Major Lourdes might enjoy the Deadwood better if she could share it with him."

Aster nodded, forcing herself to smile, though all she wanted to do was hide beneath the table. She had gone too far again. She always did. Sometimes she still found herself thinking that this was all a mistake—that Ursula really *should* be Major. She would be better suited to it. "Yes, of course. Queen Iris is very considerate. I would indeed prefer to share the adventure with Quintin when he arrives."

Out of the corner of her eye she saw Aunt Leona make an urgent gesture to Sir Rion, who hurried to stand between Aster and Iris. "If the Major is ready, I would be happy to escort you and your party to your apartments."

"Thank you, Sir Rion," said Aster. "That would be fine." But she couldn't think of anything worse. Retiring to private rooms with her mother and Ursula. What would Lady Lourdes say about what Aster had done? *Have you forgotten yourself completely, Aster Lourdes!*

"Major Lourdes," said Dev, addressing her formally for the benefit of the room. "With your permission, I will take my leave to tend to Alcor."

The traitor. Abandoning her now. "Certainly," she said stiffly, "High Keeper Dev."

Dev hurried out through the great doors, not sparing a backward glance—he was too eager to be free of politics and formality.

Sir Rion led Aster and her family through Thorn Manor, which seemed nothing but cavernous rooms covered in tapestries of still more watching Lynxes. They climbed a grand carved staircase, the stone walls intricately carved with the faces of staring Lynxes, judging Aster as she passed. The stair finally opened onto a large floor with three massive oak doors adorned with painted fern fronds. The center door, the biggest of the three, led to Aster's rooms: grand, luxurious apartments with cold wooden floors covered in ornate purple rugs. There was a four-poster bed draped with still more purple. A purple fern tea set, too, just like the one Lady Lourdes had in her rooms back in Tawnshire, sat on a small table near the massive marble fireplace.

"Are the chambers to your liking, Major Lourdes?" Sir Rion asked. "The North Tower is considered by many to contain the most spectacular rooms in all Felisbrook."

The deep purple made everything so dark. So oppressive. She felt trapped. Suffocated. "Yes, thank you, Sir Rion," was all she said.

"Thank you, Sir Rion," echoed Lady Lourdes, standing beside the open door. "That will be all."

Sir Rion bowed, and when he was gone, Lady Lourdes closed the heavy oak door behind him.

"Well?" she said, looking at Aster expectantly.

"Well what?"

Her mother was in no mood. "What in the name of Tawn was that vulgar display downstairs?"

"It was a mistake," Aster said quickly, hoping that would be enough to put the issue to rest.

It wasn't.

"Need I remind you," her mother said, "this is a political visit. You are the Major now, Aster. You cannot be a spoiled child, not in the company of our allies. Show politesse!"

"Some allies," Aster scoffed. "All of Felisbrook was ruled by Pan Leander about a minute ago, who—I don't need to remind you—was aligned with Uncle Bram!"

"*Don't* call him Uncle," Lady Lourdes hissed.

"The Minor, then!" said Aster. "If you ask *me*, there's not been enough groveling from this kingdom, given what their former king was party to! Yet I'm supposed to behave perfectly?"

"Aster!" warned Ursula. "Pan's in exile. Felisbrook has turned its back on him *and* the traitor Bram Lourdes. Don't bring the weight of the past here, not to this place and this relationship, not now. We must turn to the future."

Aster sat on the edge of the bed, her arms crossed defiantly. She knew Ursula was right. Felisbrook in its entirety could hardly be blamed for the actions of one man. She didn't know why she even brought it up.

"I'm sorry," she said. "I just…Aunt Leona, with her constant interrupting! Honestly, you'd think Iris Goreman was missing a tongue the way that woman speaks for her. Iris is a *queen*, for the love of Tawn!"

Lady Lourdes rubbed at her temples, the way she so often did when she and Aster argued. Finally, she took a long, deep breath through her nose, her eyes closed as she tried to muster an air of calm. But Aster knew Luella Lourdes' calm was a thin façade. Underneath, her mother was a bubbling volcano. "Whatever my sister's position here at Thorn Manor, it is between her and her queen. It is not for you or me to judge."

"If not the Major, then who?" Aster retorted.

"Aster Lourdes!" her mother snapped. "Is that what you imagine the role of a Major to be? The judge of all the realm?"

Aster sighed. "No, of course not. I just—didn't you find it frustrating? Having to speak through Leona as though the whole of Felisbrook were hers?"

"And what if I did? Would you be pleased if I had erupted on her like some sort of raging Hemoth?"

"I wasn't *that* rude," said Aster, looking to Ursula to agree. But her sister's eyes flashed with pity.

Was what Aster had said in the great hall really so bad?

"You don't understand," her mother said, breathless. "You don't see how your every action has consequences in the Highen you rule!" Lady Lourdes held her face in her hands. "On-High help us. What would your father say? Tawn keep his star!"

Father.

Major Jasper Lourdes.

The Death Chaser.

Aster deflated then. What would he have done, if he were here now? How would he have behaved? She thought of his booming laugh, his endless calm. Mother was right. Father would never have shouted at Aunt Leona. He would have been understanding. Courteous. Respectful of Felisbrook custom. And then he would have retired to his quarters and conferred with his Keeper, the late High Keeper Rizlan, on the matter. Together, they would have quietly, *discreetly* uncovered what was going on in the Felisbrook court.

Aster was not living up to her father's name.

"I'm sorry, Mother," she said. "And you, Ursula. I should not have acted the way I did. I'll try harder."

"Yes, you will," her mother said, walking across the room and kneeling before Aster. She took Aster's hands in hers. "You are Aster Lourdes. Daughter of the Death Chaser. The *Star Writ* will praise your rule. You just need to remember to act like it."

Aster looked at her mother's hand on hers, the grip tight and the knuckles whitening.

"A little decorum, eh?" her mother said.

Aster nodded. "A little decorum."

"Good girl." Lady Lourdes rose, patting Aster's cheek, and made her way to the door. "Rest now, my darlings. We'll be expected to do it all again at supper. And On-High knows the audience will be bigger—and twice as obnoxious."

"Bigger?" said Aster. "I don't think Quintin Wyvern will have much of an entourage with him." Quintin Wyvern was the private type.

Her mother laughed. "Quintin Wyvern is now King of Dracogart. I don't think the size of his entourage is up to him. Especially for an event as important as this."

There it was again. The importance of the Shooting Star Parade. It had been over a hundred years since a star last fell in the Highen. Even her father had never attended one.

"And anyway," her mother said, "it's not just the House of the Shadow Dragons coming."

"It's not?"

"Certainly not!" laughed her mother. "I expect the House of the Ox to get here before the Shadow Dragon. And Roarque, I imagine they won't be far behind—trust the House of the Lion never to miss out on a party. And of course, King Conri of the House of Hounds we know is already on his way." Her mother winked at Ursula. "Add to all this the rest of the Felisbrook court. It will be quite a crowd. Now rest—Mother's orders. You need to be fresh for the events this evening."

And with that, their mother left, no doubt to smoke her Celeste root in quiet.

Aster looked at Ursula, who was blushing as bright as Ursan amber. "Arthur Conri is coming here?"

Ursula pressed her palms to her cheeks and smoothed her dress. "It's a fallen star, Aster, anybody who's anybody has to be here."

Aster considered that a moment. "But not Bernadine?" Their cousin, Bernadine Lourdes, was the Head of the House of the White Bear. She was far away, at home in Whitlock. "They'll judge her for it this time. This is the second Highen event she's refused to attend. They'll all think her a coward."

Bernadine hadn't left Whitlock since she returned home shortly after the Northern Crowning. She was the daughter of the traitor Bram Lourdes. And it weighed on her.

Never mind that she'd saved Aster—and Ursula and Dev and Quintin. All of them, really. Never mind that she'd turned against her father, begged him to stop his evil campaign against the whole of the Highen. Never mind that the White Bear, Marmoral, chose her to lead the House of the White Bear. No. She was the daughter of Bram Lourdes. And the Highen whispered her name with hatred. So she hid. And Aster couldn't blame her.

"Well," said Ursula. "*You* won't. And King Wyvern certainly won't. Neither will Arthur."

Aster raised an eyebrow. "*Arthur*, is it? What would decorum say about that, Ursula Lourdes?"

Ursula pushed her little sister so that she fell sideways on the bed. "Goose! In any event, that's three Highen houses that know Bernadine Lourdes' quality."

Maybe. But Aster couldn't help but worry.

How long would Bernadine keep hiding? The only contact Aster had with her cousin was the letters they sent back and forth. She was grateful for those letters. Bernadine had lived with Aster and Ursula at the Manor most of their lives—she was a second sister, really. And Aster missed her dearly. It wasn't healthy, hiding away in the cold, alone, away from everyone and everything. Just Bernadine and her thoughts. Thoughts which, from what Aster could tell from her letters, were increasingly fixed on dark things. Grim things. Stories and legends and scholarly texts about the Moon Door, the passage of death and demons.

Ursula left—to sleep, she said, but Aster suspected she was going to prepare for Arthur Conri's arrival. Once alone, Aster sat at the little writing desk by the fireplace and penned a letter to Bernadine. Silly gossip, the thing Bernie used to enjoy so much: Lady Lourdes' face upon meeting Aunt Leona; the awkward lunch; the surprisingly meek nature of Queen Iris Goreman. She saved the best for last—Ursula and Arthur Conri. How her cousin would swoon at the thought! She had always dreamt of romance.

"Queen Ursula Conri," Aster whispered. She hated the sound of it. Hated the idea. She'd already had to say goodbye to Bernadine. Would Ursula leave her too? Then it would just be Aster and Mother.

No. There would be Dev. Always Dev. Just as Keeper Rizlan had always been by her father's side, so Dev would remain by hers.

In fact, she wanted to talk to him now. Wanted to get his read on Aunt Leona and Iris Goreman. On what the Lynx Keeper had said. *Time of great need.*

The thought of sending for him crossed her mind. But after his reaction earlier, summoning him twice in one afternoon would be pushing his patience too far.

*Bernie,* Aster wrote, *I wish you would join us in Felisbrook. I could do with one more sister.*

And then a roar, thunderous and angry and ever so familiar, rang out somewhere below.

Aster leapt up from her chair and looked toward the curtains, a sliver of daylight spilling through the gap in the middle. She crossed the room and pulled them open, revealing a large balcony. The city of

Felisbrook lay sprawled beneath the Manor, its houses and buildings crowding winding streets that ran up and up to the castle gates. She could see her convoy of Hermans and carriages and wagons below. And Alcor. He stood in the center of the castle courtyard, his massive head swinging side to side the way it did when he was frustrated.

And there was Dev, standing before the great Hemoth, his arms held out in a pleading gesture. She couldn't hear him, but she could guess at the conversation. *"I'm sorry, Alcor, they don't have lamb here. I can get you more trout!"*

No, she thought, folding up her letter for Bernadine. She wouldn't summon her Keeper.

Instead she'd go to him. She'd leave her cousin's letter with Sir Rion to have it sent to Whitlock, and after that, she would head out into the courtyard to join Dev in preparing Alcor for the evening's festivities.

He couldn't be mad about that, now, could he?

Aster left her rooms and tried to remember her way back through Thorn Manor. It was harder than she expected. The corridors were dark and narrow and cold. And everything looked the same—stone walls, tapestries, candles encased in purple glass.

Finally, she rounded a corner to discover a broad landing laid with lavish rugs. There was a pair of heavy doors hewn of twisted oak, impeccably carved with lynxes chasing each other end to end across a starry sky.

The queen's chambers.

There were hushed voices beyond the doors, and Aster crept closer. Where the doors met, there was a seam, and she peered through to see a solar—a sitting room—much the same as her mother's back at home. Inside, she could see her mother...and the shadow of someone else.

"You haven't changed," her mother was saying. "The nerve of you, asking for favors after all this time!"

"It is not a favor," the shadow said. Aunt Leona! How long had it been since her mother was alone in a room with her elder sister? Aster thought of the way her mother's hands had fidgeted nervously when they'd first seen Leona on the steps. She did not look nervous now, but Aster suspected her mother would not want to linger long.

"Felisbrook is the kingdom of your birth, Lu," Aunt Leona was saying. "Its success is as much your responsibility as it is mine."

"Preposterous," laughed her mother. "You are overreaching, Leona."

"Promises were made, sister."

Her mother's arms dropped at her sides, stiff, the hands balled into fists. "*Not* by the Major," she growled.

A long silence.

"Made all the same," Leona said finally.

"I don't recommend you come to my daughter trying to uphold the promises made by that snake...."

*Uncle Bram.* The way her voice dripped with venom—Mother only sounded like that when he was subject of discussion.

Aunt Leona stepped into view, palms open, pleading. "If you could just *speak* with Aster—"

"She is Major Lourdes to *you*."

Silence fell between the sisters. Aster's mind raced.

What had Uncle Bram promised Felisbrook? Pan Leander had been one of his closest allies in his play for the Highen. He could have offered anything.

And so what if he had? Surely the promises of a traitor to an exiled king didn't matter now.

"Forgive me, Lu," Leona said at last, her voice shifting from cold and formal to warm and familiar. It set Aster's nerves on edge. "I don't know what's come over me. Things being as they are in the kingdom, to add something as...complicated...as a fallen star over everything—I've not slept much these last few months. I've no right to ask you for anything."

*Complicated.* Momentous, certainly. Holy. Rare. But *complicated?* Why?

"The queen and I will speak to the Major ourselves," Leona went on. "When we do, I ask only that you find it in your heart to offer a modicum of support for the kingdom you once called home."

How much would Leona even allow Iris to say? Aster wondered.

"You will have my support for what the On-High will, sister mine," said her mother. "As for the rest, I suggest you reconsider your...compromise."

Compromise?

But the conversation was over. Lady Lourdes moved toward the door and Aster leapt back, darting around the corner she'd come from. Lady Lourdes emerged, letting the doors slam behind her. She stood there a moment, pressed against them, and closed her eyes, breathing deep. She pressed a hand to her stomach, breathed again, and then left, following a corridor across from the oaken doors.

Aster waited a minute. Then another, determined not to let her mother catch her eavesdropping. It took all of her discipline to stay in her hiding spot, deep in shadow. She was itching to race out of the Manor, out into the evening light. To find Dev.

And tell him what she'd heard.

Whatever was happening in Felisbrook, it had the stink of Uncle Bram all over it.

*It is a grave mistake on the part of High Keeper Wip and the Bear Highen to ignore the threat that watches from above—the moon. With this compendium, I intend to rectify it. For the On-High. For the Highen. For the souls of Man.*

—KEEPER KALAMITY,
*A Compendium of Nightlocks,* forbidden text

# FOUR

 HE moon was made of snow.

This was the theory that Bernadine Lourdes had come to believe was more true than fanciful. The moon, like the snowdrifts of Whitlock, glowed brilliant and pale, illuminating the night. It lit the earth, too—the ice and snow reflecting the moon's light, bright and twinkling.

At least, that was how things were when the moon was full.

When the door to death was firmly closed, and trouble sealed away behind it.

But tonight. Tonight it was just a sliver.

Bernadine sat in the snow on a woolen blanket, beside her a journal, a spyglass, and a quill. In her hands she held a book, and she ran her fingers over the wrinkled leather cover, a glittering moon embroidered there in gold thread. She'd had her people search the Highen for it, and at last one of her men had returned from Härkädia with her prize:

*Keeper Kalamity's A Compendium of Nightlocks*

What went on behind the moon?

She didn't really think old Keeper Kalamity had the answers, of course. He was a storyteller, a nonsense-weaver. And he had lived hundreds of years before Bernadine's time. But he was a historian, too, in his way—recording the spoken tales of regular Highen folk on the page for posterity. The stories had to have originated from somewhere, Bernadine was sure.

And in them, she was determined to find the grains of truth to help her unravel the mysteries of the Moon Door. The mysteries of death beyond it.

Marmoral, the White Bear, groaned at Bernadine's side, nudging the book with her snout. The young bear had found Bernadine again, somehow. Even here, in the freezing cold overlooking White Bear Lake where no one in their right mind should have any reason to be—Marmoral had found her. The little bear never did understand when Bernadine just wanted to be alone.

"Will you read to her again?" Keeper Gwyn called.

Bernadine turned and saw Keeper Gwyn—a stout, strong woman, arms holding a bale of hay as though it weighed no more than a feather. She stood in the open door of the Bear Holding, warm golden lamp glow spilling out across the pale snow. She smiled hopefully. "Marmoral so loves it when you read."

Bernadine smiled back, if only to be polite. Keeper Gwyn was right—the young white bear did seem to enjoy listening to Bernie read the stories of Keeper Kalamity out loud. It was still strange to Bernadine, that this little cub should be so interested in her—the daughter of Minor Bram Lourdes—the very man who had murdered the little bear's mother.

But for whatever reason, Marmoral was always trailing after Bernadine—forever snuggling as close as she could get, falling asleep on Bernadine's shoes. Even if she didn't understand it, Bernadine couldn't help but be grateful for the creature's affection. It was the only warmth in her life these days.

Marmoral nudged the book again, and Bernadine scratched under her soft, downy chin. The bear groaned happily and settled down in the snow at Bernadine's feet, chin resting on her shoes, big black eyes watching her expectantly. Bernadine sighed and opened the book, a red falcon feather marking her page.

"The Birth of the Terror Maids," Bernadine read. She closed the book, glancing back quickly to see if Keeper Gwyn was listening. There was thudding in the Bear Holding. The Keeper and her apprentice were busy at work cleaning Marmoral's stall.

Bernadine held tight to her book and looked down at the white cloud of fluff at her feet. The bear blinked at her, innocent, trusting. And Bernadine wasn't at all sure she should be reading about such things to a High Beast. "The Birth of the Terror Maids" had fast become one of Bernadine's favorite Keeper Kalamity stories. But it was not the sort of thing a proper Highen girl should be reading, she knew. It was the sort of thing most pious folk would disapprove of.

Most pious folk disapproved of anything concerning itself with Nightlocks. Unless it came from the *Star Writ*. Anything else—that was playing at dark matters indeed.

Aster had warned her, in her last letter from Tawnshire before she left for the Shooting Star Parade, not to meddle with Moon Demons. *It will only trouble your mind further, cousin. For your own peace, you mustn't chase such dark matters.* Most people feared what they didn't understand.

And that was just the trouble, Bernadine thought. She *was* afraid. To her core. She didn't understand Nightlocks any more than the next person. But she'd seen them, which was more than most could say. She'd heard them croak her name, watched them seep into her bedroom. Watched them leach away her father's soul. Watched their nightmare shadows carry him off.

Carry him behind the Moon Door.

Fear had taken hold of Bernadine the moment the Nightlocks found her in Tawnshire all those months ago. And it hadn't released her for a moment since.

She was so tired of being afraid.

So she would learn. Anything and everything she could about the demons that lived behind the moon. Then maybe she could make the fear stop.

Bernadine glanced up at the moon, just a sliver in the dark. The door to death was open tonight. Just as it had been for days. It hadn't changed for many nights, Bernadine was sure. As if stuck.

And a star had fallen in Felisbrook.

She hugged the book to her chest. If ever there was a night for mischief from the moon, surely this was it.

The bear sighed, still looking up at Bernadine.

"Are you afraid?" she asked the bear.

Marmoral chuffed.

"Don't worry, little one," she said. "I'll protect you."

*The adolescent phase in the life cycle of the Hemoth is a trial not fit for the faint of heart. For wrapped in the body of the great bear of our Highen are the will and the power and the might of the stars. When a Hemoth moves from cub to juvenile—that might takes hold, and it is the job of the Keeper to help his charge control it, lest the High Beast destroy itself and the whole of the Highen with it.*

—THE WRITINGS OF BERN,
On Hemoth Bears: The Age of Tawn, *Star Writ*

# FIVE

THE sun was setting over the High Gates, and the pink stone of the towering range glowed in the fiery orange light. *The gateway to the stars*, Rizlan had told Dev once. The High Gates were said to be the way to the On-High, so impressive in their height and beauty that they were supposed to reach the heavens.

Dev didn't understand how that had come to be the tale, given that the larger Drakkan Range could easily be seen to the east. But still, staring out at the rosy highlands of the Gates, he couldn't help but wonder: If he climbed to their peaks, would he find Rizlan waiting?

And if he did…Dev didn't like to think of the questions he'd have for the old man. Each one would be like a dagger to Rizlan's heart—Rizlan, his father and mother and teacher and friend.

Why did he take Dev away from his mother all those years ago?

How could he do it?

Didn't he think about the life he was robbing Dev of?

Didn't he care?

Dev grabbed a stone off the cobbles and hurled it as hard as he could, sending it pinging off the wheel of a Tawnshirian supply wagon.

Alcor looked up from his second wheelbarrow of trout and moaned. *Bope bope bope.*

Dev sighed and sat back down on the little crate he'd been

using as a chair. He stuck his head in his hands and tried to calm down. Tried to will the thoughts of Rizlan, thoughts of his mother, away—thoughts of the life he lived and the life that could have been. But he knew it was no use. They'd find their way back to him. They always did.

Lately, the dreams of that life were chased by visions of the moon being swallowed by the Great Lord Tawn, his sky-image made up of stars. Dev didn't know what it meant. Perhaps he was the moon, and Alcor and Aster were Tawn, swallowing him up so that there was nothing of him left....

He'd been seeing it for weeks now. And still it was meaningless. Perhaps it had to do with the fallen star? With the Shooting Star Parade? He was tired of trying to sort it all out.

Whatever the meaning, it filled Dev with dread, an unease he'd been unable to shake.

*Bope bope bope.* Alcor nudged Dev's arm with his muzzle, and Dev hugged the bear tight. Alcor, the Great Hemoth, highest of High Beasts. And the only true family Dev really had.

"What's he upset about now?" Aster appeared behind them, and Alcor pulled away from Dev, chuffing excitedly. "Did Felisbrook run out of fish for him?"

Dev stood up, wiping at his eyes quickly. When he turned to face her, she had a crinkle between her brows. "Dev, are you all right?"

"I'm fine," he said, picking up the little wooden crate and dumping it into the supply wagon, trying to look busy—too busy to talk about it. "What are you doing here, Aster? Shouldn't you be preparing for the reception this evening?"

Aster folded her arms. "Shouldn't you?"

Dev frowned. Yes, he would probably be expected to attend. Especially if that overly enthusiastic Keeper Von was going.

"Never mind about all that." Aster joined him by the wagon and leaned against it in a most unladylike fashion—not like a high-born lady at all, in fact, but more like one of her Herman Guards recently off duty. "You'll never guess what I just overheard Aunt Leona saying to my mother. She asked for my mother's support in something she's going to petition me for." Her voice was hushed—conspiratorial. He wasn't sure he had the strength for it tonight.

"Sounds like the usual Highen politics to me."

"You didn't hear it," she said. "They were talking about *promises*—promises Uncle Bram made to Pan Leander!"

That wasn't surprising. Pan Leander was Bram's second. "I imagine there were many promises made. But Bram's dead and Pan's no longer in the Highen. What does it matter now?"

"Well, exactly!" said Aster, throwing up her hands. "What *does* it matter now? Why is Leona bringing it up at all? What could she have to ask me that she's got to get my mother on her side?"

"That's dealmaking, Aster. I imagine there will be more than a few Heads of Houses asking you for favors in the coming days." Dev had never met a powerful noble who didn't need more power, more security, more influence. *Too dazzled by the glow of the crown to notice the glow of the On-High,* Rizlan always said whenever the Heads of Houses came together. Alliances were formed or broken, deals struck, promises made—all of it in effort to gain more, more, more.

Aster had no gift for this kind of maneuvering, and learning it came slowly to her. Dev had no doubt that whatever happened in the next few days, watching Aster navigate it would be grueling. "It's all part of being Major," he insisted. "You'll need to get used to it."

"I don't know, Dev," she said, dubious. "Something feels…*off* here, don't you think? I mean, what sort of *great need* could Felis-brook even have? Looks prosperous enough to me. And why would Aunt Leona not want to speak of it? Didn't you notice how she kept interrupting everyone? Kept chiming in on conversations that had nothing to do with her? I swear, Keeper Von was scared of her! She's got secrets, I'm telling you."

Dev rolled his eyes. "Who doesn't?"

"Come now, be honest. Didn't you find it all strange?"

Dev sighed. "I don't know, Aster."

"What?" she said. "What is it? You're exhausted with me. I can tell." Sometimes he hated how well Aster could read him. Yes, he was exhausted, but not with her. With…everything.

"No, it's just—Alcor's been in a mood all afternoon. He's calmed down now, but you know how he gets when his routine is disrupted." The Hemoth had been obstinate the entire way to Felisbrook.

Aster huffed. "When *isn't* he in a mood?"

She had a point there. Alcor was more and more obstinate these days. Any little thing could upset him. "The *Star Writ* says it's how they get. Hemoths. Right before they're fully grown. They get cranky. Combative."

"You mean stubborn?"

"No, I mean—he's testing boundaries. Setting his own limits. Defining the world on his terms and letting us know."

Alcor moaned, aware that the conversation was about him, and Aster scratched him affectionately beneath his chin.

"So, I'm wrong?" Aster said, eyes flashing with that curiosity and suspicion she got whenever she was working out a problem. Pity she never brought that sort of earnestness to her *Star Writ* studies. "You didn't find anything strange about the relationship between Aunt Leona and Iris?"

Dev just wanted to rest. But Aster was out to solve a riddle, and Dev could tell rest would be hard-won for him tonight. "No, I didn't. And frankly, I'm a bit surprised you did."

"How's that?"

"I found it very *familiar*, Aster. Leona was not acting very different than your own mother at these sorts of events. I found it all so…*maternal*." The word fell out of him like a bad plum, sour and bitter, and he instantly regretted it.

"Maternal?" said Aster. "What in the name of Tawn is that supposed to mean?"

"Nothing, it doesn't mean anything."

"You think my mother treats me like that? Speaking for me?"

"Well…not so much these days," said Dev. Luella Lourdes was trying hard to give her Major daughter room to rule. "But certainly when you were younger. She just wanted to help you find your voice, and that's all Leona is doing for Iris, I think."

"Find my voice?" Aster laughed. "How? By yelling over it?"

Dev pushed off the wagon and stormed over to Alcor. "At least you have a mother who loves you enough to yell at you."

Aster went quiet, watching him with that crinkle of concern between her eyes. Oh, turds of Tawn, why did he say it?

She stood up, moving close to him, voice lowered. "What are you on about?"

"Nothing," he said quickly. "It's nothing. I'm sorry, I don't know why I said that."

"Dragon spit," she said. "This is about that visit to your mother, isn't it?"

"No, it's not—"

"Don't lie to me. You've been out of sorts ever since you got back. Moody. Moping around. What happened?"

He should have known she could sense what was bothering him. He knew he'd been a miserable bore these past few months, retiring early from their nightly game of Crowns & Stones. Of course Aster would notice. And now that she'd said as much, there was no sense lying. "Nothing happened. It was just…not what I thought it would be."

"Was she unkind to you?" Aster's lip was curling, as if she were ready to fight someone. He couldn't help but appreciate it a little.

"No," said Dev. "She was very kind to me. She was just…distant. Formal. She didn't know me. At all. And it hurt to see it in her eyes. At least in my mind she could be my mother. In real life there's no avoiding what she really is."

"What's that?"

"She's…a stranger. "

Aster laughed. "Well, of course she is. That's what you call someone you've never met before. A stranger!"

Dev felt his neck flash hot with anger. "You're not supposed to say it about your mother," he said darkly.

"Wish I could say it about mine! Then maybe she wouldn't feel the need to go on about marriage all the time. Honestly, Dev, you don't know how lucky you are to have some distance from yours."

Dev blinked. He couldn't decide if he wanted to scream at her or simply turn and leave.

Of all the insensitive, ignorant, privileged things Aster Lourdes had said to Dev in their life together, this had to be the worst. Did she really think he wouldn't have given up everything for just one unguarded, raw screaming match with his own mother about who he should marry? Did she really think a few disagreements with her own mother was worse than having no mother at all?

He opened his mouth to shout exactly that, but stopped when he saw she wasn't listening. Her head was turned, focused on something happening on the far side of the castle. "Yes, of course," he hissed anyway, furiously. "I'm a very lucky sod, no need to talk about it further. Thank the On-High for the wisdom of Major Lourdes, for now I can appreciate my great motherless fortune. However will I repay you for all—"

"She's leaving again," Aster said.

She hadn't heard one single word he'd said. Just like he'd

known she wouldn't. He looked toward the movement that had pulled Aster's attention—a girl in a cloak. Beside her, he caught the faintest glimpse of a large catlike shadow. Iris Goreman and Sileria.

"Well, go on," he said, annoyed. "Off on another adventure. Follow the Lynx queen and see what sort of trouble is waiting for you in the forests of Felisbrook. I have chores to tend to."

"I'll need Alcor."

"You must be joking." But he could tell by the look on her face she was deadly serious. "You want to take Alcor through the streets of Felisbrook? You'll cause a scene!"

"Iris is bringing Sileria."

From what he'd seen of the two briefly, he was pretty sure it was Sileria bringing Iris.

"Alcor needs to rest," said Dev, with as much authority as he could muster.

It meant nothing to Aster. "What do you think, Alcor?" she said, turning to the Hemoth. "Up for a bit of excitement?"

Alcor swung his head happily from side to side and Aster grinned at Dev triumphantly.

"Iris!" she shouted, hurrying after the shadow, Alcor hurrying after Aster.

"No, hang on," said Dev, following behind. "Aster, I said no!"

The Lynx queen and Sileria stopped at a corner of the curtain wall.

"Iris, wait for us!"

"Us?" hissed Dev. Of course, he knew it was too late now.

"Major Lourdes," said Iris, with an awkward bow.

Aster nodded politely, and there was a new bounce to her step, the promise of an interesting evening filling her with exhilaration, Dev's personal problems already a distant memory. "Where are you headed this evening?"

"We're just—" Iris looked down at the lynx. The lynx stared at

Alcor, who was swaying happily beside Aster. "Sileria likes to venture out around this time, check on her forest."

"And the star, no doubt," said Aster.

Iris eyed Aster a moment, and Dev couldn't help but notice that her eyes weren't on the ground now. Finally, she smiled, amused. "Indeed."

"May we join you?" said Aster.

Iris looked up at the Manor, her lips pursed in thought. "I don't know. Leona said—"

"I won't tell," said Aster quickly. "What my aunt Leona doesn't know"—she put emphasis on the word *aunt*, claiming Leona as her own, not Iris's, and Dev couldn't help but be impressed at the strategy—"won't hurt her. Besides," said Aster, "we queens know how to keep a secret."

Iris shook her head, and Dev thought she was trying not to laugh. But then she glanced up at the Manor again, and Dev watched her mirth fall away. "What in the name of Thorn…"

Dev and Aster looked up as a shadow drifted across the courtyard. There, in the sky, just beneath the clouds, a great beast circled, black as night, with wings broad enough to blot out the moon.

A Shadow Dragon.

It dipped sideways and dropped, moving fast toward the Manor.

No. Not just any Shadow Dragon—Umbra. The High Beast of Dracogart.

Aster smiled. "Looks like Quintin's arrived."

*The Follies: The weakest of the moon's minions, no larger than a child, and incorporeal in form, the Follies speak in riddles and delight in confusion, bent on the torment of the minds of men.*

—KEEPER KALAMITY,
*A Compendium of Nightlocks*

 SIX

MARMORAL was fast asleep, her weight and heat warming Bernadine's toes through her boots. Bernadine had stopped reading Keeper Kalamity—Keeper Gwyn had left the Bear Holding hours ago, and the lamps had dimmed to nothing, so that Bernadine could hardly make out the words. She settled for watching the sky instead, stars blinking to life across the inky dark. And the moon. Silent, yawning, waiting.

"I know you're back there," Bernadine whispered. "I know you can see me."

The *you* she'd found herself talking to lately was no one in particular, but everyone at the same time—the Nightlock that had come to her aunt's rooms that night in Tawnshire. The Nightlock characters written about in Keeper Kalamity. Her father...He was there. She knew he was. Trapped behind the Moon Door, damned for all eternity.

On a night like this, when the door was open—could he escape? And if he did...would he come for her?

Bernadine shuddered at the thought, the same one that so often found her when she lay awake at night. Either she wanted him to escape the Nightlocks...or she didn't. She wasn't sure which was worse.

She'd thought about writing all this to Aster. About putting her tangled thoughts concerning her father to the page, sharing them with someone who knew him. If anyone could understand the bone-deep love of a father, it was Aster Lourdes. Her cousin hardly breathed before asking how her father would have breathed himself.

But shame kept Bernadine from being honest. Just like it kept her from joining her cousin and the rest of the Highen in Felisbrook for the Shooting Star Parade. And she had no idea if that shame would ever leave her.

She suspected it would not.

Marmoral shifted at Bernadine's feet. When she looked, the little bear was writhing, as if running in her sleep. The white cub chuffed and whimpered. A frightened sound. Bernadine reached down, pressing her palm to the High Beast's back, hoping to calm her.

But the cub started, jolted awake at the touch. She blinked up at Bernadine. And then she turned away—looking to the moon.

Bernadine followed Marmoral's gaze, followed it to the door to death, and saw it bleeding—

*Oozing—*

Black, fluid shadows, deeper than midnight, poured from the Moon Door as ink from a bottle, spilling out across the sky.

Marmoral pressed herself close to Bernadine, trying to disappear inside her skirts, to hide from whatever poison was pouring out over the Highen.

Bernadine watched as the oozing shadows shifted and writhed, taking shape—winged shape—one, then two, then three. They soared across the sky in a southeasterly direction.

Nightlocks.

Bigger than Bernadine could ever have imagined.

And then the flood.

Smaller shapes, dark little lumps of evil, tumbled forth, spilling out of the Moon Door and raining down to earth as they tried to follow the same path as the first three.

Felisbrook lay to the southeast.

*Aster!*

Bernadine scrambled to her feet, Keeper Kalamity's tales gripped in her hands, heart pounding in her chest.

The Moon Demons. They had come, just like she'd known they would.

"Marmoral," Bernadine breathed, the bear still pressing against her shins, "we'll have to go. To Felisbrook. We have to go warn Aster."

*A hungry hound will eagerly follow a closed fist, never suspecting the hand is empty.*

—HUNDFORDIAN PROVERB

 SEVEN

THE Shadow Dragon had grown. It landed, silent as a feather, on the cobbles of the courtyard at Thorn Manner. When last Aster had seen Umbra, she was the size of a large horse. Now the young Shadow Dragon stood taller than the Major's carriage.

"On-High be praised," breathed Iris Goreman beside Aster. "She's bigger since the Northern Crowning, isn't she?"

Alcor pushed between Aster and Dev, cooing happily, *bope bope bope*, and sniffing at the air around Umbra. She watched him, narrowed yellow eyes gleaming, before finally emitting a happy shriek.

"Flew here all by your lonesome, did you?" said Aster, standing before the beast.

"No, I'm here!" called a familiar voice.

Aster's heart swelled. She hurried around the back of the dragon to find a boy hanging from the sharp, scaly spines.

"Quintin Wyvern!" she cried. "As I live and breathe!"

He grunted, struggling to stretch his leg toward Umbra's tail for purchase.

"Do you need some help?" asked Dev.

"I can manage," said Quintin, though it hardly seemed true. He hadn't been very adept at getting on and off Umbra back when she was a horse's size. Now it was much trickier, and he was clearly still learning. He wore a black scalecoat and a woolen cloak and clutched a brown leather satchel.

"Is that all you brought with you?" said Aster, a bit envious. "A dragon, a cloak, and a satchel? Doesn't a king need an entourage?"

With a yelp, Quintin released the spines and slid down the dragon's side, landing hard on the ground. Aster noticed Iris Goreman raising an eyebrow. The lynx by her side watched the new arrivals carefully, ear twitching.

"They'll be here," Quintin said. "They're coming up the main road now." He dusted off his scalecoat and stood before Aster, a warm smile on his face. "Major Lourdes," he said, holding out his arms.

Aster jumped onto her old friend, hugging him tight. He was cold from his flight, ice crystals flaking off his coat, but he was solid. Real. Here with her after so long.

"It's so good to see you, Quintin!" she said, squeezing.

"King Wyvern," said Dev, with pretend formality.

Quintin laughed. "King Wyvern! Do I have to call you Honorable High Keeper, then?"

As Dev and Quintin embraced, Aster noticed Iris standing awkwardly to the side. She was chewing on a strand of her hair, eyes flitting from the Manor, to Quintin, to the dragon, to the Manor. Probably waiting for Aunt Leona to materialize and formally introduce her.

Aster hooked her arm in Iris's, not giving the Lynx queen a chance to argue, and ushered her forward. "King Wyvern of Dracogart," said Aster, "may I present Queen Iris Goreman of Felisbrook?"

Quintin bowed—it was a most gentlemanly bow, confident and chivalrous, not at all Quintin's usual shy style. Whatever etiquette they were teaching him in Dracogart was working. It seemed the crown agreed with him. "Queen Iris, I am most honored to have been invited to join you in Felisbrook."

Iris curtsied, quickly and awkwardly. "The honor is mine, King Wyvern."

"You're just in time, Quintin," said Aster, still holding tight to Iris's arm—the Lynx queen was slippery, and Aster didn't intend to let her get away. "Iris was just going to take us into the Deadwood to see the fallen star."

"Aster." Dev's voice carried a warning tone, but she ignored him.

But Quintin didn't miss it. He frowned. "You're not about to get us all in trouble, are you, Major Lourdes?"

"Who? *Me?*" She waved a hand. "Never."

Quintin laughed. "Well, if *you're* not about to get us in trouble, then I'm sure Lorc Conri will. The Hundford caravan is coming up the main road with the Dracogart retinue. They'll be here any minute."

Lorc Conri. It had been so long since she'd seen him last.

At the Northern Crowning, after she was named Major, everything had been so busy—there'd been no time for proper goodbyes. He'd written exactly twice. The letters were brief. Writing was not his talent. She missed talking to him, unguarded and equal, like they had in the Shiver Woods what felt like ages ago.

Here, in the Deadwood of Felisbrook, maybe they could be like that again.

Lorc would understand her suspicions of Leona. He was suspicious by nature. He wouldn't brush off what she'd heard—he would help her to figure out what was going on in the Kingdom of the Lynx.

Barely able to contain her excitement, Aster ran to the gates and saw the caravans coming up the main road toward the castle. It was just as Quintin said. Ornate obsidian carriages from Dracogart with sleek black horses jostled alongside the rickety wooden wagons, chestnut stallions, and hordes of boisterous hunting dogs from Hundford.

The two caravans crashed upon Thorn Manor like a sudden tide, the grounds instantly filled to bursting with Shade Guards and

Hermans, Hound Guards and hunting dogs of every size, shape, and color. They spilled out onto the streets of Felisbrook, wagons and carriages blocking the road.

Thorn Manor was well and truly full now, as was Felisbrook Town. Dignitaries and nobles who had come from all over the Highen mingled with the commoners of Felisbrook; musicians and minstrels, bakers and cooks set up to entertain and feed the gathering crowds. With the sun nearly set, torches were lit along the curtain wall of the Manor and outside along the flagged streets of Felisbrook. In what seemed like no time at all, the entire city was alive with a spontaneous celebration, a welcoming party for the weary travelers.

"Now's our best chance," Aster said. "No one will miss us in this press. Lorc'll have to catch us up later. But leave the beasts—you're right, Dev. We can't get through unnoticed with them now."

Aster slipped from the castle courtyard with the other children. Iris kept her shoulders hunched, making herself smaller, almost insignificant. Aster kept close to her, afraid Iris might disappear in the jumble altogether. The Great Lynx Sileria padded by Iris's side, and Aster couldn't help but note the advantage of being paired with a small High Beast, a quiet little lynx making herself as noticeable as a whisper. It was easy for them to move about without drawing attention.

Every dog that ran by, Aster stopped to look twice, eager to see a Starhound and the attendant Conri boys. But every dog was only a common mongrel. The Starhound pack must have been farther down the convoy.

"Tawn be praised," said Dev, marveling at the massive line of Dracogart carriages. "Did you bring the entire kingdom with you, Quintin?"

Quintin sighed. "Just about. It's a fallen star. Do you know how sacred this is to Dracogart?"

Dev looked confused. "It's sacred for the whole of the Highen."

"Yes, because of the star," said Quintin. "But it's not just about that for us. It's also about the Dust Dragons."

"Dust Dragons?" Aster had never heard of such a thing.

Quintin nodded. "No one's seen them for over two hundred years. They're attracted to the star's holy energy."

Aster looked at Iris. "Have you seen them?"

She nodded, nervous eyes flitting about the crowds. "I'll show you."

"You've seen them!" said Quintin, bursting with excitement. "What was it like? Were you there for their emergence? Were they flocking? Did they have visible wings or just the suggestion of wings?"

Iris shrugged, not liking the sudden attention. "I didn't see any wings."

"No wings? I expected as much. The few illustrations we have of them from the last star, well, the artist included wings, but that never made much sense to me, given that they are built almost like clouds—well, so they say!" Quintin's interest in the Dust Dragons was too strong for him to notice Iris's discomfort. "The whole of Dracogart is on pins and needles waiting to learn more about them. It's really a once-in-a-lifetime spectacle!" Quintin stopped beside one of the scaly wagons, the whole thing decorated with carefully carved scales of glassy obsidian that glinted in the torchlight. "That's why we bring so much in the way of treats."

"Treats?" Aster's stomach grumbled.

Quintin climbed up onto the carriage, unnoticed in the general throng. It was filled with barrels made of black creeper larch. He pried the lid off the first barrel and fished out what looked to be a little round fruit—it was like a plum, but black as coal, and glistening with whatever juice it had been soaking in inside the barrel.

Iris's eyes went wide, suddenly focused on Quintin. "Is that a shadow plum?"

Quintin grinned, happy she knew what it was. "It *is* a shadow plum! Dracogart's specialty."

"I've never heard of a shadow plum," said Aster, and she was sure she'd tasted every delicacy the Highen had to offer.

"We only get them once a year during the Festival of Tawn," Quintin explained. "They grow on Mount Draccus for just a couple of weeks. We brought the entire crop. Won't have anything for the Festival of Tawn this year, but for this—a shooting star—we had to bring them."

"We'll get to *eat* the shadow plums?" said Iris, forgetting her shyness as she moved closer to see inside the barrel.

"Oh yes," said Quintin. "More than enough for the whole of Felisbrook, I expect. Have you had one before?"

Iris shook her head. "My grandfather told me about them. He had one once, when he was a boy. When the Queen of Dracogart came to Felisbrook for her sister's wedding to the Lynx king. He said there were three days of celebrations and that the Dracogartians brought bushels and bushels of shadow plums. Enough for everyone. It had the juiciest flesh, sweet and tart and spicy, he told me." She looked up from the barrel then and blushed when she saw they were all watching her. "He's long dead now."

Quintin stiffened and Aster bit her lip to keep from laughing. Not that a dead grandfather was funny—but Iris was just so *blunt*. She'd said it as casually as if she'd been commenting on the weather.

"Well," said Aster, rescuing the silence, "if your grandfather spoke so highly of shadow plums, then I can hardly wait to taste them."

Iris smiled meekly at the ground, tucking that same strand of hair between her lips. Sileria sat beside her, eyes ever watching Aster. What was Iris's life, Aster wondered, before the lynx chose her for the Felisbrook throne?

Iris went suddenly still, standing straight and alert like a deer in the woods. And Aster became aware of new sounds in the din of the crowd. Angry voices. Jeering.

Something hit Aster's shoulder, hard, and fell at her feet with a thump. Spoiled cabbage.

"Imposter!" someone shouted, close now, and a rotten apple slammed into Iris's face, brown pulp exploding on her cheek.

Aster whirled around. "Who DARES—"

But Iris was already running, disappearing into the crowd as more shouts rose up. Dev and Quintin were beside Aster in an instant. "You all right?"

"I'm fine! We have to find Iris!"

"Who threw that?" asked Quintin.

Aster could still hear the voices, more distant now—were they after Iris? "Fraud! False queen!"

Aster plunged into the crowd, trying to find where Iris had gone. She could hear Dev and Quintin behind her, calling her name. And one voice—gruff, old-sounding—a man—shouting *"Down with Iris Goreman!"*

Aster shoved through a group gathered around a singing minstrel, and across the cobbles she could suddenly see the owner of the voice—a big, bald man, a cloth covering his nose and mouth to hide his face. He carried a sack of what must have been old food.

"You there!" Aster screamed.

When he saw her pointing, he took off down a dark, narrow alleyway.

Aster chased after him, too furious to care that she had no sharps, no blade. If she had stopped to think, even for a moment, about what exactly she intended to do when she caught the heckler, she would have realized she had no intention at all. But she didn't think, she only ran, racing down the alley until her foot caught on the cobbles and she fell face-first onto the ground. Her chin scraped stone and she winced, thinking about what her mother would say if there was a mark.

And then a laugh—deep and phlegmy. The heckler. He stood before her, and he reached into his sack and pulled out another rotten apple. "Well, well, well," he said. "If it isn't the false Major."

Aster struggled to her knees, feeling blood drip from her chin. "How dare you, churl!"

"Long live the memory of Pan Leander!" the man cried, winding back his arm. "Long live the memory of Minor Bram Lourdes!" He hurled an apple and Aster threw up her arms—

—but before it could hit her, a dagger sailed past her ear and sliced the dead fruit in two.

The heckler ran off, and a dog, tall and dark and lean, its coat shimmering with a subtle glint, gave chase, its bark deep and resonant and deadly. A Starhound!

"Argos, get back here, you great fool!" A pair of hands helped Aster to her feet. "Trouble hanging on to your boyfriends, Major Lourdes?"

A boy, a bit older than Aster. Eyes like storm clouds and tousled hair, curls in his eyes in the Hundfordian fashion.

Lorc Conri.

"How've you been, Bloomnut?"

*A handsome creature, the Starhound, with a black coat studded with the faintest glow of starlight. There is a reason the On-High blesses the whole of the Pack and not just one hound. To look upon each one is to look upon the beauty of the stars.*

—THE WRITINGS OF BERN,
On Starhounds: The Fore, *Star Writ*

# EIGHT

ASTER'S face was bloody. Her chin, bruised and raw.

Dev hadn't been able to help her. Anger surged in his chest. Why could she never wait?

Aster dusted off her skirts, leaning on Lorc Conri, who'd managed to chase the assailant off.

"Well done, Lorc!" said Quintin.

"Nonsense. The Major had everything well in hand before I came along." Lorc Conri. Prince of Hundford. He looked older now. Taller. Broader. With a face sharper and more angled—more like his brother's, King Arthur of the House of Hounds.

He smiled at Dev. "Honorable High Keeper," he said warmly, clapping Dev on the shoulder. "Shirking your duties to the Hemoth tonight, are you?"

"No," said Dev, indignant. "Alcor is just fine at the Manor."

"Where's Iris?" asked Aster abruptly. "We've lost Iris!"

"Can't say I blame her, taking off like that," said Quintin. "What sort of person throws moldy fruit at their queen?"

A dangerous one, Dev knew.

"An ally of my uncle," said Aster. "Someone who still believes in the Minor's cause."

Lorc frowned. "The Minor is dead."

That he was. But his cause—his cursed mission to usurp Major Jasper Lourdes and redefine the rule of the Highen—obviously lived on in many minds. His shadow lurked in more corners than Dev liked to think about. Pan Leander had been his second, and that had made Felisbrook the foremost of all the kingdoms after Tawnshire, standing to profit greatly from Bram's ascendancy. Now, Felisbrook was no different than the other kingdoms of the Highen—a change not universally favored.

*Promises*, Aster had said. Dev was suddenly ashamed of how dismissive he'd been. Bram Lourdes was a dangerous man in life. But in death…A darkness yawned over the back of the alleyway. Hidden spaces and nooks and crannies…How safe was Aster anywhere? How safe were any of them? He thought of the bent and crooked trees of the Deadwood, still and silent and watching.

"We need to find Iris," Aster said again.

Dev sighed. "I think I can guess where she's gone."

The Deadwood was not exactly a dead thing, Dev realized.

The trees, with their thick, warty trunks and crooked, naked branches, were very much alive—just leafless. It was the smell that gave them away. Fresh and clean, like water. Twisted oak, they were called. Gnarled and crooked and ancient, but hardy. Purple ferns littered the ground, growing up between thorny bramble and twisted roots. And birds—or bats, maybe—flitted out of every hidden crook they passed. Their feet crunched with each step—even Lorc Conri, who prided himself on being a skilled hunter, couldn't keep his footfalls quiet.

"Turds of Tawn," the Hound prince growled. "The whole place is brittle as old bones."

"Probably why it's called the Deadwood," Dev said, rather archly.

The branches on the twisted oaks were thick, heavy things, and Dev could see broken nubs where many had grown too weighty and snapped off. The trees were covered in these broken notches, and the forest floor was littered with their severed limbs. They shattered underfoot like chalk.

Dev was certain one could live a lifetime in the Deadwood and still not master its crunchy terrain.

"Iris!" Aster called into the dark, not caring who or what she alerted to their presence. "Iris Goreman! Where are you?"

They marched through the brush for what felt like ages, before finally Lorc held up a hand for everyone to stop.

"Something's watching us," he whispered, and Dev felt a chill run through him. "In the bushes across the creek there." He pointed to a pair of golden eyes glinting at them from across a babbling brook.

"That's Sileria!" Aster shouldered past the Hound prince and cupped her hands to her mouth. "Iris?"

Iris Goreman stepped out of the shadows with her lynx, her head hung low. "I'm here," she said. "And I'm sorry for all that."

Aster climbed down the bank and began picking her way across the creek. "Seemed you were ready for it."

That was an interesting observation, Dev realized. Aster was right. When the fruits were thrown, Iris had been gone as fast as a jackrabbit. He thought of her hunched shoulders as she walked beside Aster through the city streets, her shifting gaze. She'd been looking out for trouble all along.

"Have to be," Iris said with a shrug.

"How bad is it?"

Iris looked at Sileria, and the lynx's ear twitched thoughtfully. "Most of the kingdom supports my rule. The people are eager to leave behind the shame Pan Leander brought on Felisbrook by aligning us with Bram Lourdes....But there are still some who... miss the old rule."

"So they throw old fruit?" said Aster.

"It's not usually as obvious as that."

"What is it usually like?"

Iris was quiet for a while, her hand stroking Sileria's silver coat. "Usually it's...whispers. Quiet conversations in the streets about how they miss Pan, or how Bram Lourdes was right. How I'm not fit. It's quiet but...but I hear it."

Shame moved through Dev a second time. How could he have been so careless as not to consider how present Pan Leander and the Minor must be in the minds of Felisbrook? They'd received reports, of course, ever since Aster took the throne, about loyalists of Bram Lourdes and his minions—followers of the old rule that felt Aster and the new Heads of Houses were a mistake of the On-High. In the early days of Aster's rule, there had been fighting in the streets of Tawnshire, in Härkädia. Eventually, the hostilities died down and they heard less and less about unrest. But he should have guessed that just because those loyal to Bram and his allies were quiet, that didn't mean they'd forgotten. And here, in Felisbrook, where Pan Leander, one of Bram Lourdes' closest and most powerful allies, had ruled—Dev should have been prepared for this sort of hostility.

The question now was simple: How much had it infected the royal court of Felisbrook?

"I'm sorry, Iris," Aster was saying. "I'm sorry you've had to deal with all this alone."

There was pain in Aster's face, and Dev knew just how strongly the young Major meant it.

Her cousin, the new Minor, Bernadine Lourdes, was the daughter of Bram Lourdes, and she had to deal with much the same. It weighed on Bernadine. And because it weighed on Bernadine, it weighed on Aster, too. Dev knew Aster would feel the need to shoulder some of Iris's burden.

Aster was suddenly mad, turning away in a rage. "If my father were alive, none of this would have happened."

This was becoming a common refrain. Everything that went wrong in the Highen, Aster was *sure* could have been avoided if only Major Jasper Lourdes had still been with them. Dev wasn't so sure about that.

"It's not so bad," said Iris. "Your aunt has been helping navigate all the politics of Felisbrook. And I have Sileria."

Still, Iris radiated unhappiness—the difficulties of running a kingdom seemed to plague her. And Dev wondered how much she must resent her crown.

"It's not enough," said Aster, fuming now. "It's not near enough if there are people here who think they can treat you that way. You're queen, for Tawn's sake! If my father were here, he'd have all the traitors hunted down and buried beneath the Manor, that's what he'd do."

"Aster," said Dev, and Aster glared at him, nostrils flaring. Major Jasper Lourdes might have been a celebrated warrior—but he was not a vengeful man.

"Well then," said Lorc, climbing up onto a fallen log, "that's what old Jasper would do. And what about Aster?"

"What?" she growled.

"You're not your father, Aster," said Lorc firmly. "It doesn't matter what he would do. What matters is what you want to do."

Dev held his breath. Lorc Conri had just said the exact words Dev had been trying to work up the courage to say for the last six months. And now, Dev suspected, he would pay for it.

"Are you suggesting I can't make decisions for myself?" Aster said.

Lorc Conri grinned, amused at the accusation. "Of course not. I want to live."

"Quiet!" Quintin Wyvern was standing farther up the brook, on top of a large boulder, looking off into the distance. "All of you, shush."

There was a sound. Like a distant, quiet, wordless song. Dev's eyes followed Quintin's gaze, and through the gnarled branches of the Deadwood, he could see light, flickering and pulsing somewhere in the distance.

"It's the Dust Dragons," said Iris. "They like to sing."

"Come on, then!" called Quintin. "What are you all waiting for?"

And with that, Quintin took off running toward them. Iris Goreman and Lorc Conri were quick to obey, but Aster didn't move. Her fists were clenched at her side, her lips tight.

"Aster—" Dev started.

"Don't!" she snapped. "Just don't."

She stormed up onto the bank and begrudgingly followed the others, and Dev trailed along behind her, wondering what Lorc Conri's words were doing inside her mind—echoing and reverberating and twisting her thoughts and fears and anxieties into knots. He was right, of course. Dev just wasn't sure Aster was ready to hear it.

The singing grew louder as Dev stumbled through the brush, and at the crest of a large hill, the light became so bright as to almost appear as day.

Aster and the others stood, transfixed by the dazzling display before them, and when Dev looked out over the clearing, tears pricked at his eyes.

Dust Dragons. Hundreds of them. Dancing and swirling around a light more brilliant than the sun.

The fallen star.

*The heart at the center of the On-High, it beats as yours and mine.*
*It longs, it pines, it breaks, it dreams,*
*It wants through infinite time.*

—THE WRITINGS OF THE GREAT LADY BERENICE:
The Fore, *Star Writ*

# NINE

ASTER had never, in her fourteen years of life, seen anything so beautiful as this. The Dust Dragons were there, but not; incorporeal, like clouds of glittering smoke. Like the starflame that burned down the Oracle House—the starflame she'd unleashed. But no, that had been different—it hadn't *glittered* like the Dust Dragons, and it had had a frantic energy, searching, devouring. The Dust Dragons were in no hurry: they swelled and waned, coiling and twisting around a brilliant white glow.

The star.

There weren't enough words—the *right* words—to describe the sight before her eyes. Indeed, she was sure she could live another fourteen years, and more, and still not have lived enough life to have the right words in her possession. Not even a poet could capture the beauty of what they had found in the Deadwood.

Her father always seemed to have the right words. Oceans of them, cascading from his lips whenever he told stories of his adventures in the Highen. What would he have said about this? He'd seen a great many things in his lifetime—but nothing in Aster's memories of his spectacular tales could match this.

How he would have loved to see this.

The young royals stood together in silent awe, all of them rendered speechless by the floating, glittering creatures. After what might have been moments or hours, Iris Goreman was the first to break the silence.

"They sparkle," she said. "The Dust Dragons. What makes them do that, I wonder?"

"That's the earth," said Quintin. He stepped farther down the hillside, crouching down and blinking through tears. "That's why they're called Dust Dragons. They live underground, mingling with the rock and dust and dirt for hundreds of years, sometimes thousands, until they are nearly one and the same. When a star falls they emerge from the ground, carrying bits of minerals on their bodies. And when those tiny particles catch the light of the star, they sparkle."

How had Aster never heard of these creatures? They were nothing short of miraculous. She would have thought the *Star Writ* would be bursting with poetry and songs celebrating their beauty. But then, how many Keepers had lived to witness a fallen star?

"They teach you all about Dust Dragons in Dracogart?" asked Lorc.

Quintin nodded. "On Mount Draccus, there are places where you can see them sleeping—they just look like glittering rings in some of the rock. You can't tell they're dragons, just lines of sparkling color, really, but we know it's them. The glitter is never so brilliant as this."

Lorc began to make his way down the slope, and a dragon, billowing and bright, swelled up from the group, its head whipping around to face them, eyes like foggy glass. Lorc froze, and Aster felt her own body stiffen. The dragon's mouth opened, a black gaping hole in the cloud of sparkling dust. It emitted a puff of smoke before turning back to join the group.

"Do Dust Dragons...eat people?" Lorc asked.

Quintin rose. "No, not based on what I've read. But when threatened, they could kill you...like anything else."

"Could," said Lorc carefully. "So it's possible...but not inevitable." He looked at Aster and raised his eyebrow, a mischievous grin on his face. She'd wanted to see his grin for so long, the grin he wore when they were together, first becoming friends. But it was different now. He had become what some would define as—well, handsome. She felt a flush rush her cheeks and looked away, still angry about what he'd said.

His grin faded. "You're mad at me," he said, surprised. "All because I said you're not your father?"

"I'm well aware I am not my father," she snapped.

"Oh, good. For a second I wasn't sure." He turned away from her, hands set resolutely on his hips as he watched the dragons swirling.

"What is that supposed to mean?" The flush in her cheeks was searing hot. "That I can't think for myself?"

"Oh, I'm quite sure you can," said Lorc. "For example, your father would never have been so irresponsible and foolish as to think he could actually catch a Dust Dragon." He glanced back at her then, his half smirk a clear and irresistible dare.

And she felt a thrill twist in her gut.

"Catch one?" said Quintin, horrified.

"Catch what?" said Dev. "They're practically ghosts!"

Maybe Lorc Conri was right.

Maybe her father wouldn't think to do such a thing.

But Aster found she wanted to try. She knew it was impossible. But it was the chase of it that she wanted. The chase with Lorc, a master huntsman.

She tore off down the hill, barreling toward the dragons as fast as her legs would take her. She could hear Lorc Conri behind her, his feet crunching deadwood. The trees thinned at the bottom of the hill, and when Aster and Lorc emerged, they stared at the Dust Dragons crowding together, closer to the light, swelling like storm clouds.

Aster gave them a wide berth, rounding the left side of the

clearing, opposite where the dragons were gathering. "Go right," she told Lorc. "We'll corral them."

Lorc laughed. "And then what, Major Lourdes?"

She had no idea. She glanced back at the hill and could see Quintin and Iris and Dev watching at the top. Dev had a point—how did one catch a ghost?

"Dev!" Quintin was frantic. "You've got to call her back."

As if it were so simple.

"Catching a Dust Dragon is not just reckless," Quintin said. "It's profane! It will offend the On-High themselves."

Dev wasn't so sure about that. After all, he was the High Keeper, the one who was supposed to know the most about the will of the On-High and what they found offensive. If they cared so much about Dust Dragons, he would have thought there would be more about them in the *Star Writ*.

Then again, if they were so rarely seen, how much could the old Keepers write?

"Do you think they can?" asked Iris, crouched beside her lynx. She was watching Aster and Lorc with interest—obviously a hunter herself, the young queen had clearly been intrigued by Lorc's challenge. And yet she'd stayed behind. Why?

"I don't know!" said Quintin. "Dust Dragons are not flesh and bone like you or me, so I'm not saying it'd be easy. But this is Aster we're talking about! If there's a way to do it—"

Dev looked to the lynx—Sileria. The High Beast hadn't moved. She only stood, stoic and silent. Watching. But there was something in the tightness of the beast's neck—she was more alert now. Which meant she sensed something of trouble in the air.

Dev glanced up at the moon—a thin crescent, just a sliver in the sky. The door to death was wide open.

"Dev!" Quintin pleaded. "Call her back, please!"

"What makes you think she'll listen to me?" Aster had made it clear how little she cared about anything Dev had to say these days. Even when it was important to him. She *could* listen, if she wanted to. When it came to Dev, she never wanted to.

Lorc Conri, though—listening to him seemed to come easy enough to her.

"Well, you're her Keeper, for one!" said Quintin as the mass of swirling Dust Dragons began to grow, their chests puffed and the fins around their jaws fluttering aggressively. "You're the conscience, she's the courage. Major and High Keeper, that's how it works! Don't you think you should do something?"

A pair of Dust Dragons, larger than the rest, billowed out of the group, screeching and stretching their smoky wings. A warning.

Aster and Lorc were making their way through the bramble, low and crouched, so concealed by thorn and brush that Dev could just make out the top of Aster's head. She knew how to hunt. It was a favorite pastime of hers, and Lorc was a Conri, renowned the Highen through for their woodsmanship. But as Dev watched the larger Dust Dragons scream at the sky, dust streaming from their nostrils, he was deeply aware that these creatures were no boar or deer. Could Dust Dragons smell?

Sileria stepped forward, her shoulders hunched like she was preparing to flee.

The trouble, Dev realized, was about to find them. But not from above.

Iris Goreman was standing beside Sileria, her head turned in the same direction as the lynx's. "Down there," she said, and pointed at the brush around the far left of the clearing. A line of smaller dragons were slinking their way through thorns—right toward Aster and Lorc, whose focus was elsewhere.

"Aster!" Dev shouted. "Lorc!"

"They can't hear us," said Quintin. "The dragons, they're too loud!"

The chain of smaller dragons slunk quietly closer, covered by the brush, their glittering forms transformed into nothing but shadow.

Dev took off down the slope, racing toward Aster and Lorc. Quintin was behind him, the two of them shouting and clapping, but the stalking dragons paid them no notice, slithering and winding like creepers through the trees. The two large Dust Dragons puffed out their chests, impossibly large as they hovered in the air over Aster and Lorc. Aster clutched her sword tight, ready to strike should the massive beasts drop on them, but it was the beasts slinking in from behind she needed to mind.

The first of the slinking dragons, an arm's length from Aster, compressed itself low to the ground, ready to pounce. Dev leapt, hurling himself at Aster, and Quintin leapt at Lorc, both of them knocked to the ground as the slinking Dust Dragon hurtled out of the brush. Dev landed on Aster with a painful thud, and she cried out beneath him. "Dev! What are you doing!"

But there wasn't time. The dragons were banking back around, coming to collect them, more now joining the group. Dev grabbed her by the arms and hauled her to her feet. "Run!"

The other hidden Dust Dragons burst from the brush like a wave of raging, frothing sea, the sound an incredible shrieking wind through a tunnel. A pair of arrows—Iris Goreman's—blasted through the heads of the two Dust Dragons in the lead. She stood at the edge of the clearing with Sileria, nocking more arrows, but she needn't have bothered. The arrows passed harmlessly through the creatures, like birds through a fog, the dragons stopping only for a moment to gather their disturbed mists back together.

"The trees!" Lorc shouted as they ran. "Hide in the trees!"

But as Dev looked back, the dragons' speed was too much for

them—they bore down on the children, mouths gaping as they dove onto them. Aster screamed—Dev dropped to the dirt, covering his head as if that could protect him from the mouth of a ghost.

And then silence.

The howling, shrieking, windlike noise of the angry Dust Dragons was gone.

And what remained was Dev's panicked breathing, the breath of Aster in front and Quintin at his side. Dev opened his eyes.

The light was dimmer—the glow of the star faded. And the dragons—

They hovered overhead. The glasslike, clouded orbs of their eyes blinking at something just behind Dev. He turned and saw a pair of naked, milky-white legs.

A girl.

A girl with silver hair to her elbows. Naked as a newborn baby.

*Be wary of strangers, and do not turn your back on them—that is where they stab.*

—THE WRITINGS OF WIP,
The Crowning of the Major Olan Farr: The Ring Wars, *Star Writ*

# TEN

THE dragons were transfixed. Staring, calm, and settled.

Aster got to her feet, and Dev followed her lead, the two of them blinking at the stranger in their midst. Dev glanced back to the trees, where Iris and Sileria were watching, Iris's mouth agape, just as surprised as they were. Lorc and Quintin rose out of the brush, Lorc's focus on the dragons.

"Is that it, then?" Lorc said quietly. "Just like that?"

The girl tilted her head, blinking curiously at Aster, as though the dragons were of no consequence whatsoever.

"Did you do this?" Aster asked her. "Did you...calm them?"

The girl's head tilted the other way, and she regarded Aster a moment before her eyes flicked to the dragons overhead. Dev watched as she took careful stock of all their faces, all their nervous glances skyward. Finally, the girl grinned and looked up at the dragons.

She made a sound.

Her tongue pressed to her teeth, she made a series of short gasplike hisses—like compressed steam escaping a kettle—and the dragons dispersed, returning to the starlight, dimmer now, circling the glowing, shattered rock.

When the children looked back at the girl, she was grinning wider, pleased with herself. She spoke a string of strange words. Words neither Dev nor any of the others could understand.

Whoever she was, the tongue she spoke was not from anywhere in the Highen.

The girl kept on speaking, her brow furrowing and her tone becoming angrier, more insistent.

"Where in Tawn's name," Aster said, "are her clothes?"

Dev supposed it was as fine a question as any, given the circumstances, but the girl didn't seem to like it at all, because she made a gesture, right at Aster—and whatever it was, it didn't look very polite.

"Watch yourself," Aster warned. "I am the Major Aster Lourdes and I will have respect!"

The girl didn't understand, but she seemed to grasp Aster's mood; she rolled her eyes and made the gesture again. Shouting and pointing at the Dust Dragons.

"How dare you speak to me this way?" said Aster, and before she had the chance to give the stranger a piece of her mind, Dev stepped between them.

He held up his hands to the girl, hoping it meant the same wherever she came from as it did in the Highen—*peace*. The girl eyed him suspiciously, and he pressed a hand to his chest. "Dev," he said, and pressed his chest again. "Dev."

The girl blinked, not comprehending. Dev pointed to his fuming Major. "Aster." And introduced the rest of them in turn. He could feel the royals bristling at his abandonment of formal titles, but given the communication limitations, he thought it for the best.

The girl's brow furrowed as she took in the information. Dev pressed his chest again—"Dev"—and pointed at the girl.

Her eyes narrowed, and her lips pursed, and Dev couldn't tell if she didn't understand, or just didn't want to answer him. After a long moment, she nodded firmly. She pressed her hands to her chest just as Dev had done and spoke slowly, clearly, so that there was no mistaking her name. "Seren."

"Seren," Dev repeated. And she nodded, satisfied.

"Where did she come from?" Aster asked. She was looking at Dev, as if he had the answer. This small victory of learning the girl's name was not enough for his Major. And he wasn't at all sure the answers she was demanding would be quick to learn.

Sileria appeared beside Aster, as if from air, her appraising eyes taking in the stranger among them. Sileria watched everyone, Dev had come to notice, everything, with a practiced, detached focus that had a way of making him feel less than adequate. But this was not the gaze Sileria used on Seren now. The lynx's eyes were wide— was that fear? Dev's nerves fired beneath his skin.

Iris appeared behind the lynx, and she watched the High Beast warily, clearly aware of the same shift in Sileria that Dev had noticed. "I don't think the girl is from Felisbrook," she offered. "I've never heard language like that here."

"No," agreed Dev. "I don't think so either."

"Then where!" said Aster. "And *why* doesn't she have clothes?"

Where indeed? He'd never heard a tongue like that, not ever, and he'd been acquainted with all the official languages of the Highen. Whatever the girl, Seren, was speaking, it was either not of the Highen, or so obscure as to be completely unknown. Either answer would have surprised him. For a language to go completely undocumented by the *Star Writ* ... But if she was not of the Highen, then where exactly had she come from?

The girl, Seren, for her part, seemed to have lost interest in a conversation that she couldn't understand, and she began to pick her way through the brambles, back toward the swirling dragons.

"In Hundford," said Lorc, watching her go, "they tell stories about a pair of sisters raised by wild Starhounds in the woods. Celestina and Lupa. They were naked like that. In the drawings, anyway. They were supposed to be blessed with some sort of magic. Like light witches."

"You think this Seren is a light witch?" asked Quintin, alarmed.

"Raised by wild Starhounds?" asked Aster, dubious.

Dev had similar doubts. Light witches hadn't been documented for more than three hundred years, and what had been recorded was unreliable at best. As for Starhounds, they simply didn't run wild across the Highen. They lived in Hundford and Hundford alone.

Lorc only shrugged.

Iris shook her head, unconvinced. "Sileria and I know every inch of the Deadwood. There are no Starhounds here."

"Of course there are no Starhounds here," said Aster. "This is Felisbrook!"

"Maybe not Starhounds, then," said Lorc. "What about the Dust Dragons?"

"A girl raised by Dust Dragons?" Quintin looked scandalized. "It's not possible. They live underground, sleeping. Like smoke in the rock. She couldn't have been!"

Dev couldn't help but agree. "And anyway," he said, "she may not speak our tongue, but she's speaking *some* sort of tongue. She has people."

"Who, then?" Aster demanded.

"I don't know," said Dev patiently. "But whoever did raise her, they've left her here vulnerable and alone. She must have—"

"They?" interrupted Aster, and Dev felt an old anger surging in his chest. "Who is they? Another Highen, do you mean?"

"I haven't the faintest idea. It will—"

"The Ring?" she said, not listening again. He closed his eyes and took one slow, deep breath. "Could she be from the Ring, do you think? Speaking a tongue from there?"

"I couldn't say," said Dev calmly. "As I was explaining, it could take me quite a lot of work with her to learn about her past."

"Work with her?"

"Well, yes," said Dev. "We can't leave her here, like this."

"No, I suppose not." He was glad she was willing to listen to him on that at least. If Seren was indeed from the Ring, or even somehow all the way from the Waters, then it was possible she was some sort of spy—or a Haven seeker, forced to flee her homeland in search of safety. Either way, leaving her alone would not be wise.

"Wait," said Iris, comprehending. "You want to bring her back to Thorn Manor?"

"Like Dev said, we can't leave her here!"

"I don't know…" Iris's hands were fidgeting in front of her again, nervous, agitated. "I don't think Leona would like that very much."

"Whose manor is it? Leona's or yours?" Aster snapped.

Dev watched Iris deflate, her hands ever wringing. He suspected Iris Goreman wasn't sure of the answer to that. And truth be told, Dev wasn't sure either. Luella Lourdes' formidable sister ran Thorn Manner as a captain would a frigate.

"Why does she need to know?" asked Lorc.

"What?" Aster's voice was clipped, but she watched the Hound prince with earnestness, eagerly awaiting whatever scheme he was concocting. Dev forced himself to take another deep breath.

"Well," Lorc said, "until we know who she is, where she comes from…I don't see why there's any reason to alert the whole of Felisbrook that she's even here."

"You want to keep it a secret?" asked Aster.

Lorc shrugged. "Not a secret, just…not a thing worth mentioning."

"I agree with Lorc," said Quintin. "We don't know anything about this girl, except that she seems to have a special way with Dust Dragons. That in and of itself is strange enough. But given what we know about the state of Felisbrook now, I'm not sure it's a good idea to do anything that might…raise tensions."

Dev had to agree. If the kingdom was as divided as it seemed, bringing this preternatural stranger with an even stranger relationship to Dust Dragons to Thorn Manor unannounced and unplanned, right on the eve of the Shooting Star Parade, with the whole of the Highen gathered there…well, he couldn't imagine what the result would be.

Aster nodded. "Everyone is on edge here. Old grudges are alive, and no doubt *some* are seeking opportunities for power plays, what with all the Heads of Houses together at once." The way she said *some* left little doubt who she meant. Leona Lourdes.

Iris paled.

"Sorry, Iris," said Aster. "But you said yourself the kingdom is in turmoil. How are we to know who we can trust and who we can't? There are too many voices trying to whisper in royal ears. We need time to figure out this girl and what all this"—she gestured around—"really means."

"Voices whisper everywhere," said Lorc grimly. "Shout, in my experience."

"Leona is loyal to me," insisted Iris, knowing exactly who Aster was talking about.

"I hope so," said Aster. "But who else can you be sure of?"

Iris said nothing.

Quiet as a shadow, Sileria stepped away from Iris, slinking past Dev as she made her way toward the swirling dragons, following Seren. Iris moved as if to follow, but stopped short. She watched, eyes wet and confused, as her High Beast trailed at someone else's feet.

Even Dev, with his limited knowledge of lynxes, had to admit he found it unsettling. He couldn't imagine Alcor, or Argos or Umbra, abandoning any one of their chosen companions to follow a stranger in the woods. And what unnerved Dev more was the question—if Alcor had been here, would he have followed Seren too?

"We can bring her in through the kitchens," offered Iris, gaze suddenly determined. "And keep her in the servants' quarters. That way we can consider this matter privately." Whatever pull this Seren stranger had over the lynx, over the Dust Dragons and whatever else, it was clear to Dev that Iris Goreman was going to get to the bottom of it.

"No," said Aster. "That's too exposed. We'll keep her in my chambers. That way we'll have more control over the situation."

The Major had a point. The servants' quarters would be bustling with chambermaids and cooks and porters. Any one of them could notice a strange girl speaking a foreign tongue and report it to Leona. In Aster's chambers, they could conceal her better from the Manor.

So it was agreed. And as the sun set on Felisbrook, the five friends prepared to head back to Thorn Manor.

Seren, much to everyone's surprise, didn't take much convincing. In fact, when Dev said her name again and beckoned her to follow them, she was more than happy to go. Excited, even, as though he and the young royals were leading her to a grand adventure. Quintin offered her his cloak, and the girl laughed, as though it were a marvelously funny gesture, but took and wore the fine garment anyway.

The Dust Dragons, on the other hand, were less willing to part with Seren's company. A few of the smokelike creatures followed at a distance, leaving behind the dimming starlight that the rest stayed to protect. Quintin was most alarmed by this; understanding the behavior of dragons better than any of them, he seemed to have difficulty accounting for what about Seren would make them risk leaving the fallen star, the thing they'd been waiting for for two centuries. He kept asking Dev, as if he might have an answer.

The problem with being High Keeper, Dev was quickly coming to realize, was that everyone seemed to think he had an answer for everything.

The dragons slunk through the brush behind the group and slithered around tree trunks, accompanying them nearly to the edge of the Deadwood, where the lights of the city burned. It was the light that sent them back into the trees, the glow of man's lanterns too much to contend with. But, Dev suspected, they wouldn't be too far away, so long as Seren was in Felisbrook.

How long, Dev couldn't begin to guess at. How long would Seren find all of this amusing? How long before she grew bored, as she had with the conversation in the Deadwood, and simply abandoned them?

How much time, Dev wondered, would he have to learn anything about Seren at all?

*There are two things of greatest complexity beneath the On-High's skies—the mystery of where the Lynx hides its secrets, and ladies' fashion.*

—THE WRITING OF RIZLAN,
The Crowning of the Fifty-Third Major: The Lunar Offensive, *Star Writ*

# ELEVEN

THORN Manor was buzzing with excitement.

The courtyard was ablaze with brilliant torchlight and lanterns strung along strings. The Manor's many small arched windows were lit with millions of tiny candle flames. The air was heavy with the smells of a thousand foods and the sounds of excited voices as servants and soldiers and nobles alike hurried about in a flurry of activity, preparing for the banquet that was sure to begin any moment. Aster could guess her mother was running through the halls, yelling at everyone she came across to find the Major so that she could get dressed in time. She did look forward to seeing what heavy filigreed gown her mother had picked out for her—something fine and masterfully made to raise her spirits.

They passed through the gates easily enough—one wave of Aster's hand and the soldiers bowed, not bothering to count the heads of the children in her company. But passing through the doors of the Manor—that would be different. The Manor was filled with people who knew her, knew *all* of them—and it would take only one look from Ursula, or her mother, or Aunt Leona, for Seren to be discovered.

"The kitchens," said Iris, leading the way around the west side of the Manor.

They hadn't even rounded the first corner when a roar shook the cobbles and Alcor came bounding toward them, nearly toppling

Dev with his giant muzzle. Umbra and Argos were right behind him, followed by a gaggle of guards and servants carrying buckets of food, grooming brushes, and oils. The servants and guards all shouted questions—which scented oils for Alcor's fur, what foods for Umbra's meal, how manicured need their claws be. Everyone was frantic; the children's absence had clearly hindered whatever preparations they were supposed to be making for the High Beasts.

Umbra had stopped nuzzling Quintin, and Aster noticed her long neck go rigid, her head tilt as she blinked at Seren. Alcor, too, had noticed the stranger and was inching his massive frame closer, his nose sniffing the air around her—*bope bope bope.*

It was like the Dust Dragons.

Whatever quality Seren possessed that had called the Dust Dragons to her, it was having a similar effect on the High Beasts.

And that, Aster knew, would be a problem if they lingered.

"You must forgive me," said Aster, shouting over the din, "but I am late to preparing for the banquet." She linked her arm pleasantly with Seren's, as though they were dear old friends. "My ladies' maids have been pestering me for hours, and so I really must go dress. I trust all of your concerns can be handled by the good High Keeper."

"Aster!" Dev gaped at her in surprise, but what else was there to do? Surely he saw how this provided the perfect distraction for hiding Seren?

"Direct your questions to High Keeper Dev," she repeated. "He will see to it all of your needs are met. King Wyvern and Prince Lorc will also, I'm sure, be able to instruct you on the care of their sacred animals." Before the group of shouting men could devour him, Aster caught sight of Dev's face. She was getting tired of his disapproving scowls. And really, what was there to disapprove of this time? How else were they to get Seren out of there? Let him be mad, she thought as they hurried along the manor wall. She could defend her actions perfectly well if he decided to make an issue of them. What mattered now was getting Seren to Aster's rooms undetected.

Leaving the boys, Iris and Sileria hurried Aster and Seren through the kitchens, the servants and cooks too busy with their work to pay them any notice, and up through a narrow corridor that led to the main hall with the lynx tapestries.

"Your stairwell," said Iris, pointing to the left, "it's just this way."

"Queen Iris." A voice echoed suddenly through the dark chamber. The girls spun to see Aunt Leona standing halfway up the great staircase. "I've been looking for you."

Aster glanced back at Seren—her silver hair was obscured by the hood of Quintin's cloak, but her ankles and bare feet were exposed, and the mere fact that she was wearing a hood indoors was strange.

Aster took a tiny step, obscuring Seren from Aunt Leona's view, though the fearsome woman hardly seemed interested in what Aster was sure she took to be a servant girl. Leona's deep-set eyes fixed on Iris.

"You did not attend our scheduled meeting in the East Tower."

"Er, yes," said Iris, moving to go. "I've just been helping our Major....I'll be with you in a moment."

"Queen Iris," Aunt Leona said firmly. "I must speak with you now."

"Yes, of course," said Iris, ushering Aster and Seren to the stairwell. "Let me finish here with Major Lourdes and I will come meet you in—"

"I'm afraid I must insist." Lady Leona's voice was quiet but firm, a purr that carried just the slightest hint of a threat. "The matter is of great urgency."

Iris's hands began to fidget. Aster knew if she pressed the matter, she would risk Leona's ire. "Thank you very much for a marvelous tour of your fine city, Queen Iris," said Aster, as formally as she could. "Forgive me, Aunt Leona, for detaining your queen; there is just so much of Felisbrook I was eager to see. I realize now I have kept her from her duties for far too long."

"Not at all, Major Lourdes," said Aunt Leona, though her tone and sneer said otherwise. Her eyes flicked past Aster to Seren, who swayed like a child, waiting for further instruction. "Who is that?"

"Who?" said Aster, feigning confusion. "Oh, that's Sssss…" Her mind raced, hunting for a name that sounded like something the common girls of Tawnshire would have. "Sil…my lady's maid, Sil." Aunt Leona's eyes narrowed, regarding Seren with increasing suspicion. Aster made a small curtsy. "Sil is to help me dress for tonight's events. I must take my leave now."

She spun on her heel and pulled Seren along to the stairwell, leaving Iris alone to face her aunt. If Leona was even a little bit like her own mother, Aster wasn't at all sure that had been enough to satisfy her suspicions. She could only hope the matter Leona needed to speak to Iris about so urgently proved to be a bigger distraction. Where exactly Leona got the nerve to speak to her queen that way, Aster would never understand.

Then again, Dev was right in that it wasn't so different from the way Lady Lourdes spoke to her daughter.

Aster pulled Seren along, racing up the stairs and across the open hallway to her rooms. There was no sign of her mother, or Ursula, who was probably off with Arthur Conri. A dress had been laid out for Aster on the bed—a typically Tawnshirian blood-red satin gown, intricately threaded with gold in a fern-leaf pattern to honor Felisbrook. The shoes were matching red, with bows framing two massive rubies, and heels that Aster knew would, unfortunately, hurt her feet. At least the garment was chosen; that meant there would be no one to come and dress her, as it was known she insisted on gowning herself.

Still, there was no telling how long they had before a maid or porter or Sir Rion came knocking. Aster opened her wardrobe, pulling out dresses and robes and corsets and stockings—anything that might fit Seren and make her stand out less.

She grabbed a forget-me-not-blue silk gown, inlaid with pearls and silver thread. It had always been a bit big for Aster, but with Seren's height, it just might fit. "We'll try this," said Aster, though she suddenly wasn't sure clothing would be enough to camouflage *this* stranger.

Seren was on Aster's bed, jumping up and down and grinning as if she'd never felt anything like it.

"What are you doing?" Aster said. "Stop it! Get down from there!"

Seren stopped and stared at Aster. "Sssssssss," she said, hissing, and Aster flinched.

"Stop it."

"Sssssssssss," the girl repeated. She blinked hard, then she spoke again, with greater effort this time. "Sssssssstop. It."

"Yes," said Aster. "Yes, stop it. You're upsetting me."

Seren's efforts to speak were scarier than her hold over the Dust Dragons. Aster was suddenly keenly aware of how alone she was, alone with this strange girl she didn't know anything about.

"Sssssstop it," Seren said again, and giggled as she returned to jumping. "Sssstop it. Stop it. Stop it."

"Turds of Tawn," said Aster, dropping the clothes beside her red gown. "Yes, stop it!" She reached up and grabbed Seren by the arm; the girl laughed all the more as Aster pulled her down off the bed. "Carrying on like some sort of wild Nightlock! People will think you've never seen a bed before. Here, get dressed." She thrust the blue gown into Seren's arms.

"Bed?" Seren asked.

"Yes, bed," said Aster.

Seren pointed. "Bed."

Aster scoffed. "*Yes*, it's a bed."

"Dressed," said Seren, trying out another of the words Aster had just spoken.

"Dressed, yes," said Aster, jabbing her finger at the blue gown. "Dress. It's a dress."

"Dress," Seren said, holding up the garment.

"On-High save us, do we need to name every object in the room?" Aster didn't have time for this—the banquet was starting and her mother was probably tearing down every tapestry in Felisbrook looking for her right that moment.

Seren pulled the dress onto her head, still wearing Quintin's cloak.

"No! Not like that!" growled Aster. She pulled the dress off and ushered Seren to the changing screen. "You'll need to take off the cloak, *then* put on the dress. Surely this is not your first time wearing clothes?" Seren just blinked at her, not understanding. Aster growled. "Fine, then! Observe." She gathered up her red gown—a gown she truly despised, and her mother knew very well that she despised it—and ducked behind the screen. She pulled off her frock and hung it over the top. "Tunic off first," she explained. "You will do this with your robe. And then…" She hauled the heavy dress over her head, grateful there were no chambermaids to force her to wear a corset, as was the fashion. She stepped out from behind the screen. "All done!" she said, holding open her arms and curtsying. "Fashionable and refined, you see?"

Seren frowned, unconvinced.

"Yes, well," said Aster, adjusting the neckline, "it's not my favorite either. But we're not really in much of a position to make a fuss about it, are we? Not if we don't want the whole of Felisbrook to find out about you…whoever you are."

A knock sounded at the door, and Aster and Seren jumped.

"Go, go on," whispered Aster, hurrying Seren behind the screen. "You put that on. I'll go see who it is."

"Put on," repeated Seren.

"Yes, yes, good, good," said Aster, shoving the girl out of sight.

She hurried to the door. "What do you want?" she barked, hoping her tone would scare off anyone who wasn't as big a problem as her mother or Ursula.

"Aster, it's me."

Relief flooded Aster's heart and she opened the door to Dev, who stood with his hefty copy of the *Star Writ*, sporting the same scowl she'd left him with. "Come in come in come in," she said, grabbing him by the arm and pulling him over the threshold. "Finally, I thought you'd never get here."

"Whose fault is that?" he said.

"Oh, stop," said Aster. "If you had a better idea for how I could get out of there with Seren you didn't share it."

"You didn't let me—"

She wasn't in the mood for one of his lectures, especially about this, since, as far as she saw it, there was nothing else she could have done. "The way Alcor was moving for her? I thought he'd follow us into the Manor if I didn't act right away."

"Alcor?" said Dev.

"Yes!" said Aster, surprised he hadn't noticed. "Dumb beast was sniffing at Seren, practically ready to jump in her lap. And he wasn't the only one. That Shadow Dragon was looking mighty curious herself."

Dev dropped the massive tome on the bed and began flipping through pages.

"Suppose I'd stayed," Aster went on, "and the High Beasts started following her around like the Dust Dragons?"

Dev looked up from the book. "Where is Seren?"

Aster motioned at the screen. "Changing."

Dev went back to his book.

"First the Dust Dragons," mused Aster. "Then the High Beasts. What's that all about, I wonder?"

"I'm not sure," Dev admitted.

"Or perhaps the greater concern should be: What else is going to like the smell of her?"

"What do you mean?" said Dev.

"I mean, suppose we're at the banquet, and, I don't know, the nobles start following her around all trance-like—They *are* animals, of a sort—"

"Seren can't go to the banquet!" said Dev, half-laughing.

She shrugged. "Not if she can't get the gown on, I suppose."

At that moment, Seren emerged from behind the screen, her left arm and shoulder squeezed out of the hole meant for her neck. Aster laughed and hurried to help, readjusting Seren's limbs so that the dress hung properly. Seren ran her fingers along the fabric, luxuriating in the feel of it.

"It looks good on you," said Aster approvingly. "You can keep it."

"Aster!" said Dev impatiently. "You *cannot* bring her down there in front of all those people. I'm serious. She's not even wearing shoes."

"I know that, Dev!" snapped Aster. "But she needed something to wear." Seren swished her skirts, giggling at the sound as she moved about the room, then climbed back onto the bed and began to jump. Aster didn't bother stopping her. "Quit pecking at me like I don't have any brains of my own."

Dev said nothing to that, only looked away, his nostrils flaring like he had something more to say. This sullenness of his, this irritability, was getting tiresome. She'd tried to be patient since he'd returned from finding his mother, tried to be understanding. But it had been months of this now. And Aster was about out of patience.

When he looked at her finally, he eyed her hair. "Is that how you're going down there, then?"

"What?" she snapped. "You have an opinion on ladies' fashion now, do you, High Keeper?"

"You're not supposed to be calling attention to yourself."

"Bit hard to do when you're the bloody Major."

"You know what I mean."

"This is not my first ball. I know what I'm doing."

"Your hair is in knots."

"So what if it is?" she snapped. "You think my father gave a flying dragon fart about the state of his hair?"

"Yes, actually! And your father never had to hide an outsider in his room from the whole of a fraying alliance, last I checked! You have to be on your best behavior tonight, Aster. You have to make it so—"

"Have to, have to, have to. Since when does a Keeper give orders to his Major?" demanded Aster, grabbing a brush and running it over her long amber curls.

"Since when does a Major refuse to even *listen* to that Keeper!"

Aster stopped. Since when did Dev shout like this? Since when did he look at her that way? Like he...hated her? She had to fix whatever this poison was that was spreading between them.

There was a groan of creaking wood from the bed, and Dev and Aster broke eye contact, both of them keenly aware of Seren, watching them.

"Assssssster," Seren said, trying Aster's name in that strange and echoing voice. "Lisssssten." Seren was pointing at her, sliding down off the bed. "You lisssssten. Assssster."

Her name. Hissed through that voice that turned words into something else, swallowed them down into a mysterious abyss and returned them, a thousand times older and stranger than before. It made Aster's blood run cold.

Was Seren agreeing with Dev? Why? When did Dev ever speak that Aster did not listen to him?

But Dev had forgotten their row completely. His eyes were wide as saucers. "She spoke! That—that—*that was a sentence!* Or nearly!"

"Barely."

"So fast," Dev said. "She's learning so fast! Did you teach her to do that?"

Aster shrugged. "I taught her how to say *bed*."

Seren pointed to the bed. "Bed!" she said, and then pointed to her gown. "Dress. For Seren!"

"HA!" cried Dev. "She's learning from just hearing how we speak!"

Seren nodded. "Yes. Seren learn."

"On-High be praised," Dev breathed, burying his fingers in his hair.

Seren was learning fast, Aster had to agree, but she found she didn't feel that was a cause to celebrate. If anything, it left her with a nervous feeling. "What does this mean?"

"I have no idea!" Dev laughed, flipping through the *Star Writ*. "But it's miraculous, if anything, don't you think?"

Aster chewed her lip, not sure how to answer that.

"And who is responsible for the miraculous?" Dev asked, though Aster got the sense the question was rhetorical. She answered anyway.

"The On-High?"

"Seren," said Dev, holding up the *Star Writ*, "do you read, where you come from?"

Seren blinked at the pages. "Read?" she said.

"Yes!" said Dev, pointing to the words. "Letters? Books?"

Seren looked to Aster, not understanding, and Aster felt another swell of nervousness turn her stomach. Where had Seren come from that she'd never seen a book?

A knock sounded at the door. "Aster!" bellowed a husky, furious voice.

Mother.

Silently, Aster grabbed Seren and dragged her back to the changing screen. Seren hid happily, grinning as though this was all great fun. Aster waved to Dev to join her, but he had already decided to hide behind a curtain, his feet poking out the bottom.

"Dev, no!" Aster hissed. "Get over here."

He waved at her to be quiet, but the spot was too obvious, her mother would spy him in an instant. Aster hurried over and grabbed him by the shirt, pulling him back to the changing screen just as the door flew open.

"Aster!" Her mother burst into the room like a raging Härkädian bull, snarling, practically foaming, nostrils flaring. Her dress was woven glow-creeper silk, fitted and radiant, her hair pinned atop her head with gold-plated purple fern leaves. When her eyes found Aster clinging to Dev's arm, her snarl disappeared, and she stood straight, appraising them both with a cocked brow and cool, shaded eyes.

"High Keeper Dev," she said, purring dangerously like the lynx of her homeland. "I didn't expect to find you here, when my daughter should be dressing."

Dev turned a worrying shade of red and Aster felt her own cheeks flush. "Mother!" she said. "The High Keeper has matters to discuss with the Major that supersede party gowns and hairpins!"

"Of course," said her mother coolly. "I meant no disrespect to the important office our young Dev holds. I only meant that the Felisbrook celebrations have begun and our Major's presence is expected."

At a hint like that, Dev would usually bow and excuse himself, but given the circumstances, Aster was left with no option but to be the one to leave. "Oh, I am forever tardy when it comes to these things!" she said, smacking herself on the forehead. "But as you can see, I am ready and willing. Shall we go down, Mother?"

Aster linked her arm in Lady Lourdes' and ushered her out the door, closing it behind them with a bang, sealing Dev and Seren inside.

Lady Lourdes let go of Aster, appraising her daughter with thin lips. "What was that all about?"

"What was what?"

"The Keeper. In your rooms. In the study is one thing, or in the stable, but—"

"He is *High* Keeper, you should remember, Mother." Aster made for the stairwell, annoyed already by her mother's suspicious tone. "And High Keepers discuss Highen business with their Majors in private regularly, in case you have forgotten."

"He's a Keeper, Aster."

Aster turned back. "Of course he's a Keeper. He's always been a Keeper. What about it?"

Lady Lourdes crossed the atrium and cupped Aster's cheek gently. "Some things, my ferocious girl, are not meant to be."

Aster recoiled, suddenly grasping her mother's meaning. "On-High save us, Mother! Dev is my best friend! We weren't *kissing*! Get your mind off matchmaking and betrothals before you lose it completely!"

Lady Lourdes sailed past Aster, not the least bit embarrassed—in fact, she seemed to look at Aster with...was that pity? "Forgive me," she said, "my little Major." She descended the steps, her iridescent train billowing behind her. "Best not keep them waiting any longer," she added. "Your people are expecting you."

Aster sighed. "Yes, I suppose they are."

"Aster..." Her mother stopped and Aster turned. There was a notch of worry between her mother's brows.

"What is it?"

Her mother looked away, fidgeting with her sleeve, and Aster could see her mind working. Finally, she met Aster's eye, smiling in a forced way that made Aster's stomach swell with nerves. "Nothing, darling. Just…remember who you are tonight."

Aster nodded. "My father's daughter."

Her mother took her hand. "You are the Major Aster Lourdes. And you know what is best for your realm. Yes?"

It was Leona. Whatever her aunt had told her mother. Promises. They had Luella Lourdes worried.

Aster squeezed her mother's hand. "My realm."

*Eyes the color to match the purple fern,*
*for me alone, his eyes will burn,*
*with dimples and strength, patient and kind,*
*the On-High I pray, grant this great love of mine.*

—FELISBROOK SUPERSTITION,
typically spoken as the ring finger is wrapped with the
frond of the purple fern of Felisbrook, recorded
in the Writings of Drew the Dreamer

# TWELVE

$B$ALLS were a loud and tiring affair. As a little girl, Aster had loved them, mostly because she was rarely allowed to attend. But now...

Trumpets blared—the favorite instrument of Felisbrook royalty—as Aster and her mother entered the ballroom. She'd hoped to slip in, her tardiness unnoticed, but Sir Rion had intercepted her and her mother and insisted on announcing them.

The room was filled to bursting with nobles and dignitaries from all over the Highen. And all of them had their eyes on Aster. She remembered what Dev had warned her—best behavior. Turds of Tawn, she hated how right he always was.

"Major Lourdes!" Ursula waved from the middle of the room, her arm linked in none other than Arthur Conri's. He was very handsome. Tall, with russet-brown hair like Lorc's and kind green eyes. The dimples that formed on either side of his mouth when he smiled spoke to an easy and forgiving nature, while the hardness in his jaw spoke to an iron will.

"She's coming to announce it," her mother muttered through a practiced smile, "be gracious and don't forget to hug her."

"Announce what?" asked Aster.

"Major Lourdes!" Ursula was flushed, giddy with excitement in a way Aster hadn't seen since she was little. "We've come to ask for your blessing!"

"My blessing?"

Her mother nudged her. "Marriage, Aster," she whispered. "They want you to bless their marriage."

"Marriage?" Aster nearly choked on the word. It shouldn't have been a surprise. Ursula had said this was possible. But here? Now? Aster hadn't prepared for it at all.

"Aster?" asked Ursula, gripping tight to Arthur's hand as though he might be taken from her. But it was Ursula who was being taken from Aster. Ursula who would have to leave Tawnshire. Become a Hundford lady: riding horses, hunting with dogs, wearing fur cloaks. What sort of place would Tawnshire be without Ursula Lourdes? Arthur clasped his other hand over their intertwined ones. Both lovers watched Aster with expectant eyes.

Aster blinked. "My—my blessing…"

What if she didn't? Would Ursula have to stay, then?

"Aster," her mother said, a warning tone behind her regal smile.

"My blessing," Aster said, and she saw her sister's face fall. Saw Arthur Conri go pale with every second Aster stalled. "I…I…"

She couldn't do this now. Couldn't face it. Didn't want to. Who did they think they were, anyway? Springing this on her, like a snare on a rabbit.

"On-High be praised!" Aunt Leona's raspy voice was unmistakable, and the older woman, heedless of the tension, swooped in between Aster and Ursula with a glowing smile. "What a blessing it is to have such a joyous announcement tonight." Beside her stood Keeper Von, hands still wringing like a squirrel with a nut.

"Joyous," agreed Keeper Von. "Joyous occasion."

Behind them, doing her best not to be noticed, stood Iris Goreman. But not being noticed in that dress would be hard to do—a purple silk gown draped in the way Aster's own mother preferred, adorned with glittering red carbuncles and gilt thread. Sileria sat at her side, watching the group with interest.

"I remember well the day the Major Jasper Lourdes asked for

your own mother's hand," said Aunt Leona. "It was at the Festival of Tawn, was it not, Luella? Near Blue Marble Bridge. Yes, of course, I remember. He came parading through the streets with the magnificent Mizar. Don't you remember?"

Her mother blushed. "I remember."

Aster kept her focus on her aunt, unable to meet Ursula's eye. But oh, she could feel it. Could feel her sister's gaze, burning into Aster's heart, feel the ache of betrayal radiating from her. Was it betrayal, to withhold her blessing from Ursula and Arthur Conri? Or was it more of a betrayal to give it when she didn't mean it? Why had they not discussed this at length first? She knew she and Arthur were very good friends, but marriage—Ursula was barely eighteen. She needed to talk about this with her sister.

"Oh, I'd never seen such a mighty creature in all my life," Aunt Leona went on. "That Mizar was such a presence. And the White Bear, too, Alurea, she was there. With the detestable Bram Lourdes. I believe they were both being crowned, Major and Minor that very day, were they not?"

Her mother's blush drained, the mere mention of Uncle Bram turning her to ice—as Aunt Leona must have known it would.

She was playing at something, Aster was sure, and her gaze narrowed.

But Aunt Leona didn't seem to notice the shift in temperature of the group, because she went on, "Speaking of the Minor, we had very much hoped to see Minor Bernadine Lourdes tonight, but she has refused our invitation."

There was a lengthy silence as Aunt Leona waited for comment, the implications of Bernadine's absence loud and nagging.

"Marmoral is still very young for a White Bear," offered Ursula, her cheeks red with all of the emotions Aster could see churning inside her. "The Minor did not think the journey would agree with her."

"Ah yes, young High Beasts are indeed the most vulnerable, as surely our own High Keeper can attest," said Aunt Leona.

"Where," asked Keeper Von tentatively, "is the High Keeper?"

"He was tired," Aster said quickly.

"Is he ill?" asked Aunt Leona.

Iris's eyes went wide, and she shook her head behind Leona and Keeper Von.

"No," said Aster, suddenly unsure of herself. "Actually, I don't know." Perhaps if he were ill he wouldn't be expected to make an appearance. Then again, if he were ill, Aunt Leona might insist on sending bone broth and ginger tea to his rooms, which would mean servants, which would mean more opportunities for someone to discover Seren.

"Oh, I very much hoped to have him here," said Keeper Von. "There is so much to discuss—"

Aunt Leona placed a staying hand on Keeper Von's arm. "We had hoped," she said, "the High Keeper would honor this most sacred event with his presence."

"Aster," said her mother quietly, holding her wineglass in front of her mouth, "it *is* rude of him not to be here."

Aster picked at the sleeve of her dress. What was she supposed to do now?

"Shall I send a Herman to collect him?" offered Arthur.

"Oh no, he doesn't like it when I do that."

"Then how do you propose we summon him?" said her mother, impatient. "Starflame?"

"I'm sure Sir Rion—" started Keeper Von.

"Yes, of course!" said Aunt Leona. "Sir Rion can claim him from his room." She waved a hand and Sir Rion, who'd been standing by the pies, jumped to attention.

Iris grimaced.

"No, no," said Aster, waving her hands frantically. "No, he's not there."

Aunt Leona cocked a suspicious eyebrow. "Where is he?"

"He's…" All eyes were on Aster. And suddenly a poorly thought-out lie felt more dangerous than the truth, so truth it must be. "…in my chambers."

Her mother took a large glug of her wine, but not before releasing a scornful "Ugh."

Aunt Leona's and Keeper Von's eyes went wide, and even Ursula and Arthur exchanged glances.

"A Keeper?" said Von, on the edge of being scandalized. "Alone in his Major's chambers?"

Aster's cheeks flushed hot, and she wanted to scream. Perhaps an unpredictable lie would have been less trouble after all.

"That is most unusual," agreed Aunt Leona.

Keeper Von stepped closer to Aster, voice lowered as though the conversation were just between them. "Is this a common occurrence?"

Iris placed her head in her hands—this was fast becoming a disaster.

How was Aster even supposed to answer that? Yes, of course it sounded unusual when they put it like that, but what were all these people *thinking*? She thought of her mother—*He's a Keeper, Aster. Could she not merely have a friend without causing a scandal?* Surely her father had never had to answer this sort of suspicion.

"I'm not sure," said Ursula, dropping Arthur's hand and moving beside Aster, "that I take your meaning, Keeper Von." Her sister was standing in that regal Lourdes pose, that straight and formidable stance that allowed her to look down her nose at whosoever found themselves at the end of it. "After all, the Major has many important things to discuss with the High Keeper, as is the way of the Highen, and they find themselves in close quarters often. It is the way our kingdom stays strong and well governed. It has always been thus."

Even without Aster's blessing, Ursula had not abandoned her.

Was that because of her loyalty to Aster? Or to the Highen? Or maybe even to Father. No matter what the sisters argued about, he always told them, they were sisters first.

Perhaps this issue with the blessing would be forgiven more easily than Aster thought?

Keeper Von bowed, sensing his misstep, but not ready to let the matter rest. "Yes, of course, Lady Ursula. I only meant that for our Major and our Keeper to be alone, it suggests a certain intimacy that, forgive me—"

"Forgive what?" said Ursula, forcing the Keeper to shrink back a little. "Unless of course your implications are against the honor of your Major, which I am sure you would never question." Aster wondered again if Alcor should have chosen Ursula instead for Major. Because right then, Aster would have followed her anywhere.

"Come now, Ursula," said Aunt Leona, "Keeper Von only means to celebrate the Highen's good fortune in having a Major and High Keeper who are so close, who truly know each others' minds. Indeed, a Major and his…excuse me, *her* Keeper…are very much like a marriage, don't you think?"

Aster wanted to sink into the earth and die of humiliation. Never mind that her father and Keeper Rizlan had indeed been the closest of friends! Was it because Aster was a girl? Was that why they had to speculate? The unfairness of it—the stupidity of it!—made her hot with anger, and she opened her mouth to say something tart, something that would cut like glass.

A bark broke the silence, and Argos the Starhound bounded into the center of the group, leaping and licking at Aster and Ursula and Arthur and drawing looks of disapproval from Leona and Keeper Von.

"May I have this dance?" Lorc Conri, dressed in a handsome cream doublet, embroidered with shimmering green thread, appeared between Leona and Von. Behind him stood Quintin, a midnight-blue sash hung smartly across his chest over a scalecoat tunic; he offered his hand to Iris.

Lorc bowed, his own hand outheld, and Aster, grateful for the distraction, took it eagerly.

The group parted and the boys led Aster and Iris onto the dance floor. Aster could feel the heads in the room turning to watch. She glanced back at Aunt Leona and Von, who were sulking at the interruption, and at Ursula, who was comforting Arthur Conri, his handsome face grim and drawn. But her mother looked happy enough—beaming, even, giddy at the sight of Aster dancing at a ball. And, Aster realized, this was indeed her first dance—at least the first one with someone besides her father or Ursula.

"So I guess I'll soon be calling *your* sister, *my* sister," said Lorc by way of small talk.

"You know?"

He laughed. "Doesn't everybody?"

"I didn't."

"Right," agreed Lorc. "A Major has much more important things on her mind."

"I didn't mean it like that."

Lorc watched her, and Aster was instantly uncomfortable at the scrutiny. "You don't seem happy."

"Are you?"

He shrugged. "I don't think it matters how I feel one way or another."

That was a backward sort of answer. "So you're not happy?"

But Lorc had decided to move on. "Turds of Tawn," he said, "Quintin Wyvern is quite the dancer."

Aster looked over to see Iris—clearly terrified, but, despite not having grown up in the nobility, dancing the Twigatian Spring Step as gracefully as a swan, with Quintin in the lead. His form was impeccable, and he moved with a grace and confidence and a practiced admiration for his partner that was delightful even to Aster.

"That he is," agreed Aster, just as Lorc stepped on her foot. "Ah! What are you doing?"

"Dancing!" He beamed.

"Is that what you call it?" she laughed. His form was undisciplined, and he added steps where none were supposed to be.

"What?" he said. "Not staunch and serious enough for you, Tawnshire?"

"If that's a crack—"

"I wouldn't dare. You're welcome, by the way. For the rescue."

"Yes, thank you," she said, because she *was* grateful. She didn't think she could survive any more questions from her aunt and Keeper Von. But the question she had answered hadn't gone over well at all. "Though I fear you may have been too late. They're sending someone up for Dev. Suppose they find Seren?"

"Do you want me to go warn him?"

"Could you?"

The Twigatian harps fell quiet as the Spring Step came to an end, and there was applause and laughter as Aster and Lorc bowed to each other. "I'm no king," said Lorc with a wink. "No one will miss me."

She had to envy him that. As she watched him go, weaving through the crowds, unnoticed by the stately heads he passed, she couldn't help being jealous of his freedom. How easy it was for him, without the weight of a crown on his head.

"Major Lourdes!" Quintin, Iris Goreman on his arm, found Aster on the dance floor as the musicians started up what sounded like a Tawnshirian jig. "Would you enjoy a shadow plum?" he asked, offering his other arm.

"Please!" she said, as brightly as she could, though her nerves made her feel less like eating dessert and more like vomiting. She couldn't see Sir Rion anywhere in the hall, and worried what that meant for Lorc's chances. She linked her arm with Quintin's and allowed the Dragon king to escort her and Iris off the dance floor.

Quintin, astute as ever, leaned close. "Is something wrong with Seren?"

"Lorc's gone to handle that," she said quietly. "I feel ill."

"Well then, I *insist* you partake in a shadow plum," said Quintin. He led them to the far side of the ballroom, to a grand table attended by Shade Guards and piled high with all manner of delicacies and confections. "There is nothing in the whole of the Highen that can set your stomach at ease like a shadow plum."

"Quintin Wyvern," said Aster, "since when did you become such a salesman?"

"Major Lourdes," he said, "I assure you, shadow plums sell themselves. Sir Bren!" He waved to a portly old man who was tending a tower of oozing, syrupy black plums. "Queen Iris and our Major have never tried shadow plums!"

"Well!" the man boomed, eyes lighting up eagerly. "Best put that to rest, eh, my king?"

"Indeed." Quintin smiled. "Sir Bren tends the shadow plums from harvest to festival. It takes all year, ensuring each fruit is perfectly marinated in the syrup."

Iris licked her lips, watching with anticipation as Sir Bren worked. "What is the syrup?"

"It's taken from the sap of the creeper larch the plums come from," he said. "They mix it with water and spices and soak the plums for the whole year."

The plums glistened in the candlelight, swollen, plump, and blacker than Umbra herself. The juice that oozed down Sir Bren's fingers and wrists was dark as night, and the flesh of the fruit nearly disintegrated when the large man handled them. They looked spoiled. Dying, unhappy things.

"Why soak them at all?" Aster asked, her stomach turning.

"Ah!" said Sir Bren, a plum on a skewer in one hand, as he pulled a torch from its rest beside the table with the other. "To withstand the breath of dragons!"

At that, he touched the torch to the plum and the little black fruit ignited with a flare that made Aster and Iris flinch, Aster yelping. Quintin laughed and the nobles standing nearby laughed too, and applauded. Aster watched, bewildered, as the flame burned on the plum and the smell, sugary and tart, filled the air. Sir Bren handed the flaming plum to Quintin, who gave it to Iris, whose eyes were wide and glowing with the fire.

"Don't forget to blow it out before you eat it," laughed Sir Bren, fixing another plum to its skewer. When the second plum was burning, Quintin gave it to Aster, and she stared, not quite sure what to do with such a strange food.

Iris, trying to hide her excitement, blew, but not hard enough, the flame only flickering. Quintin laughed and bowed before releasing one quick and decisive blow, extinguishing the flame. Aster held her plum out for him, and he obliged, putting out the fire with another decisive puff. The plum was blistered and bubbled, with a frostlike sheen over parts of it.

There was a crunch as Iris bit in, tarlike juice smearing her cheek. Her eyes lit up, like she couldn't believe what she was eating, before she went back for more, devouring it hungrily.

"You see!" said Quintin. "There is no finer food in all the Highen than a shadow plum!"

Curious, Aster bit into the strange little fruit. There was a satisfying crack as her teeth shattered the fire-crisped sugary crust that covered the skin, followed by an explosion of sweet, warm, spicy flesh, like cooked apple and mulled wine, the juice spilling down the corners of her mouth.

"On-High save us!" said Aster through stuffed cheeks. "This is extraordinary!" She'd never tasted anything so perfect and strange, and she wished Dev were there to try it for himself. The flavors might make him faint with delight.

"It's the fire that makes them so special," said Quintin. "The Shadow Dragons dig up the plums from under the rocks where the larch grows, and when they find them, they are too tough to bite into, so the dragons roast them with their flame before they eat them."

"If this is what dragon flame does to fruit," said Iris, "then I'd like to be a Shadow Dragon."

Was that a joke? Did Iris Goreman tell jokes now?

Aster and Quintin exchanged looks and laughed, the three of them enjoying their treat until there was nothing left but sticky fingers and messy cheeks.

"So, Quintin," said Aster, wiping her mouth with a handkerchief. "Where did you learn to dance like that? Your mother?" The plums and the company had momentarily eased her mind, just as Quintin had promised.

"She was a good partner," he said. "But it was my father, actually. He always insisted a gentleman of Dracogart must know how to lead when a lady called him to it."

"He was a very chivalrous man, your father," noted Aster.

Quintin nodded with a sad smile. "One of the last."

"Not the very last," she said. Quintin blushed at that, and Aster thought how nice it was that there were Quintin Wyverns in this world.

At the side door of the hall, Aster saw Lorc, weaving through the crowd toward them. Aster could tell from the look on his face that whatever he was about to tell her would not be good news. Suddenly, her spicy shadow plum felt like fire in her belly.

"He's gone," Lorc said when he joined them. "The door was locked."

"Did he leave with Seren?" said Aster.

"I don't know. Neither of them answered my knocking, so I assume—"

"Isn't that him over there?" asked Iris.

Over by the main doors, where the nobles of Felisbrook were flowing in and out, Dev appeared, awkward and stiff in his formal robes. He craned his neck, searching over the crowds until his eyes found Aster. He made his way, as best he could, through the festivities, and Aster realized that the Keeper's robes were nearly as heavy as the crown. The High Keeper was forced to stop and shake hands with many dignitaries and politicians who wanted to wish him well.

"Where is Seren?" Aster asked when he finally joined them by the shadow plums.

"She was asleep when Sir Rion came up, but I was able to keep him out of the room. Seren was snoring so loudly, I thought I could pop down quickly before she noticed I was gone."

How quickly was quickly enough? He'd already wasted valuable time exchanging pleasantries with the nobles. "But the door is secure?" she asked.

"I'm sure of it."

"Suppose she climbs out the window?" asked Lorc.

"From that height?" said Dev. "She's not *that* strange."

Lorc frowned. "Isn't she, though?"

Aster glanced around the room and noticed eyes on them, well-to-do men and women of the Highen observing the intense conversation between the royal children, no doubt concocting nasty gossip as they spoke. "Stop looking so conspiratorial," said Aster, waving them back. "People are staring."

Another dance song Aster recognized, the ever-popular Härkädian Line, began to play, and Quintin took that as his cue to break up the group.

"Iris," he said, demonstrating admirable chivalry as he bowed and offered his hand, "would you care for another dance?"

"Will there be more shadow plums at the end?"

"All you can eat."

Iris accepted, and the two glided onto the dance floor together.

"Prince Conri?" said Aster.

Lorc grinned and bowed, dramatically lower than Quintin, in a great show of propriety. "If the Major Aster Lourdes calls me to it, I am honored to oblige…unless, of course, it's Dev's turn."

Dev frowned. "I'm a Keeper."

Lorc laughed, confused. "Do Keepers not dance?"

Dev looked away, as if the very idea was repugnant. "No."

And Aster couldn't help but be offended. She remembered the way Dev had talked to her in her rooms, how angry and unhappy he'd been with her. He was unhappy with her all the time now. "Yes, why *would* you want to dance with me?" she said. "I probably can't hear the beat, can I?"

Dev rolled his eyes. "That's a bit dramatic, isn't it?"

Aster felt a surge of rage in her chest. "You tell me!" Careful not to shout, her voice a savage snarl. "You're the one who says I don't listen!"

"Right," said Lorc, taking a step back from them both. "I'm just going to go and—"

"No," said Aster. "You don't need to go. You are taking me to dance…since obviously no one else will."

"Is he taking you?" asked Dev. "I wasn't sure, since you didn't let him finish talking."

A heat rushed to Aster's cheeks, and her fists balled at her sides.

"Peace, friends," said Lorc, placing a hand on both their shoulders. "It doesn't look like we'll be dancing either way." He pointed to where Iris was being pulled away from Quintin by Aunt Leona, Keeper Von already nearly upon Aster and Dev.

Dev groaned beside her.

"High Keeper!" said Von. "Glad to see you up and in good health."

Dev was curt, not hiding his disdain. "I am well, thank you."

"Major Lourdes," said Aunt Leona, shouldering past Keeper Von, arm linked with Iris's. "May we speak with you, privately? Both of you."

Beyond Keeper Von and Aunt Leona, Aster saw a vision in blue skip into the great hall. Seren. Dev gulped beside her as Seren swished her skirts and picked up different foods from the nearest table, trying a bite and putting things back in revulsion. Her feet were bare.

"Privately?" said Aster, throat dry. "Can't it wait till after the ball?"

Her eyes met Lorc's, but he was already moving, collecting Quintin to intercept the strange girl, whom people were starting to notice.

"I'm afraid," said Aunt Leona, her grip on Iris's arm tightening, "the matter has become too urgent to wait."

*The Esurience: The most common of the Moon Demons. Stronger and larger than the Follies, the Esurience are similarly incorporeal. They are mindless and ravenous for the souls of man. Witnessed attacks most commonly come from the Esurience, as they travel in packs and are attracted to the same thing—the souls of the wicked.*

—KEEPER KALAMITY,
*A Compendium of Nightlocks*

 THIRTEEN

BERNADINE rode hard, her white Whitlock mare's breath ragged from the effort.

Cadewyn was not used to traveling such long distances. Marmoral clung to Bernadine's chest. The little cub had not wanted to leave Bernadine, and in her haste to warn Aster there had been no time to convince the bear to stay behind without her. Keeper Gwyn would be beside herself. Bernadine could only hope the note she'd left would be enough to ease the Keeper's worries. But then, Bernadine had to doubt it would be. She doubted herself, even— bringing such a young High Beast on the road alone. Perhaps she should have brought the Frosmen with her. Staring ahead at the deserted road, the shadows of the pine forest that grew in the High Gates reaching out as if to grab her, she wondered—how well could she protect Marmoral from the threats that lay between Whitlock and Felisbrook? Especially on a night like this, when she knew there were Nightlocks about? How well could she even protect herself?

Marmoral grumbled into Bernadine's chest, and the little bear began to wriggle, her movements threatening to topple them both off Cadewyn's back. They were, all three of them, Bernadine knew, tired already. But Felisbrook was still so far, the High Gates another hundred miles of rocky foothills and pine forest.

*So far,* Bernadine thought—they would need their rest if they were to survive the journey.

Regretfully, she brought Cadewyn to a stop, and she held tight to Marmoral, sliding off the mare. They would rest just off the road. An hour or two. Enough so Cadewyn could catch her breath and Marmoral could nap properly before they set out again.

Off the road, not far into the pines, there was a little clearing. Close enough that they could hear anyone coming, but far enough and covered enough that a little fire wouldn't be seen. Her father had taught her the importance of seeing and not being seen.

She sat against a pine while Cadewyn drank from the stream and Marmoral snuggled up and went straight to sleep. In the quiet, Bernadine glanced at the waning moon. Still and quiet, its demons all spent. How many had spilled forth in the rush of shadows? Had her father spilled out among them? "Oh, don't come for me, Father," she whispered.

She wanted to see him, and she was terrified his spirit would sense it. Would see her secret wish like a beacon in the dark—and then he would appear.

And then what? What could she say to the man who had done all the horrible things that he had done? To the man who did those things and didn't even think about what doing them would mean for his family? Mean for her?

Bernadine was a pariah now.

Minor. Queen of Whitlock. Yes. But what did that matter when the whole of the Highen didn't want her? She was only given these titles because of Marmoral. An infant bear. The Highen didn't choose her. The Highen didn't want her. Bernadine knew it. And she couldn't blame them. She was the daughter of Bram Lourdes, after all. His blood ran through her veins.

How could the Highen trust her?

How could what was left of her family trust her? Aster and Ursula and Aunt Luella? Aster wrote her still—frequently. No matter how long Bernadine took to respond, Aster was quick with another letter. It was as if her cousin refused to let Bernadine fall into the shadows.

No matter how much she wanted to.

Bernadine hardly knew herself anymore. She used to like fine dress and sunny days and daydreaming about all the things awaiting her in the future. Now all those things were the interests of another lifetime. Another Bernadine. This Bernadine—she preferred the dark. Preferred the shadows of the night so that she could keep watch over a moon she never used to pay much attention to at all.

A moon that held her father.

Bernadine swallowed the pain swelling in her throat. She didn't want to go to Felisbrook. Didn't want to face all the judging, disapproving faces. Especially Aunt Luella—who still blamed her for her father's plots. Bernadine didn't think she was wrong to.

She had to go. She knew that much. She'd seen the Nightlocks escape.

But she didn't want to.

The little White Bear shivered. It was too cold; Marmoral was used to a fire tended by the Keepers in the Bear Holding.

She leaned down and hugged Marmoral, the fuzzy slumbering cub grunting at the sudden disturbance. They had each other. Bernadine and Marmoral. And that could be enough, couldn't it?

Them and Aster.

And even if the Highen didn't want her, she would serve them. Because Bernadine was not, and would never be, her father.

*Issuance: Dev—Kingdom of the Ox, Härkädia*
  *Parentage: Adileigh of the Bog Pine region, peasantry*
*Charge: Alcor, Hemoth Bear, son of Mizar*
*Guardian: Rizlan of Tawnshire, Keeper of Mizar*
*Age: The Lunar Offensive, Year Seventeen*

—THE BOOK OF KEEPERS,
The Bear Highen: *An Archive*

# FOURTEEN

DANCING, Lorc Conri had suggested. The thought was infuriating. Dev followed Leona and Keeper Von up the servants' stairs near the kitchens, Aster at his side, Iris trailing gloomily behind. They'd gathered Lady Lourdes and Ursula, too, Aster's closest advisors, and Sileria, the High Beast, who stalked behind at a distance.

His mind should have been on Seren. On her barefooted presence at the Felisbrook ball. And he wasn't at all sure Lorc Conri and Quintin Wyvern would be able to control her, since if there was one thing he'd learned, it was that Seren did not abide control.

But his mind was stuck on dancing.

Of course he couldn't dance. When would he have had time to learn? What with all the studying, and meditating, and advising, and lessons, and actual *keeping*, there wasn't time for dancing. And even if there had been, who would have taught him? Rizlan? He'd laugh if he weren't so angry.

Why *was* he so angry?

He wasn't sure. After all, Lorc had only meant to include him in the fun. He hadn't been trying to point out the difference between a Keeper and a prince.

But even if he hadn't meant to, he'd done it. Princes danced with young ladies. They wore fine clothes and moved with confidence, knowing the steps. Keepers stood out of the way.

Was that it, then? Was he jealous of Lorc? Jealous of the Hound prince, who could dance with Aster while Dev couldn't even if he wanted to?

He did want to.

He wanted to float about a crowded room with the Major, impressing the court with his chivalry and grace. Wanted to laugh with his best friend and eat shadow plums and become excited by music he knew the dances for.

But no, he wasn't jealous of Lorc for all that. He liked Lorc. They were good friends.

His anger grew from the same root it had been growing from for months now. His anger over things that could have been. His anger with Rizlan, for taking him from his mother. If Rizlan had never come for him, perhaps Dev's mother would have taught him how to dance.

The stairs came to an end at a wide-open corridor and a pair of great wooden doors, and Leona unlocked them, revealing a luxurious sitting room with portraits and tapestries—these were the queen's royal chambers. Dev was suddenly aware of how far they must have been from Aster's rooms—from Seren, if Quintin and Lorc had managed to get her back there. His stomach clenched—it would be very hard to convince Seren to go if she didn't want to. When Dev had tried to get her to put on shoes, she'd hissed at him like a cat—a big one. And when he'd tried to be firm, she'd tossed them over the banister.

The sitting room was dark and wood-paneled and there were not enough seats for the group. Aster, Ursula, and her mother took the sofa by the table, Leona seating herself in a magnificent chair near the fire, purple fern patterns carved into the armrests.

"At last, we come to it," said Leona.

"Good," said Luella. "I've had about enough of the cloak-and-dagger theatrics."

Leona's eyes flashed, and the tension between the sisters was uncomfortable to behold. "I remind you, Lulu, that you are only here because you are the mother of our Major and the Major permitted your presence. It is not your consultation we seek."

"And I remind you, Leelee dear, that you are not now, nor have you ever been, Queen of Felisbrook, and would do well to remember that you have no power or influence to ask of the Major anything at all."

Dev had always thought the disagreements between Aster and Ursula were bad, but imagining a young Leona and Luella in this Manor together—it was a wonder the place was still standing.

"Mother, stop it," said Aster, getting to her feet. She looked then at Iris Goreman, who was standing with her hair in her face by the door, Sileria seated at her side, watching. "Iris, what is happening here? What does Felisbrook need of me? If you know what this is all about, why don't you just tell me?"

Iris kept her eyes on her feet, and Sileria stood, moving to put herself protectively between her queen and the eyes upon her. "We need a Keeper," Iris said, her voice barely above a whisper.

"A Keeper?"

Dev felt a twinge in his gut.

"Yes," said Leona, her chin resting on the back of her slender fingers. "Our enthusiasm in your coming to our little celebration, both you and our High Keeper Dev—it has not been solely because of the fallen star."

Felisbrook's time of great need, Von had said.

"It's Faline," said Keeper Von. "She is one of our Great Lynxes here in Felisbrook—Sileria's own mother and, indeed, the mate of our former High Beast, Thorn."

Thorn. The fallen lynx, slain by Pan Leander's own hand.

"She will give birth any day now," said Von. "Any moment, truly!"

"And," said Leona, "we have no Keeper to pair with the next Great Lynx of Felisbrook."

Dev felt sick.

"I fear," said Von, "we've already allowed the hour to grow dangerously late. Our young High Beast will be exceedingly vulnerable if we don't act."

"You need us," said Aster slowly, "to provide you with that new Keeper."

"Among other things."

"Leona," Lady Lourdes warned, but Leona held up her hand.

"I'm afraid the situation in Felisbrook, however," she said, "is much more complicated than having or not having a Keeper. That is a routine matter, in comparison—as routine as the changing of generations."

Dev breathed deep through his nose, trying to calm the sick feeling in his belly. As if anything could be more complicated than finding a new Keeper.

"How do you mean?" asked Aster.

"It's no secret that Pan Leander was a close ally of the Minor Bram Lourdes," said Leona, and Aster's mother tensed at the mention of his name. "And as such, the Minor made certain promises to Pan. To Felisbrook."

"What kinds of promises?"

"To make Felisbrook the seat of the Minor."

Ursula almost laughed. "The Minor has always been of Whitlock. It is ordained by the On-High."

"Even so," said Aunt Leona, "the promise was made. Please don't misunderstand us; the Kingdom of Felisbrook honors the will of the On-High and has no interest in pushing the question of the seat of the Minor any further."

"And yet you're still talking," said Aster's mother scornfully.

"Yes," said Aunt Leona, "because the seat of the Minor comes with immense power. Power brings prosperity. Trade. Influence. Growth. Coin. There are many within the kingdom who feel... despondent in losing out on the promises made by the Minor."

"The Minor was a traitor," snapped Ursula.

"That he was. But now Iris is the one holding his bag of empty promises. She represents only what we have always had—Pan represented a future where we had more. With the kingdom divided between those loyal to him and those loyal to the Highen, Iris's rule is in a precarious position. And Pan is not dead, as you know. He could return at any time. Iris must be strong enough to resist him."

Lady Lourdes leaned forward on the sofa. "Perhaps you have not been diligent enough in weeding out and punishing his followers."

"I'm sure I don't need to point out," continued Leona, "that if Felisbrook is thrown into unrest—even war—many of the other kingdoms may become destabilized. How does that affect the whole of the Highen? We need our Major to do her duty and support Iris's rule, bolster it."

"How?" asked Aster.

"Give Iris a place on her privy council, for a start. We propose an official title," said Leona, and Dev could feel the mood in the room shift. Titles bestowed upon Heads of Houses had been out of fashion for hundreds of years. The only title that endured was Keeper of Crowns, the treasurer of the Highen.

How could Leona expect Aster to hand out titles again like the Majors of old? She was asking Aster to give Iris a position and an influence *above* the other kings and queens.

No. Every Head would want the same. Such a decision would introduce very serious problems.

"What did you have in mind?" asked Aster.

"Oath Guard."

"Leona!" Luella Lourdes roared. "I told you, you go too far with this!"

"That is the level of *need* here, sister."

"There hasn't been an Oath Guard in a thousand years!" cried

Ursula. "You can't possibly expect to have Iris set with such an extravagant title?"

"And even if Aster *were* to do something so reckless," said Leona, "surely you see how the title should go to Arthur Conri. It is a military position. The boy not only aided in the battle against Bram, he is marrying Ursula!"

Leona raised her chin, her eyes hard. "Keeper of Crowns, then."

"No," said Ursula. "That position has already been promised to Quintin Wyvern when old Ser Paley of Roarque relinquishes it."

"Then break that promise."

"How dare you?" said Lady Lourdes. "Do you really mean to come in here and tell the Major what to do with her own council?"

"Stop!" Aster shouted. They quieted. "You have asked me, now, for two very large things. A title and a Keeper…"

Leona nodded. "That is what we need to secure Iris's rule and stabilize the kingdom. She must be shown to be legitimate. To have power."

Dev shook his head, fighting the bile rising in his throat. "No," he said, "no, I won't do it."

"What?" Luella Lourdes asked, as if noticing him for the first time.

"Have the titles," Dev said, "but I won't call a new Keeper to serve."

Von, for his part, looked confused. "But you're High Keeper. The On-High can tell only you where to find the infant that will become a keeper."

"I won't go!" Dev said, pacing the room like a caged beast. The idea of a baby, somewhere in the Highen…of taking him from his mother, just as Dev had been taken…He would not.

Leona rose from her chair. "Well, that is frankly absurd. You are the High Keeper of the Bear Highen. It is your sacred duty to the On-High themselves!"

"Dragon spit," said Dev, his heart racing. "There is nothing in the *Star Writ* about wrenching children from their mothers' arms—believe you me, I have looked."

"Hang on," said Ursula, hands raised for calm. "No one is talking about wrenching babies from their mothers."

"No, no one talks about it! But that is how it is done! This thoughtless, heartless practice set forth by Keeper Thuban a thousand years ago. Thuban! Who, I think we can all agree, had indulged in Celeste root a little too long for his mind to be quite right near the end. It's not as if this practice were set forth by the On-High themselves. Just an old man whose writings were incoherent half the time!"

Keeper Von paled. "Blasphemy!"

"It's not blasphemy if it's true!"

"Spare us your theories on the histories of Keepers," growled Leona. "Felisbrook is in desperate need of a Keeper, and this practice, like it or not, has been the only way since the Star Majors!"

"Well, maybe it's high time we come up with another way!"

The room went silent then. All of them blinking at Dev as if he'd just pulled his own head off his shoulders. All of them except Aster. She stood, still and quiet, staring into the fire.

"Aster," said Dev, pleading, and there were gasps from Leona and Von. Lady Lourdes held her face in her hands.

"Major Lourdes," said Leona, "if the High Keeper will not go, you must order him to. You are the Major. Your word is Highen law."

"Leona is right, Aster," said her mother, rubbing at her temples. "Your duty is to the Highen, whatever the High Keeper's concerns."

Aster turned, her face a tangled frown—whatever her thoughts on the matter, it was clear she had many. And Dev felt his anger grow—she should have only one.

*Amberberries grow on the highest cliffs of the High Gates mountain range. The reflected light of red sunsets on pink speckled stone heats the berries and concentrates the juices for use in the most brilliant custard for amberberry tart. But beware, the amberberry is so delicious in its flavor that many who taste it cannot resist scaling the cliffsides again to have another bite. And more often than not, fall to their deaths.*

—THE WRITINGS OF THUBAN,
Delicacies of the Bear Highen: The Star Majors, *Star Writ*

# FIFTEEN

SEREN of Whoknewwhere might not have spoken the language, but she had no trouble making herself clear. And that, for Lorc Conri, was proving to be a big headache.

"Shoes bad," she said, stuffing her face with her fourth cloudberry tart as a Roarsh noblewoman looked on in horror.

"Not all bad, Seren." Quintin, bless him, was made of infinitely more patience than Lorc. "Perhaps you would be happier in a sandal."

"A sandal," said Lorc. "This time of year?" The windows had started to build up frost in the morning. A sandal would be just as conspicuous as bare feet. At any rate, they were doing themselves no favors by having this conversation in the middle of the Felisbrook great hall. Lorc linked his arm in Seren's. "Come on."

"Come?" asked Seren. "Seren not come. Seren stay. Seren likes tarts."

Her speech was improving with everything they said to her. She'd be able to argue like a proper scholar by day's end.

"I can see that," said Lorc, "so let's take a few for the road." He began loading his arms with tarts, and Seren clapped, pleased, as the Roarsh woman watched, unblinking. "Six, seven, eight, there we are."

"She's gone," said Quintin, and Lorc turned to see the barefooted girl skipping across the dance floor to the table that held a pair of crisp roast boars. "Hurry up!"

Lorc looked down at the tarts in his arms. "Do we still need the tarts?"

"Yes!" shouted Quintin.

With a groan, Lorc did his best to balance the load, hurrying through the crowd without spilling as curious eyes followed him. They caught up to Seren, stopping her before she could wrench off the whole hind leg of the boar for herself.

"Right," said Lorc, "hungry thing, you are!"

"I'll make her a plate." Quintin was already piling slices of meat onto a silver platter, and Seren helped herself as he did, stripping off pieces of skin and licking her fingers.

"Finish up, will you!" said Lorc, feeling the eyes of all the Highen nobles on their backs. "We've got to get her out of here before people start asking questions."

"Lorc!"

Ugh, what now?

Arthur made his way through the crowd, his jaw clenching and unclenching with concern. "I've been looking for you."

"I'm a bit busy right now, Arthur."

His brother looked offended, as though the idea that Lorc could be busy with anything was unexpected. "With what?" Arthur glanced down at the armload of tarts. "What's all this?"

Lorc's mind raced—any explanation for an armful of cloud-berry tarts would be a bad one, and when he didn't answer, Arthur looked behind him, at Quintin trying to pull Seren's hand away from an open flame burning beneath the gravy. "Who is that?"

"No one."

He could tell by the way Arthur's lips pursed that that had been the worst answer he could have given.

"No one, just Quintin Wyvern," he added. "What of it? You've seen a king before."

"But who is *she*?" Arthur said, more slowly, deliberately... suspiciously.

He had to say something. If only to make his brother's questions stop. "She's a...an Oracle. You know how they are."

Arthur nodded slowly, the word *Oracle* explaining her behavior enough for the moment. "But she doesn't wear the robes."

He'd have to change the subject. "What do you want, Arthur?"

Arthur craned his neck, peering over Lorc's head to get a fuller view of Seren. "And where are her shoes?"

"They were hurting her feet—she couldn't dance in them."

"Lorc!" Quintin yelped. Lorc turned, dropping the tarts onto the plate of boar to help Quintin keep Seren from crawling under the table. He ducked under the tablecloth and saw her reaching after a pair of fancy feathered shoes.

"Yes, I saw you dancing earlier with Major Lourdes," Arthur was saying behind him. "That's why I wanted to talk to you, actually."

Panicked, Lorc raised himself and grabbed a fistful of tarts. "About dancing?" he said as he ducked back under. "Seren!" he hissed. "Seren, look! Tarts!"

She glanced back and scowled at him, her adoration of cloudberry tarts apparently spent already, and turned back to her new interest—the feathered shoes of an unsuspecting Twigatian nobleman.

"About the Major," said Arthur. "Does she...like me?"

Lorc popped back out from under the cloth, waving at Quintin, who was hurrying along the other side of the table to intercept Seren. "Of course she does. You were at the battle against Bram."

"Right." His brother's voice was heavy, disappointed. But Lorc didn't have time to deal with whatever Arthur's troubles were right now. "Well, it's just...my engagement with Ursula. She seemed a bit...unenthused."

Lorc's eyes darted around the room frantically, looking for anything that might be more interesting for Seren than the feathered shoes. "Arthur, I think maybe we should discuss this later."

"I'm sorry to burden you with it, brother."

And then Lorc saw it—shadow plums. He ran over to the Dracogart chef, Arthur following. "I'd thought—with the festival—the timing of my proposal would be perfect. And that it would be welcomed."

"Uh-huh." Lorc snatched a skewer and dunked his whole arm into the vat of sticky fruit, coming up with a speared plum, sleeve glazed and dripping.

Arthur was too heartsick to notice. "Have I made a mess of this? Tell me the truth—you always do."

Lorc raced back to Quintin, who was talking animatedly with the Twigatian nobleman, leading him away from the table.

"You know Aster," Arthur went on as Lorc reached for a candle. "You're her friend. She's never once spoken to you of my...well, of me and Ursula?"

Lorc lit the plum on fire and dropped to the floor, lifting the cloth right in front of Seren's face. She laughed, delighted, eyes fixed on the flame.

"That's it," said Lorc, guiding her out from under the table.

Seren ran her fingers through the flame and giggled, as though tickled by the fire.

"Lorc?" Arthur said. "She's never said anything?"

"Lorc!" Quintin was back, having successfully removed the man with the feathered shoes from Seren's path. "That was close—we should get out of here now."

"Right," Lorc agreed, abandoning Arthur. "This way, Seren, follow the fire."

"Fire," she repeated. "Seren like it much."

"That's it!" He led her through the crowd, her hand reaching for the burning plum, Quintin showing them out through the kitchens. "You can have this plum, Seren," Lorc said, "just as soon as we get outside."

"Outside. Into the night," she said eagerly.

"Yes!" said Quintin. "The night! Very good, Seren. This way."

They'd come to a little side door, and they spilled out onto the cobbles, Seren all but pouncing on the plum. She licked at the flame as if it were a lollipop, and Quintin cried out, lunging for the plum and blowing it out before she could burn her face.

"Quintin!" she snapped, face furious. "Flame was mine. Mine. Seren!"

"I'm sorry!" he said. "I just didn't want you to hurt yourself."

"Lorc!" Arthur stood at the kitchen door. "I need to speak with you about this."

Turds of Tawn, did it ever end?

"Arthur," said Lorc. "I've never spoken to the Major about you and her sister. I'm sorry the meeting didn't go very well, but she's got an awful lot on her mind right now, and anyway it's not as if—" He was thrown sideways, his knees and elbows scraping along the bricks as the hulking, heaving flank of Alcor pushed by him.

The bear groaned and huffed, trying to get at Seren, who backed away, protecting her plum. Argos bounded around Alcor, barking and jumping like a pup.

"Argos! Silly beast, what's all this?" said Lorc as Umbra landed on the other side of Seren, her scaly face sniffing at the sour-looking girl.

"Mine!" Seren shouted at them, not the least bit intimidated. "Seren's treat. Not for you, you beasts!"

Arthur helped Lorc to his feet. "What in Tawn's name are they doing?"

But Lorc wasn't sure. They weren't after the plum. Alcor could have lunged and snatched it from that distance easily enough. No, it was Seren they were interested in.

"Umbra," Quintin called, trying to push the dragon back. "What's got into you?"

The Shadow Dragon didn't acknowledge Quintin at all. Bewitched. All of them.

"Who is this girl?" Lorc asked, more to himself than anyone else.

"Indeed," said the Hound king. "What's this all about? The girl—her name is Seren?"

"Do *try* to keep up, Arthur."

The Hound king stared at him, not comprehending. And Lorc couldn't blame him. Lorc couldn't make any sense of the situation either.

Whoever Seren was, she was someone the High Beasts wanted very much to know.

And that sent a shiver of worry down his spine.

*There is no creature so lonely as the Lynx of Felisbrook.*

—HUNDFORDIAN SAYING

# SIXTEEN

"LEAVE us," said the Major Aster Lourdes firmly. "All of you."

Iris didn't wait to be told a second time. The tension in the room was palpable, and she could think of nothing better than to escape, leaving the Major and the High Keeper to their argument. She was the first to the door, Sileria at her side, spilling out into the hallway.

Keepers. Felisbrook needed one. Leona and Von had made that abundantly clear. They'd been banging on about the Keeper crisis in Felisbrook for months. And Iris had put off their concerns. Every day they reminded her about the division in Felisbrook—about how Iris sat at the heart of that division. As if she needed reminding. Felisbrook itself reminded her! Why *had* she put off requesting a Keeper for so long?

Mostly because she wasn't well suited to diplomacy. Leona knew that. Iris was afraid to speak with the Major, with the other Heads of Houses. Afraid to fail in negotiating delicate matters of state, as everyone in the kingdom no doubt expected her to. So she avoided it.

And now look where that had got them. She'd made such a mess of things.

And High Keeper Dev. If he refused to find the new Keeper... Iris shuddered to think what Leona would do.

A screech sounded beyond the Manor walls—the Shadow Dragon.

Iris met Sileria's eyes and frowned. Something was wrong.

The two padded down the hall to the open air of the parapet walk. In the courtyard below, Iris could see the Dragon king and Lorc Conri fending off the Hemoth Bear and the Shadow Dragon, who were trying to get close to an angry Seren.

"What on earth…"

"Iris!"

Iris spun at the sharp voice of Leona, who was marching toward her. "Where are you going?"

"I was just…" She moved back inside the hall, trying to keep Leona from witnessing the scene taking place below. Sileria yowled quietly, annoyed.

"You were just," said Leona, "going to find that Hound prince and Dragon king."

Iris swallowed. How was it Leona always seemed to be able to read her mind? The woman watched her more closely than Sileria. Leona closed her eyes and breathed deep—never a good sign. "Iris, you need to remember, these people—those *boys*, even the Major— these are not your friends."

"I thought they were our allies."

"Yes," agreed Leona.

"Allies are friends."

Leona raised a correcting finger. "Allies are tools, Iris. You do not befriend a hammer."

Iris bit the inside of her cheek and glanced down at Sileria. The lynx hissed in annoyance.

"This is very important to us, Iris," Leona said, urgent now. "If you want your people to look kindly on you…"

Iris looked away. She hated it when Leona reminded her that her people were not happy with her. Would anyone ever let her forget? Just for one blessed moment?

Leona softened then, eyes full of concern. "I heard there was trouble in the city this afternoon?"

*False queen*, the heckler had called her. How could Iris blame him when part of her thought he was right? She didn't feel like a queen at all.

"You were not hurt?" Leona asked.

Iris shook her head. Not physically, anyway.

Leona nodded, satisfied. Her advisor *did* care for her, Iris knew. She pushed because she wanted what was best for her.

And then Leona pressed her palms together, a pleading gesture, and Iris braced herself. "Do you not see," her advisor began, "how Felisbrook would suffer if the Major had been injured?"

Iris nodded. Aster hadn't blamed her for the attack, but it didn't change the fact that something terrible *could* have happened to the Major in the city. And if something terrible happened to the Major in Felisbrook…well, it would be even more terrible for her people.

"I do," Iris said.

"Retire to your study for now," said Leona. "I will summon you when the Major has come to a decision."

"But I—"

Leona raised her chin, daring Iris to argue, and the young queen stopped herself. She glanced back to the parapet. Sometimes it was easier not to argue with Leona. "Yes, thank you, Lady Leona."

Her advisor smiled and patted Iris on the cheek. "Fear not," she said. "The Major will deliver us a Keeper, you'll see. And name you Keeper of Crowns. And the people will love you for it."

Iris nodded and watched Leona go.

Easier not to argue. And beg forgiveness later.

When she was sure her advisor was gone, Iris made for the parapet with Sileria, racing down the servants' stairwell and out into the courtyard, where Alcor and Umbra were shoving each other, trying to get closer to Seren.

The Great Lynx ran out into the fray, putting herself between the dragon and bear. Sileria was almost never gone from Iris's side, and her sudden distance made Iris uneasy. Especially when the dragon puffed up her chest.

"Sileria!" Iris ran after the lynx—but before she could reach her, Quintin Wyvern slammed into Iris, taking her to the floor as the Shadow Dragon released her flame, bright white and searing hot and everywhere.

It was over as quickly as it began, and when the night was dark again Iris shoved the Dragon king off, scrambling for Sileria. The lynx hissed at the dragon, furious but, to Iris's relief, unharmed.

"The flames are frightening," Quintin admitted, dusting off his pant leg. "But Umbra only does that to be intimidating. Never to actually roast anything."

"You sure about that?" Lorc Conri and his brother, the Hound king, stood on nimble legs, ready to dive at a moment's notice. The Shadow Dragon smoked and sparked as Alcor growled at her, forcing her back from Seren. Seren, for her part, was not afraid. She looked irritated. Protectively blocking the shadow plum she carried.

Seren. All this—High Beasts behaving like starving street dogs—was because of her?

The distant sound of screams rose up from the city, becoming louder and louder beyond the curtain wall. The Tawnshirian Hermans and the Felisbrook Fern Guard milling about the courtyard froze, heads turning skyward.

"On-High save us," breathed King Conri.

When Iris looked up, she saw them—Dust Dragons. Dozens of them. Glittering and swirling, churning over the Manor like a gathering storm.

They'd come for Seren. She was certain.

"Maybe we should get her back inside?" said Quintin to Lorc Conri.

Iris's pulse quickened.

"Yes," said Lorc, watching the swirling cloud. "Maybe."

Just then, there was a piercing wail from above: the Dust Dragons were shrieking in the night.

"What is that?" asked Quintin, pointing to the thing the dragons were suddenly swirling away from.

A shadow.

Winged and fast and smaller than a dragon.

It landed on the castle turret, and Iris had to squint to see. Not a bird. A gargoyle? The creature's face turned down, looking right at them. Its eyes were bright and yellow as flame.

And then it dove.

"Seren!" Lorc shouted, sprinting for the barefooted girl. He was right, Iris could see. It was diving for her.

Iris ran, Quintin too, all running for Seren, to get to her before the shadow, Arthur Conri shouting at them as he ran after.

But before they reached her, light and sparks and smoke engulfed them all—the smell of burnt sugar and earthworms, the feel of dust and warm light.

*Waste not your time, Keepers of the Bear Highen, dwelling on the dark-ness of the Moon. Stand in the light of the On-High, with true hearts and clear minds, and the minions of death cannot touch you. Those who turn from the light, the Moon Door is eager to claim you for its armies.*

—THE WRITINGS OF THUBAN,
On the Mysteries of the On-High: The Star Majors, *Star Writ*

# SEVENTEEN

WHEN they were alone, Dev collapsed on the nearest chair, trembling with nerves and anger. He could feel Aster's eyes on him—surely she could see what this was doing to him?

"What would you have me do?" she asked.

"Give her the titles," he said. "All the titles! Anything but a baby."

"That's not a solution, Dev!" she said in frustration. "A new High Beast will need a new Keeper, do you agree with that?"

"It will need a Keeper, yes," said Dev. "And there are plenty of grown Keepers who can care for a kitten before its true Keeper must be put to work."

"But the Keeper and the Beast must always be together," said Aster.

"Must?" repeated Dev, rising out of his chair. "*Must?* Says who? A man who died a thousand years ago? He won't say much about it if you change things now!"

"I can't just change our law," said Aster.

"You are the Major!" said Dev. "You're the only person who can!"

"Just because you want it?"

"Because it's the right thing to do!"

Aster folded her arms impatiently. "So a thousand years of Highen way has been wrong, and you, Dev, you are the one to save us from ourselves?"

"So what if I am?"

"Is this back to that thing with your mother?"

Dev felt a shadow fall over his soul. "*Thing?*" Was that all it was to her?

"Yes, the thing about how she wasn't what you expected. You would have me change a thousand years of Highen law to what? Prove something to *her?* Some woman you didn't even know existed a year ago?"

Dev wanted to grab the nearest purple fern vase and hurl it across the room. "I am not looking to prove *anything* to her."

"What, then!"

She didn't understand, it was all over her face, in the crease between her brows, in the squint of her eyes, in the purse of her lips. It was nothing to her—everything he felt, everything he'd struggled with. It was all just…nothing. And how could it be something, be anything, to Aster Lourdes? A girl who, since the day she was born, had had everything.

"Don't you understand? I don't *know* her!" he shouted. "No Keeper who is chosen for lifetime service to a High Beast gets to know their mother. Their father. Their family! Not me. Not Keeper Von. Not even Rizlan! Do you know how that feels? To have nothing and no one but an animal who means more to everyone than you ever will mean to *anyone?*" She looked away then; at least she had the decency to do that much. Of course she didn't know. Couldn't know. "Why would I do that to another child when I know how it feels to live with that…that longing?"

She closed her eyes and breathed deep, gathering her strength before she spoke, as calmly as he'd ever heard her. "Dev, I cannot just go changing Highen law because it doesn't suit you. If it were my father, he—"

"You're not your father!" cried Dev. "It doesn't matter what he would do, Aster!"

Her eyes flashed. "You only say it doesn't matter because you know even *he* would not do this."

"No. I say it because he *can't* change it. He. Is. Not. Here. There's only you. And there's only me. And I am *begging* you: If you care about me at all, you will not ask me to do this."

She snarled and stormed away, back toward the fireplace. She paced, and Dev hated that she had to think this long about what he'd said. "You know I *do* care," she said finally. "But I can't change this just because of how much I care about you."

"You can," he said, pleading. "On this issue, Aster, please. This *one* time. You can. I have never asked you for anything. But I am begging you. *This.* Don't make me do this."

"I don't think we have—"

"You don't think?" he said. "Or Jasper Lourdes doesn't think? Because honestly, Aster, I'm ready to visit the Oracles and ask the On-High to call upon his star, since it sounds like I can expect more help from a ghost than from you!"

She stared at him, her eyes wet and pained. Her nose wrinkled as she fought back the tears. "That's not fair," she said.

"Fair?" he shouted. "I'll tell you what's not fair. I need a Major! And instead I'm stuck with you!"

Her face fell—her pursed lips and furrowed brow smoothed to out to nothing. Not anger. But still, tears fell down her cheeks. She looked at him as if she'd never seen him before.

And maybe she hadn't.

Not the real him.

The real hurt.

Because she only ever saw what she wanted.

Finally, she opened her mouth to speak—

And there was a scream. Otherworldly, eternal. Somewhere outside the massive windows.

A scream they'd heard before.

When Dev looked, he could see a glint rushing past beyond the curtains. Aster was already running toward the sound, pulling open the drapes to the balcony, revealing a deluge of Dust Dragons, hordes of them, rushing past like a floating river of stardust. They were shrieking.

In the courtyard below, soldiers and servants were running in a frenzy, voices rising in the night as fires erupted in the city beyond the gates.

"What's happening?" said Dev.

"Nightlocks," said Aster softly, and she pointed to winged shadows in the sky.

Dev glanced up at the moon—a sliver. The door to death was open.

Aster ran to the far side of the balcony. "Seren!" she shouted, and Dev could see the strange girl, see Alcor and Umbra and Argos and Sileria, the four High Beasts encircling her, trying to protect her as a rush of Dust Dragons rained down on them, engulfing them in shimmering dust.

And a shadow—

—a Nightlock?—

—swooped down after the dragons, driving toward the heart of the swirling mass.

Alcor roared, and there was a screech from Umbra, and the black shadow sailed up and out of the cloud, climbing up over Thorn Manor. Dev caught the shape of it, wings like a Shadow Dragon, but its body—

Dev paled.

—was it human?

"Dev!" Aster roared. "What under the On-High was that thing?"

He didn't know. Never in all his years of reading *Star Writ* scripture had he read of any Nightlock like that.

"Another one!" Aster pointed to the sky, where, indeed, another humanlike creature was barreling down toward the cloud of Dust Dragons. It disappeared into the shimmer and shot back out, as if spat into the night, repelled by the dust; it twisted and writhed in the air before righting itself and disappearing over the spires of the Manor.

Movement flickered in the corner of Dev's eye, and when he looked, he caught sight of a third. "Aster, there!" he shouted as the creature sped silently past the North Tower, disappearing into the dark.

"Dev, what is this?" Aster said, her voice frantic. "Is this another moon war?"

Dev didn't know how to answer. The last moon war, the Lunar Offensive, had been won by her father, over thirty years ago. An army of Nightlocks. Organized. This was chaos. This was...rogue. Back in Jasper Lourdes' time, the Nightlock army, ten thousand strong, had attacked the seat of the Highen, Tawnshire. What would the Nightlocks see fit to attack in Felisbrook? And in such a small number? Four? Five?

And then a bang sounded above them, and Dev was struck in the head as clay shingles rained down from the turret. When he looked up, his heart seized in his chest as three pairs of glowing yellow eyes met his.

Women.

Almost.

Scaly and leathered like dragons, with dark felt wings larger than their bodies, talons on their toes, and massive clawed fingers gripping the roof's edge. The small one on the left laughed, razor-sharp fangs gleaming white in the dark. The large one in the middle scratched at the laugher, and the small one recoiled, hissing and whimpering.

"Dev." Aster's voice shook somewhere behind him.

The large one in the middle gripped the roof's edge tightly, her neck bobbing downward, her head tilting like an owl's as she stared at Aster, alone and vulnerable at the edge of the balcony.

"*Major…*" The creature's voice was like steam from a kettle, like the rattle of a snake. Her forked tongue flicked suddenly and licked at her own eyeball, making Dev's stomach turn. "*We have use for you, young one.*"

The big one leapt, dropping down from above, engulfing Aster in her massive wings.

Aster screamed. Dev leapt for her, but a sharp pain ignited in his shoulders as a second creature's claws dug into him and hurled him to the floor of the balcony. He scrambled to his feet, to get to Aster—

But she was gone.

The balcony was empty.

And Aster—

Dev could hear her screams, wild and panicked, as the creatures carried her off into the night.

He gripped the balustrade, part of him desperate to launch himself into the sky, launch himself after the disappearing shadows. Disappearing with Aster.

"Aster!" he screamed uselessly as the creatures were swallowed up by clouds in the night. Out of sight. Gone. Aster gone with them.

Where would they take her? To the world of death beyond the moon?

Dev's insides began to heave. And he fell to his knees, throwing up the contents of his stomach onto the stone.

Cries rang out in the night over Felisbrook.

And they would ring out over the whole of the Highen before morning.

The Major, Aster Lourdes, was gone.

# THE STAR AND THE BIRD
# WHO STOLE THE SONGS

## THE WRITINGS OF BERN, THE FORE: *STAR WRIT*

ONCE there was a crow who wished for a beautiful song. The crow longed to sing as the lullabird and the light finch and the jewel dove. And so it stole their songs for itself. But songs are easily bruised if they are not handled with care, and the crow held them so tight that it crushed the sound until it was nothing but mournful, shrill cries. Just like the crow's own song.

Without their songs, the lullabird, the light finch, and the jewel dove began to fade from the world. And the crow so missed the sound of their songs.

One day, the crow saw a star walking among the poppies. "I wish to give the lullabird back its song," the thieving crow said to the star. "And the light finch and jewel dove. I have made a terrible mistake. I have held their songs too tight and ruined them."

"Why did you take their songs in the first place?" asked the star.

"Because their songs were so beautiful and so precious to me, I wanted them for my own for always. And now, all of our songs are ugly, mournful things. And there is no more joy among us."

The star, being a kind and eternal being, considered this. At last she said, "But what am I to do about this predicament?"

"You can grant me your star magic, and restore their songs to me so that I may return them," said the crow.

The star, kind and eternal as she was, considered the bird's words again.

But the Great Lord Tawn, who had been listening to the crow, saw the deceitful game at hand. "If you were meant to have the power of the stars," Tawn said to the crow, "then you would be a star. If you were meant to hold beautiful songs then you would be a lullabird or a light finch or a jewel dove. You chose to take what did not belong to you. And still you ruined the songs with your self-ishness. And now, you would dare fool this star into giving you the songs that should go back to the lullabird, to the light finch, and to the jewel dove, only to keep them for yourelf! This is the end of it, I say. Star magic stays with the stars. And crow song stays with the crow."

Enraged, the crow pecked out Tawn's right eye.

When Tawn was left to nurse his wound, the crow turned on the star. "You will give me your power and you will fix my stolen songs," it squawked.

"But if I give you my power," said the star, "what will become of me? A star without its power is no star at all. And a star that does not shine cannot burn in its place in the heavens, or watch over the mortal world." But the crow didn't care about the nature of stars. "Give me your star magic," the crow screamed, "or I shall peck out your eyes too!" And Tawn, furious at having lost his eye, gathered his mighty strength and gobbled the crow up before it could take the poor little star's eyes. And the star repaired the songs of the lullabird, the light finch, and the jewel dove, and returned them to their owners, restoring the songbirds to the world. And when all was set right, the little star returned to its home in the heavens.

For some choices are mistakes. And some mistakes are forever.

*Do not fear the power of the Moon. For yes, it is strong enough to pull back the sea ... and yet it can never hold the tide for long.*

—THE WRITINGS OF THUBAN,
On the Mysteries of the On-High: The Star Majors, *Star Writ*

# EIGHTEEN

ASTER'S bleeding shoulders ached, gripped in the talons of the creature. She'd given up yelling at her abductor long ago, her throat hoarse from screaming, but still she thrashed. The world yawned into forever below; a fall from this height would surely splatter her to jelly. But jelly was better than a life condemned behind the Moon Door. The talons of the creature dug deeper into her flesh, the razor points of the claws piercing nearly to the bone.

She tried to think, her mind a haze of pain and terror—whatever waited for her behind the Moon Door, once it had her, she would never find her way back out. And would she be changed right away? As soon as her mortal body crossed into the moon's realm, would it be transformed into something else? Like the Moon Demons? Would she find herself with wings like her abductor? And fangs like a wildcat and eyes that glowed yellow in the dark? Would she remember her life before the moon? Would Uncle Bram be there waiting?

No—she gritted her teeth, growling away the thought. She couldn't wonder at that. She had to focus. Keep her wits on the here and now if she hoped to see her Highen again. What would her father do?

He'd have had a dagger on him, for starters. He was never without some sort of blade. And in her heart, Aster knew she, too, should have been smart enough to insist on keeping something beneath her skirts. But her mother had never approved of her concealed weapons; she insisted that it bred mistrust and poor grace, and that Hermans would keep her safe. So she was woefully unprotected.

The world below was closer now, rising up to meet her, jagged black teeth hungry for a taste. The peaks of the Drakkan Range. They were well into the mountains now, Felisbrook miles to their backs.

There was a screech from one of the creatures flying on their left, and Aster watched as the winged monster dropped low into the mountains like a hawk upon a field mouse. The creature on the right hissed but was silenced with a deep and resonant growl from Aster's captor. The right one hissed again and dropped into the peaks, following the first. There was a scream in the dark below, and Aster tried not to wonder at what poor animal had just met its gruesome end.

The cold had seeped into Aster's bones, and the air in the sky was hollow and frigid—lonely. She remembered Quintin speaking of the cold in the sky—how his people wore scalecoats, a special armor fashioned from dragon scales that kept the cold at bay when they rode the backs of Shadow Dragons. She wished she had such armor now. She could do nothing to warm her frozen toes, frostbitten fingers. All she could do was dangle helplessly.

The mountains reached higher, until Aster's feet brushed rock, bashed boulders so that her ankles throbbed. The creature didn't seem to mind, and Aster looked up to see the moon, just as far away as it had always been.

The creature banked right and circled around until they were headed toward a ledge with a large cave on one of the mountain's slopes. Aster was thrown down, hip and shoulder slamming the hard rock while the creature landed primly at the cave's opening, folding its wings before disappearing inside.

Aster peeked over the ledge—the height was dizzying, the rocks below swallowed by the murk of the night.

This was not the Moon Door. What purpose could a Nightlock have for a Major in the mountains?

She thought of the animal screaming in the dark below, and an answer came quickly and terribly to her mind—*Supper, Aster.*

No. Not like this. As a Major, she'd imagined her own death a thousand times. Usually as a grown, mighty warrior in glory on the battlefield. Not like this—barely old enough to court, guts devoured by a hungry, scavenging Nightlock hidden in the Drakkan Range.

She stumbled to her feet, her bones near gelatin as she tried not to look back over the edge. She clung to the rock and worked her way to the cave opening.

And the creature—this thieving, hideous, abducting Nightlock—shuffled near the back wall, the crunch of leaves and twigs sounding from where its massive talons stepped. The creature scuffed its black talons on the stone and sparks ignited, lighting a small pile of tinder at its feet so the cave lit up with a golden glow from the flames.

Aster's heart raced, her body trembling—from the terror or the frigid mountain air?—probably both. But she would not die here. Not at this beast's feet.

"I am the Major Aster Lourdes," she said, with as much strength and command as she could muster. "And you will return me to Thorn Manor of Felisbrook."

The Nightlock fiddled with the twigs, flapping one massive wing gently so that the flames grew brighter. When it was satisfied, it sat back and stared. Its eyes were like a dragon's, narrow pupils set in a color as pale as the moon. And never once did they look at Aster.

"Did you hear me, Nightlock?" said Aster, her temper flaring. "You *will* take me back to my people."

There was a hissing sound as the creature huffed through its nose. It shifted around the fire, heading back toward the mouth of the cave, toward Aster. Her nails dug into the stone and she braced herself for an attack, but the creature took no notice of her at all. It shuffled by, its massive wings weighing down its human-like body so that its back was bent, and its gait, with its large taloned feet, lurched and swayed awkwardly. It stepped to the cave's edge, claws gripping tight to the stone. Was this it, then? This Nightlock beast stole her away in the night, flew her to the top of the Drakkan Range. And for what? To ignore her?

"Speak to me!" Aster screamed. "I know you can speak!"

The Nightlock glanced over its shoulder, those pale reptilian eyes meeting Aster's, and unfurled its giant wings so suddenly that Aster screamed, flinching away.

When Aster looked back, the creature was airborne, flying off into the night.

And Aster was alone, in the frigid peaks of Mount Draccus, with nothing but a tiny fire in a cave to keep the cold at bay.

*And with a mighty blow, the Major Jasper Lourdes struck down the leader of the moon's armies, a Nightlock so great in its size as to match that of the mighty Hemoth, and with its death rattle the Nightlock horde was banished back behind the moon. The Highen was safe again.*

—THE WRITINGS OF RIZLAN,
The Battle for Tawnshire: The Lunar Offensive, *Star Writ*

# NINETEEN

THE pain in Dev's back was like nothing he'd ever felt—a deep, throbbing cold where the creature's talons had dug down into the fat. The surgeon's hook penetrated his flesh, working to sew the wound together. The agony was horrible.

But it was nothing compared to what he was feeling in his soul.

He should have seen it. Should have known this would happen. His vision—a moon swallowed by the starry image of Tawn. Was it trying to warn him about the Nightlocks?

He sat in a chair by the fireplace, gripping the arms as the surgeon worked. Aster's chair. Aster's fireplace. Aster's rooms. The rooms the creature stole her from. And Dev had been powerless to stop it.

"Tell us again," Ursula was saying. "What exactly did the creature say, Dev?"

People had convened around him in the hours since Aster was taken. Lorc Conri had been the one to find him, bleeding and draped over the balustrade. Arthur Conri and Ursula Lourdes had appeared almost at the same time, and the three had dragged Dev inside, Ursula sending Lorc for the surgeon and Arthur for the two Ladies Lourdes. Soon after, there was a great flurry of activity, but Dev had barely noticed. The pain had swallowed him up, rendering it hard to make sense of anything around him. Eventually he became aware of the frantic voices of Luella Lourdes and Lady

Leona, of the stammering nervousness of Keeper Von. There were Hermans, and Shade Guards. Hundfordian soldiers. And always Lorc Conri, pacing like a caged dog.

All of it because Aster Lourdes, the Major, was gone.

What had Dev said to her before the creatures attacked?

*I need a Major!*

And the last ones he'd spoken before she was ripped away?

*Instead I'm stuck with you.*

"Dev," Ursula said again, crouching before him. "What exactly did the creature say?"

He winced as the surgeon dug in again. "It said, *We have use for you.*"

Ursula took hold of his hand. "Those were its exact words?"

He thought a moment, trying to remember. He'd been so focused on those eyes—yellow, inhuman.

"It...it whispered *Major* first. And then it said, *We have use for you, young one.*"

"What use?" demanded Luella Lourdes. "Devils and their riddles! What do the beasts want with the Major?"

Dev shook his head, at a complete and utter loss. The surgeon dug in again, and Dev groaned but accepted the pain. He'd said such awful things to her. Things he knew would hurt her. Words he chose specifically because he *knew* how they would wound her. And when the creatures fell on them, when she needed his help, he'd failed her.

"Speak!" Luella shouted, rising to her feet. "You're the High Keeper, for Tawn's sake! You have to make sense of these devils!"

"I...," he started. But what could he tell her? What sense was there to be found in the senseless? He knew of the On-High, of light, of their will—or tried to know, anyway. But the Nightlocks? They were darkness. They were evil. They were death. He'd not studied such things.

"Mother," snapped Ursula. "That's enough." She began to pace, her fingers twisting as she thought. "*Use for you*," she said. "That can only be good for us. I don't imagine the creature would call Aster *useful* if its intentions were merely to…" She stopped, swallowing the words Dev knew she couldn't bring herself to say. *Kill her.*

The surgeon fished around in his kit and pulled up another thread and a fresh hook. Dev took a deep breath.

Lorc pulled a dagger from his coat and handed Dev the leather scabbard. "For the pain," he said. He hadn't looked at Dev. Not in the eye. Not since he found him bloodied and collapsed on the balcony…alone. Without Aster.

Dev took the sheath, not sure it would be of any use, until the surgeon set about his work again. Dev groaned and bit down hard on the leather, trying not to scream.

"It called her Major, you said," Ursula went on. "It knows her status. Her importance. It must have sought her out for a very particular reason."

"But what reason?" asked Arthur Conri. "What would a Nightlock need from a Major?"

"I don't know," Ursula admitted. "But whatever it is, it must require that my sister be alive. Otherwise what use could she be?"

Dev straightened. Ursula had a point. Nightlocks didn't care about man's politics. Why not take any mortal? They must have needed Aster specifically. But what use was there for the living behind the Moon Door?

"I d-don't relish being the one to ask the obvious," said Keeper Von, "but…what if the Major is…forgive me…a Moon Demon already?"

Lady Lourdes screamed, and Leona held her sister tight as she cried.

Dev's own stomach dropped—the idea of Aster, bright and ferocious and hopeful, her life stolen by the Moon Door and her body broken and distorted into a Nightlock...Dev's throat began to swell, his eyes burning with tears.

There was a crash, and everyone looked over at Lorc Conri, who'd kicked a vase holding decorative ribbon staffs to the floor.

"The Hermans are willing, my lady," said Ravus, the captain of the Herman Guards, to Ursula. "We are ready to go after the Major, to fight for her against the Moon Demons."

"The Shade Guard will go," said the Shade Guard captain. His declaration was echoed immediately by the captain of the Fern Guard of Felisbrook. And the Hundfordian guard captain after that.

"Valiant," said Von. "But...with all due respect...go where? To the moon?"

Luella sobbed all the more, and Leona cut Keeper Von a furious glare. "Pity's sake, Von."

"He's right," said Lorc, staring out into the night. He was seething. Dev had never seen him look so angry. Like he could take on an entire army. "If they've taken her beyond the Moon Door, she's past our reach."

"Lorc," said Arthur gently.

"What? You've seen what they do, Arthur. You were there when they came for Bram Lourdes!"

Arthur said nothing, and Dev tasted bile in his throat.

They had all been there. Had seen the shadows pour from the moon and descend on Bram Lourdes, watched them drag him, like a swarm of wormy darkness, back up into the night and behind the full moon. To be damned. To be changed. For all time.

But those Nightlocks...they'd been little more than shadows. Whispery things like the Dust Dragons. There, but not. One foot here, the rest of them in a world beyond.

The Nightlocks that came for Aster..."This was different," said Dev. "These Nightlocks...they weren't like normal Nightlocks."

"What do you mean?" asked Ursula.

He thought of the large one, of the focus in her eyes and the scales on her leathery skin. "They were...more solid. Corporeal. Flesh and bone. A thing you could reach out and touch."

"A thing you could kill?" asked Lorc Conri.

Dev nodded.

"So what are you saying, Dev?" asked Ursula. "Are you saying these creatures...they aren't Nightlocks?"

Was that what he was saying? He didn't know. His body, his mind, his heart, they were all so sore and broken—scattered in pieces across the memory of a night gone so terribly wrong. Aster was gone. He'd yelled at her. Told her she was no Major. He'd made her cry. And he hadn't saved her. And he didn't know what had taken her. She was *gone* and he couldn't begin to guess where they'd taken her.

He felt helpless and hopeless and lost, and all these people, people he'd never had to manage without Aster around—they all wanted answers he couldn't give.

"Dev?" said Lorc Conri. "The creatures that took Aster. Were they Nightlocks or not?"

"We are."

The surgeon stayed his hand, and every muscle in the room went stiff. For a new voice had entered their midst. A voice like steam escaping a kettle. The hairs on Dev's neck stood on end.

All eyes fixed on the windows, and Dev twisted in his seat to see—the gauzy curtain fluttered in the open doorway that led to the balcony. And a shadow, large and dark, loomed beyond.

The creatures had returned.

Ursula was the first to move.

The heir of Jasper Lourdes, every inch her father's daughter, stepped boldly out onto the balcony, and Dev got up to follow. "Aster?" he croaked.

Arthur and Lorc were with them in an instant, passing through the curtain to the cool Felisbrook air. A creature was perched on the balustrade. Just one of them. The big one that Dev had seen snap at the smaller one. Its yellow eyes watched him before it turned its attention to Ursula.

There was a gasp from Lady Lourdes as she and Leona and the gathered soldiers shuffled closer to the door, none of them daring to cross the threshold into the night.

"What have you done with the Major?" shouted Lorc, his fists balled at his sides, his feet shifting beneath him like he might throw himself forward at any moment. Arthur pressed a steadying hand on his shoulder.

"I seek the one who speaks in the Major's stead," said the creature.

No one spoke. In the Major's absence, it was supposed to be the Minor who ruled. But Bernadine Lourdes had not come to Felisbrook.

Everyone looked at Ursula, and she lifted her chin, as poised and regal as Dev had ever seen her. He remembered a thousand years ago, when she faced down Bram Lourdes on the steps of the Oracle House—composed, unafraid.

"I am Ursula Lourdes," she said, "sister of the fifty-fourth Major, Aster Lourdes, and daughter of the fifty-third Major, Jasper Lourdes, the Death Chaser."

The creature hissed, baring its teeth.

"I demand you return my sister at once or face the wrath of the whole of her Highen. The Bear Highen. Forged by the On-High and—"

The creature laughed—or at least, Dev thought it was a laugh. A low, hollow rattle, like glass beads sliding around the bottom of an empty caldron. "Save your demands, Ursula Lourdes, sister of the Major, before you talk so much I'll have no time to deliver mine."

"Yours?" asked Ursula. "Who are you, Nightlock?"

The creature leaned forward, its face hovering inches from Ursula's. "Malice," it hissed. "Do you know me, sister of the Major?"

Ursula shook her head.

"With my sisters, Avarice and Despair…Together, we are the Terror Maids."

Dev felt a chill work through him. He had never heard of the Terror Maids. Had never known Nightlocks to have names.

"What is it you want, Malice the Terror Maid?" asked Ursula.

"We seek the girl," said the creature Malice. "We know, my sisters and I"—and her head tilted to look at Lorc; then twitched again, to look at Dev—"that you harbor her."

Seren.

"A girl?" said Ursula. "What girl?"

Dev could feel Lorc's eyes on him. On the secret they were keeping. He looked back at the Hound prince. Lorc's jaw worked, chewing on the words. They had the girl. They could hand her over right now. Put an end to all of it.

"Deliver us the girl and you may have your Major back."

"What girl?" demanded Ursula. "I cannot deliver what I cannot identify!"

"She is here," the Nightlock assured her. "The Dust Dragons followed her here."

The Dust Dragons. They had spilled into the courtyard. Dev and Aster had watched them engulf Lorc and Iris and Quintin and…the Dust Dragons. They had come because of Seren?

Lorc stepped forward, readying himself to speak, but Dev shook his head. Lorc stopped.

Ursula stood before Malice, unaware of the looks passing between Lorc and Dev. "What is it you want with this…girl?"

The creature looked away, as if bored with the conversation. She snorted, like a bull, before sucking her teeth and saying, "She is no true girl."

"What is she?"

Malice's yellow eyes flared as she looked back to Ursula. "She is what we need," she said impatiently, fangs flashing.

Ursula stepped back. "If I am to deliver this girl to you, how will I know where to find her?"

"The Dust Dragons," said Malice, her claws detaching from the balustrade as she turned her back to the group. "I will return tomorrow. Have the girl by then." The creature spread its massive, leathery wings.

"No."

Dev's breath hitched in his throat, and there was a yelp from Luella Lourdes behind him. The creature Malice looked back over her scaly shoulder. "No?"

Ursula stood there, defiant in the face of the beast.

"A day is not enough time," she said. "Even if I find what it is you are looking for, I don't yet know if trading her for my sister is in the Highen's best interest."

"Ursula," warned Luella, gripping tight to Leona.

"Give us a sennight."

The creature hissed, fangs bared.

"A sennight ensures the time we need to find your prize," Ursula continued, "and to confer with the Major's closest advisors on what you have asked for."

The creature dropped from the balustrade, shaking the floor and sending shingles hurtling from the roof. She stood over Ursula, massive wings closing around her. "Suppose we consume the Major in that time? My sisters are very hungry for souls...."

"*My* sister will not be easy to kill. She is the daughter of the Death Chaser."

Another snort from the creature. "Where is the Death Chaser now, Ursula Lourdes?"

Ursula said nothing, and Dev swallowed the vomit rising in his throat.

Finally, Ursula said, "My terms are set. Refuse, and I assure you I will find the girl and hide her in an Oracle House constructed just for her keeping, surrounded by starflame and guarded by every priestess and light witch in the Highen I can find, so that no Nightlock will ever set eyes on her as long as she lives."

The Nightlock was still, looming over Ursula for what felt to Dev like an eternity. And then she laughed—that awful death-rattle laugh. "Very well, sister of the Major. We have an arrangement." Malice turned and leapt up onto the balustrade again, wings fanning open. "You have seven nights."

And with that, Malice the Terror Maid flew off into the darkness.

To where she was keeping Aster.

*"I see you hiding in the trees," said the Shadow Dragon to the Lynx.*

*"The other High Beasts passed me by," said the Lynx. "They did not see me hiding."*

*"Nothing can hide from the Shadow Dragon," said the Shadow Dragon.*

*"Nothing escapes the Lynx," said the Lynx.*

*The Shadow Dragon nodded. "This is good."*

*"This is good," agreed the Lynx.*

—THE WRITINGS OF BERN,
On the Emergence of the Great Lynx: The Fore, *Star Writ*

# TWENTY

SEREN'S glare was a terrible thing.

The strange girl stood before Quintin, his back pressed to the stable door as he barred her exit. Her gray eyes seemed to hide a rage that would flare up suddenly, like an ember in ash. He held his breath and considered moving. But he couldn't. He'd promised Lorc he would keep her here, in the stables.

What was taking the Hound prince so long to return?

"Move!" Seren screamed.

Quintin winced, waiting for whatever she might do. When he didn't burst into flames, he opened his eyes and saw that same terrible glare. "You cannot go out there," he said, as authoritatively as he could muster. It didn't sound convincing even to him. "We need to stay here until they come for us."

"Seren not stay!" she shrieked, so loud and shrill Quintin was sure the guards would hear.

Umbra and the other High Beasts stood behind Seren, traitors all, siding with her against Quintin. How had this girl managed to sway even his sweet, loyal dragon?

How had she gotten them to do any of the things they'd done?

The Dust Dragons. Quintin had never imagined he'd be able to get so close. And because of Seren, he'd found himself at the center of a whole horde. A warmth radiated off them like a hot summer breeze. And the smell—like burnt sugar. And the color! Bright and

glittering and magnificent. The Dust Dragons had protected him . . .
no. They had protected *her*.

Protected Seren from the Nightlocks.

And now the High Beasts. What was it about this girl?

The Shadow Dragon hissed, and Alcor growled, low and threatening.

Quintin groaned. "Iris!" The Lynx queen stood at the other end
of the stable, taking a bow and quiver from the wall. "Would you
help me here?"

The Lynx queen sat down on a stool and looked back at Quintin, at Seren and the beasts. She said nothing for the longest time.
Only watched. And Quintin wasn't sure how much more she
needed to see before she decided he did, in fact, need help.

And where was Lorc, anyway? And Dev? And Aster? How long
did they expect Quintin to control all the High Beasts at once?

Why was it that Quintin always got stuck with babysitting
duties when this group decided to get into trouble?

"Where do you want to go?" Iris asked, finally. Seren turned, her
glare momentarily directed at the Lynx queen.

"What?"

"Where do you want to go?"

"I want to leave," growled Seren.

"All right."

Quintin gaped. It was not all right. And he was about to say
as much, but Iris held up a hand to stop him, her attention on the
silver-haired girl. "Where will you go then?"

"Anywhere," said the girl. "I want to go where the days are long
and the air is hot."

"You want to find a desert?" asked Iris.

"I want to feel water on my toes," Seren said brightly, excited.
"And snow in my hair."

Was her speech improving? Quintin wondered. She spoke better by the minute.

"Do you have snow," Iris asked, "where you come from?"

Seren laughed, as though the question were ridiculous. "No."

The kingdoms to the south did not see snow. Perhaps Seren was Roarsh. Or Twigatian. Then again, Quintin did not know any Roarsh or Twigatians who could influence High Beasts the way Seren seemed to.

"No," Seren said again, leaving Quintin to sit on the floor in front of Iris. The High Beasts shifted, Alcor collapsing on the stone floor behind her. "The Infinite do not abide things as small as weather."

"The Infinite?" asked Iris. "Is that your people?"

Seren nodded. "My family."

Iris looked to Quintin, but all he could do was shrug. He had never heard of any people called the Infinite.

"Do you miss them?" Iris asked.

"No," said Seren bluntly. The three of them were silent then. Until finally, Seren frowned. "I am tired now," she said. "No more talking." She waved a hand, dismissing them the way a queen might dismiss a servant, and lay back on Alcor. She closed her eyes, and as soon as she did, she appeared to be sleeping comfortably.

The rest of the High Beasts succumbed to slumber one by one, and when they were all asleep, Quintin left his post at the door and tiptoed closer to Iris so as not to wake the group.

"Bravo, Iris," he said. "I don't know how you managed it."

"Managed what?"

"Getting Seren to listen to you like that."

"I didn't," said Iris. "I listened to her."

Quintin blinked. Had he *not* been listening?

Iris shrugged. "There've been a lot of people talking *at* her since she arrived at Thorn Manor. Lots of people telling her what to do. This place doesn't have much patience for listening. I imagine she's pretty tired of it. I know I am."

Quintin was surprised to hear Iris Goreman speak so plainly. So honestly.

"Sorry," she said, glancing sideways. "I know I shouldn't speak so. We're not friends, please forget I said such things."

"We're not friends?"

"We're allies," said Iris.

Quintin laughed. "I always thought that was another word for friend."

"So did I," said Iris, brightening.

"There you have it, then. We are friends. So don't be sorry," said Quintin. Iris nodded, looking down at the quiver in her hands. "You don't like being queen?" he asked.

She sighed. "No one likes me being queen."

Quintin remembered the voices in the crowd when they'd gone out in the city.

"The people don't respect me very much. Sometimes I— sometimes I just wonder if Sileria made a terrible mistake. Stupid cat." She searched for her next words for a long time. "I guess I'm just...I'm just not the kind of queen they expect me to be."

"What kind of queen is that?"

"I don't know," said Iris. "Whatever kind Leona is working so hard to make me."

"Ah, Leona." She clucked over Iris like an angry hen. Quintin had seen it since that first night in Felisbrook. Advisors. Quintin had his own experience with advisors—Furia. But this was not the same. Leona cared deeply about Felisbrook—it was evident in just how much she supported her queen. But still, with all her clucking, Quintin doubted there was any room for Iris to just be Iris. "Perhaps that's the problem."

"What do you mean?"

"Who says Leona understands what kind of queen Felisbrook needs you to be?"

"She grew up at Thorn Manor," said Iris, a little defensively. "She was raised to be a queen herself."

"Yes, *herself*," said Quintin. "Not *yourself*. And is she queen? No. One ruler to another, Iris Goreman—Felisbrook does not expect you to be a certain *kind* of queen. It just expects you to *be* queen."

Iris looked away, considering his words. But she said nothing.

Silence opened up between them, and Quintin felt his heart begin to race. Had he offended her? Perhaps he had overstepped.

*Turds of Tawn.*

He wished Lorc would show up already. What could possibly be taking so long? Quintin would have thought Dev at least would have been back to check on Alcor by now.

"Do you think they forgot about us?" Iris asked.

No. When it came to High Beasts, Quintin's friends would not forget.

Which meant something must have gone terribly wrong.

*A Highen without a Major will collapse. It is a truth as sure as the setting of the sun.*

—THE WRITINGS OF WIP,
The Ring Wars, *Star Writ*

# TWENTY-ONE

ASTER'S rooms erupted into chaos when the creature left. Lady Lourdes was screaming at Ursula for making a deal with a devil. Ursula and Arthur Conri were shouting orders at Hermans and Shade Guards and Fern Guards and Hundfordian soldiers to scour the kingdom for a girl with Dust Dragons.

Only Lorc Conri of the House of Hounds and the Honorable High Keeper Dev stood outside the chaos, two boys quiet and still together on the balcony.

"Where is Seren?" Dev asked through gritted teeth.

"With Quintin and Iris," said Lorc. "In the stables."

The boys slipped out of the room easily enough; the throngs of people moving about, yelling and arguing over who would go where and who was in charge of who, were too busy with the mobilization of the Highen's armies to notice.

The boys hurried down the servants' stairwell, Lorc leading the way. "What's Ursula playing at?" the Hound prince seethed. "Making deals with that…that monster? What even is it, Dev? Terror Maids? Tell me honestly, have you ever heard of such a thing?"

"No," said Dev. It was the only answer there was. He'd never heard of Terror Maids. Because he'd never studied Nightlocks. Because there was so little about them in the *Star Writ*, except for the roles they played in the battles of the great Majors of the past. Who a Nightlock was. What a Nightlock was. These were profane things that Dev, and every other Keeper, had never considered worth knowing.

And now—Dev could hardly forgive himself.

"Here I thought Nightlocks were supposed to be ghosts," Lorc hissed as they came to the open atrium at the front of the Manor and made their way to the kitchens. "Or shadows. Dark clouds of devils flitting about the world, feeding on the souls of sinners and bad men."

Dev had thought so too.

"That thing was as solid as granite, Dev!" Lorc nearly shouted.

"I know."

"Well that's a relief," said Lorc, throwing open the door to the kitchens with a slam. "Glad to hear you know *something*."

The Thorn Manor cooks looked up from cleaning their pheasants, and Dev hurried after the Hound prince, who led them to a door at the back. The night outside was dark and cold and alive with the sounds of more soldiers barking orders. Dev ran out in front of Lorc, facing the Hound prince and blocking his path. "What's that supposed to mean?"

"You're a Keeper, Dev!" Lorc growled. "It's your job to know the ways of these things!"

"It's my job to know about Hemoth Bears!" Dev shouted. "It's not my job to know about Nightlocks and—and *bat ladies*. My job is to serve Alcor!"

Alcor. Dev felt a sudden surge of panic.

"Where *is* Alcor?" In all the chaos, he'd forgotten Alcor completely, and it made him faint with terror. He'd never forgotten Alcor. Not for one moment in his entire life.

"Relax," grumbled Lorc. "He's in the stables too."

"With Seren?"

"Yeah, with Seren. Alcor, Umbra, Argos. Even that pissy Sileria. None of the High Beasts will leave her side. It's like she's got them all bewitched or something. Like the Dust Dragons."

"Are the Dust Dragons still here?"

"No, and thank Tawn for that, but you can bet they haven't gone far. Her and these animals, Dev...Honestly, if Seren had been at the Northern Crowning, I reckon she'd have been chosen for all the thrones in the Highen. I've *never* seen High Beasts so enthralled with a person, not even their own chosen ruler. What in Tawn's name have we brought to Thorn Manor?"

"She's just a girl, Lorc," said Dev, defeated and tired.

"Dragon spit. You heard the Nightlock. She's not a normal girl. So what is she, then? A Nightlock? Tell me, Honorable High Keeper. Did we just trade Aster's life for a bleedin' Nightlock?"

"We'll get Aster back." They had to—whatever the Nightlock wanted, whatever Seren was, it was the key to Aster's return. But why, Dev couldn't stop wondering, did the Nightlock want Seren so badly?

"I know we will," said Lorc darkly, before turning for the stables. "I'll make sure of that."

Dev stopped, Lorc's attitude beginning to grate on his nerves. "All by yourself, then? You think I don't want to find her too?"

Lorc spun and got into Dev's face, his teeth bared, more wolf than hound. "Why didn't you want me to say anything?" he demanded. "Back there, on the balcony when the creature asked for the girl? I should have given her to them!"

"I didn't stop you," said Dev.

"Yes, you did!"

"Did I cover your mouth? Did I force you into silence?"

"Why didn't you want me to tell them where Seren is?"

Dev stepped back. Why didn't he? If Lorc had spoken, if Lorc had told the creature to find Seren in the stables and it had made off with her, would they have gotten Aster back? Would she be here, with them now? "I...I don't know."

"Because we don't know what we have." Ursula stood behind

them in the doorway of the kitchen, her arms crossed impatiently, glaring at them suspiciously. Arthur Conri stood just behind her, an eyebrow raised in disapproval. "Well, Honorable High Keeper," Ursula said, "Hound prince. What have you lot gotten us into now?"

*And at the end of his life, the first Shadow Dragon lay upon the earth and closed his eyes forever, his soul returning to the stars. His body became one with the lands of the Highen, the spindles of his spine forming the black peaks of the Drakkan Range.*

—THE WRITINGS OF BERN,
On the Founding of the Highen: The Age of Tawn, *Star Writ*

# TWENTY-TWO

THE cold was alive in the Drakkan Range. A slow, quiet thing, but ravenous for warm bodies, slowly freezing any heat it could find.

Aster huddled close to the fire, her teeth chattering. The pathetic pile of tinder that the Nightlock had gathered was all but spent, and Tawn knew where to find more in the obsidian range. But she felt the cold closing in. Felt its frigid grip tightening around her. She'd need more wood soon.

She should leave. Before the Nightlock came back.

If the Nightlock ever came back. Maybe this was the creature's plan all along. To leave her to freeze in a cave on a mountain peak where no one would ever find her frozen body.

Why, though? What was the point of that?

But then, she thought, the creature was a Nightlock. Why would she understand it?

There was a sound—the scratching and scuffing of taloned feet at the mouth of the cave. When Aster looked up, she saw two of the creatures: the smaller ones that had flown on either side of her and her abductor. Their eyes gleamed in the dark, and they watched her eagerly.

"Back at last, I see?" Aster said. "I hope you brought wood. Or brush. Or something to burn. I'll freeze to death out here. You wouldn't know anything about it, would you? Do the dead and the damned feel anything at all?"

The creatures said nothing. They didn't make a sound, and Aster wondered if she should have checked her tone. She was angry—furious—but she doubted very much the Nightlocks cared.

The creatures began to slink into the cave, stalking toward her like hungry lions. Aster leapt up from the fire. "Stay back," she said. "I'm warning you."

She inched deeper into the cave until the rock pressed against her back.

There was nowhere to run.

The creature on the left hissed, jagged white fangs glinting in the firelight.

"Such a young little thing," it said.

"Such a pretty little thing," said the other.

"So bright. So innocent. Not a single blight on a soul so young." The creature smacked its lips and Aster recoiled.

"You're not going to eat me, are you?" she blurted out.

The creature's eyes were wide, as if it could devour Aster whole just by looking at her. "We haven't drunk a soul in nearly four hundred years," it said, before closing its eyes and breathing deep. It shivered, making a rattling sound not unlike a viper's. "And my, but yours *does* smell delightful."

"You stay away from me," said Aster, wishing it had sounded more threatening than it did. But her throat had dried up; her voice was barely a whisper. And her knees—did she *have* knees anymore?

The creature moved closer, but the other stopped it. "Avarice, remember what Malice said?"

Malice. The big Nightlock that had abducted Aster. It had a name.

"Just a taste," said the thing called Avarice. "Malice doesn't have to know."

They smiled at each other, glistening fangs bared. Aster had never seen faces so grotesque and menacing. And their smell—like sulfur and doused, smoking embers. So bitter.

Her stomach churned as the creatures nodded in agreement. "Just a small taste."

Aster grabbed a rock, for all the good it could do.

The first creature pounced, its talons sinking her shoulders and pinning her to the ground. Aster squirmed and thrashed, trying to swing the rock, but the grip on her shoulders impeded her movements. The second moved in, its fetid breath like a thousand years of rot and putrefaction. Aster screamed, struggling against the beasts, but it was no use. They were strong—impossibly strong. Alcor himself would not have been as immovable as the Nightlocks, their bodies cool and solid like stone.

Aster squeezed her eyes closed and held tight to everything that made her Aster—her dreams, her hopes, her fears, her memories. Held them tight inside her heart and hoped her will would be strong enough to keep the Nightlocks from drinking her soul.

And then there was a shriek—shrill and spectral and furious, and the grip on Aster's shoulders came free and the Nightlocks were thrown off her.

Malice had returned.

Aster scrambled to a corner and curled into a ball, peeking out from behind her arms. Her heart thundered in her chest, and her breath came in panicked, ragged bursts—but she was still Aster. The creatures hadn't harmed her. Not yet.

How long before they tried again? Or—worse—was she a prize meant for the big one? For Malice to drink for herself? Aster trembled, watching the hulking Nightlock puff out its chest, its massive wings spread wide between Aster and the other two.

"I said, *she is not to be drunk!*" Malice bellowed.

The one called Avarice stayed where it was thrown, its face a furious snarl, its body submissive, while the other pleaded, "But we are starving, sister!"

"*And you'll starve some more!*" the hulking Nightlock roared, the other two flinching from her rage. She heaved her mighty weight around, turning away from the other two. "Need I remind you," she growled, "we have greater ends than this measly meal of a girl."

Aster watched the beast shuffling twigs she had brought into the cave, building up another tiny fire. Malice, Aster decided, was the ruler of this tiny world. Aster understood rulers. And good rulers…well, effective ones…understood how to communicate with other rulers. Her father had always been a tactful negotiator.

Aster steeled her nerve and rose. Clearing her throat, she tried to dislodge the fear that had dried her voice to a whisper. The Nightlock's moonglow eyes flicked to her, and the serpentine glare narrowed.

Aster spoke, as clearly and confidently as she could. "What do you want with me?"

"Nothing," the creature snarled, turning back to the little fire. "You're just the means to our end."

"A tool?" asked Aster, aghast.

"You are," the creature agreed.

"For what? What could you possibly want from the Bear Highen?"

"A girl," said the smallest of the three.

"Shut up, Despair," hissed Avarice, and the little one cowered.

"Aye," said Malice, scrubbing her talons on the rock, igniting a spark that lit the tinder. "A girl. That is all."

"What girl?" asked Aster, baffled. What could a Nightlock want with a girl? Want so badly they would make off with the Highen's Major to get it?

"The girl we need," said Malice, as though the answer were obvious.

"But *who* is the girl you need?"

"You needn't worry about that, Major Lourdes," said Malice, and Aster detected a hint of amusement. "Your role in this is to pay for her. Delivering her is not your problem."

"Not my problem!" blurted Aster. The other two Nightlocks hissed at her and bared their teeth, and Aster held her breath. Malice, without looking at her sisters, raised a claw for silence.

"I just...," said Aster, adjusting her tack, "I do feel this is somewhat my problem, since...I'm...here."

Malice's brow, a scaly, stone-riddled ridge, rose on one side. "You are here," Malice agreed. "And that is your function. To be here. Until you are not needed any longer."

"And then what? Will you kill me or return me to my people?"

"That depends on your people."

Aster frowned. "Depends on whether they find the girl you need."

Malice nodded.

*Seren.*

Her silver hair and strange tongue. The way the Dust Dragons followed her. Was that the girl the Nightlocks were after? But why? What could she possibly matter to monsters? Whatever the reason, Aster hoped Dev would know—and that he would keep her safe. If they wanted her, they must not have her.

Aster stared at the massive Nightlock, her eyes focused and glowing in the dark. A Moon Demon. Malice watched Aster with such intensity, the young major wondered if she could see into her innermost heart. Nightlocks drank souls—surely they could see them. Aster's skin crawled at the thought.

"And what if I don't want to play this role for you?" she ventured.

The Nightlock grunted and went back to the flames. The fire grew beneath the creature's breath, and she seemed to forget Aster altogether, focused on her task.

"Hear me, Nightlock," said Aster, moving closer and crouching by the fire. Malice looked at her then, eyes flashing like candle flame, and Aster felt, at last, that the creature was seeing the Major that Aster wanted her to see. "What if I choose not to stay here? In this little prison you've carved out for me?"

The Nightlock grunted thoughtfully, eyes ever on Aster. Trapped in the creature's gaze, Aster realized suddenly that she hadn't blinked. Didn't blink. And Aster felt another wave of terror.

"If you try to flee, Major Lourdes," said Malice, rising to her feet, "the mountains will kill you. Rest assured."

"I'm not afraid of the mountains."

Malice grunted. "Afraid or not, they'll kill you all the same." The creature turned away and shuffled for the mouth of the cave. "Your only refuge on these slopes is this...*prison*...that we have fashioned for you. You have no choice but to stay." The Nightlock stretched out her wings. "Sisters," she snarled, and the other two Nightlocks joined Malice at the cave's opening. "Let us find meat to eat."

"We want her soul," hissed Avarice.

"But you shall have only meat."

With that, the three Nightlocks flew off into the night, leaving Aster alone with the little fire yet again.

The mountains, Aster knew, were deadly to unprepared men who tried to scale their slopes. But Nightlocks with soul-thirsty sisters were deadly, too—and the risk of losing her soul tied Aster's stomach in knots. She'd rather take her chances and be killed by the mountains—the Highen's mountains, her mountains—than by Malice and her sisters.

If the Nightlocks were after Seren and planned to use Aster as ransom, they would be disappointed.

Aster had no intention of remaining a prisoner. She was her father's daughter. And the Major Aster Lourdes would never be held captive for long.

*The Cunning: Tricksters like the lesser Follies, the Cunning are power-ful enough beings to take a corporeal form. They disguise themselves in pleasing designs to lure mortals near. By the time the mortal realizes the rules, it is far too late to escape the Nightlocks' clutches.*

—KEEPER KALAMITY,
*A Compendium of Nightlocks*

# TWENTY-THREE

THE stables at Thorn Manor were dark structures of Draccus stone and twisted oak, the stalls tightly packed together and quiet in a way that made Dev uncomfortable. Felisbrook horses, it seemed to Dev, were silent as the grave.

Lorc led Dev and Ursula Lourdes and Arthur Conri around corner after corner. They came to the last wing of the stable, tucked into the shadows of the Manor's curtain wall. Lorc knocked twice—waited, his fingers tapping the door as if timing something—and knocked twice again.

The door opened, revealing Quintin Wyvern standing on the other side. When he saw Ursula and Arthur Conri, the Dragon prince stiffened.

"We're beyond secrecy now," said Lorc by way of explanation, shouldering his way inside.

Quintin looked to Dev. "Where's Aster?"

Dev breathed deep, willing himself the strength to explain. "Gone," was all he managed as Ursula drifted past them and let herself inside.

Quintin grabbed Dev's arm. "What do you mean, gone?"

"The Nightlocks have taken her prisoner."

"Prisoner. What for?"

Dev patted the Dragon prince's arm—there was too much to explain in whispers—and followed the others inside. The stables were sparsely lit—four candles burned, clustered in the corner where the massive orange form of Alcor lay snoring. The door banged as Quintin let it close, and he was beside Dev again, eyes wide with confusion and concern. "Dev, what do the Nightlocks want with the Major?"

But Dev didn't need to answer.

"Ursula Lourdes," said Lorc Conri in a grand voice, swooping his arm toward Alcor, "allow me to introduce Seren of Nowhere, the great treasure of Nightlocks and Terror Maids and lover of tarts."

The strange girl was fast asleep, content to lie in the crook of Alcor's hind legs, her breath keeping time with his, the High Beast's mighty shoulders rising and falling as he dozed. At her feet lay Argos the Starhound, alert and still. Even Umbra, the Shadow Dragon, who usually preferred to keep her distance from the other beasts, was lying next to the Hemoth, her head arched above the group, keeping close watch.

Only Sileria stayed outside the group, sitting by Iris Goreman, who sat on a stool fletching her arrows with feathers and silk.

Ursula regarded the girl, dozing soundly in a heap of High Beasts. "Alcor...," she started, but her voice seemed to fall away. Dev watched as Ursula crouched down, placing her fingers over her mouth in horror or amazement, Dev wasn't sure.

"This is really her?" said King Conri, considerably less moved than Ursula. "This is the girl the Nightlocks are after?"

Dev nodded. "We believe so."

The Hound king frowned. "Because of the Dust Dragons? Remember, Lorc, how they surrounded *you*—"

"Who gives a filth about the Dust Dragons?" snapped Lorc, and Dev could see from the tension in his folded arms, the tightness of his jaw—his rage was ready to boil over. "Do you not see the High Beasts?"

"I do, thank you, little brother," said Arthur patiently. "But the Nightlock specifically said we would find her with Dust Dragons."

"The Dust Dragons did follow us for some time after the Night-locks left," said Quintin quietly.

"And where are they now?"

"Gone," said Iris Goreman, looking up from her arrows. "The bear and the dragon chased them off."

"They're still out there, though," said Quintin. "I've seen their dust flutter just above the curtain wall."

Dev watched Ursula, crouched on the floor. Her eyes were wet, and he was sure she was feeling the same twinge of betrayal he'd felt, seeing this stranger tucked into Alcor's paws. Alcor was *their* High Beast. His, Ursula's, and Aster's. They'd saved him from the Minor. He'd saved them from everything else. They were family, the four of them. And yet, with part of that family gone—Aster, his chosen Major—Alcor slept like a cub, this strange girl warm and safe in his embrace.

"Spit on the Dust Dragons," growled Lorc, his narrowed gaze on Argos. "Have you ever seen a High Beast so...so at *ease* with someone who wasn't their chosen companion?"

"No," said Arthur, moving closer to Argos. He reached out his hand, and the dog gave it a disinterested lick before turning back to Seren.

"No," agreed Dev.

Arthur looked down at Argos, *his* High Beast, and Dev could see a similar sadness pass across his face. "Where did she come from?" he asked.

"She was in the woods," said Quintin. "With the Dust Dragons. Dozens of them."

"But where did she *come* from? Her people? Is she from Felisbrook?"

"We don't know," said Dev. "She hasn't been able to tell us."

Lorc grunted at that. "Or chooses not to."

"She doesn't speak?" asked Ursula.

"She speaks. Just not our tongue. She's learning, though."

"Learning?"

"I've been teaching her," said Dev. "Well, we all have."

"She's a quick study," said Quintin. "She's speaking about as well as any of us now. Well, speaking to Iris, anyway."

Iris quickly busied herself with the fletching, uncomfortable at the sudden attention.

"She's speaking to you?" Dev asked, a little surprised. Why should Seren speak more to Iris Goreman than anyone else?

But Arthur Conri brushed the question aside, stepping between Dev and Iris. "Well?" he said. "Have you learned anything? Anything that might help us understand where she comes from? Why the Nightlocks are after her?"

"She—she speaks mostly in riddles," stammered Iris. "She calls home 'the Infinite.'"

Dev had never heard of anywhere called the Infinite. And it was clear from the confused faces in the room he wasn't the only one.

"What about her people?" asked Lorc. "Her family?"

Iris shook her head. "Same thing. 'The Infinite.'"

"Why did she tell you that?" asked Dev.

Iris shrugged. Sileria sat ever watchful at her side—the only High Beast who hadn't abandoned their chosen person completely for the stranger. What was so special about Iris Goreman that Seren should speak to her? That Sileria should never leave her even when High Beasts, it seemed, couldn't care less about their chosen?

Ursula stood then, her brow furrowed, her eyes wet and focused on Seren. "She's a girl, though," she said. "She's just a girl."

Lorc laughed, a hollow, bitter sound. "Is she? Everyone keeps saying that. I don't think so."

Ursula looked at Dev, ignoring Lorc. "What could the Night-locks possibly want with a young girl?"

"If you're asking the Keeper," Lorc cut in again, "don't bother. He knows about as much as we do."

Dev winced at that. Lorc was right. He didn't have answers, though everyone seemed to think he should—even he himself thought so. If High Keeper Rizlan had been here, Dev would have looked to his old mentor, along with the whole of the Highen. But Dev was High Keeper. And nothing in his education had prepared him for this.

"I don't know of any passage in the *Star Writ* that mentions a Malice or Terror Maids," he admitted.

"And we don't have time to comb through what Dev has missed," said Lorc.

"I've missed nothing," Dev insisted. "It's not there."

"So what do you propose, Lorc?" asked Arthur.

"I'll go after Aster," Lorc said. "I'll go into the mountains and find her and bring her home."

"All by your lonesome, will you?"

"I'll go," Dev put in.

"And do what?" asked Lorc. "Brush the coat of any animals we encounter?"

"I can handle myself just fine, Lorc Conri."

"Didn't look like it when I found you on the balcony," Lorc shot back.

Dev winced. He hated that Lorc was right—again. He'd been found bloodied in a heap.

"Dev," said Ursula, gently, "I'm not sure going into the mountains is wise."

"But how else are we going to get Aster back?" he said.

"We have…," said Ursula, looking at Seren. "We have options."

"You can't just hand Seren over to a bunch of Nightlocks," Dev said. "We don't know what they'll do to her."

"What they'll do to *her*?" shouted Lorc. "What about what they'll do to Aster? What they may have already done!"

Alcor growled, low and threatening, picking up on Lorc's

hostility, at the way it was focused on Dev. Argos didn't miss it. The Starhound growled back, teeth bared at the Hemoth.

"Lorc—" warned Arthur.

"They might kill her!" cried Lorc. "They might drag her behind the Moon Door!"

"*Enough!*" commanded Ursula.

But Lorc wasn't about to take commands. "How about it, High Keeper? You reckon there's something in your *Star Writ* about what Nightlocks can do to a Major?"

"Do you think I'm not just as worried as you?" Dev shouted back. "Just as afraid? Whatever you're feeling right now, Lorc Conri, it isn't *half* of what I am. You don't know her like I know her! You don't know how she thinks! How reckless she can be! I am sick to my stomach and willing to do just about anything to find her!"

"Except give them what they want," said Lorc darkly.

"Except that! Stop blaming me for not delivering Seren on the balcony. You had your chance, and you *didn't*—because you *know* that delivering her to them would be sentencing Seren to death. You would never do that, and neither would I."

"You are loud boys, you are." Seren sat up, scowling at having been woken from her slumber. "This body needs rest." Dev was shocked to hear the flow of her words—a bit stilted, yes, but much more confident than when he'd left her. Seren noticed Ursula, and her head tilted in that inquisitive way she had. "Hello."

"Seren," said Ursula.

"Yes," she said. "I am Seren."

The two girls, princess and stranger, regarded each other a moment. And finally, Ursula looked away, looked at Dev. She walked to him, her back to Seren, her voice nearly a whisper. "You cannot go to the mountains. I need you here."

"Aster needs me to—"

"Aster needs you here," she hissed. "We cannot save her if we do not know what *exactly* it is her captors want. I need you to work with Seren and learn more about her. About what these...Terror Maids want from her."

"Me?"

"You're the High Keeper, Dev."

"I told you—we don't study Nightlocks."

"Even so," she said. "You're the only one with the training to understand the mysteries of the On-High, and their realm extends to the Moon Door. If not you, then who?"

"But I—"

A bang sounded at the door.

"Ursula Lourdes?" asked a gruff voice—one of the guards.

"What do you want?" Ursula called, irritated by the interruption.

"My lady, is that you?" The guard knocked again, and Ursula nodded at Arthur, who opened it to reveal a pair of panicked-looking Fern Guards.

"Oh, my lady, we've been searching for you everywhere," the first guard said.

"What is it?" said Ursula shortly.

"The Minor has arrived at Thorn Manor," said the first guard.

Ursula's eyes flicked to Dev.

"She is asking for the Major," reported the second. "Lady Leona commanded we find you straightaway."

Bernadine Lourdes had come to Felisbrook.

*And the White Bear Gwyneira brought down her mighty claws, tearing into the frozen wastes of Whitlock to forge the depths for the frost pearls to grow. And thus the great lakes of Whitlock—the Gouges—were formed.*

—THE WRITINGS OF BERN,
On the Founding of the Highen: The Age of Tawn, *Star Writ*

# TWENTY-FOUR

IF Bernadine could have sunk like a rock into the black, cold depths of White Bear Lake and be swallowed forever by the watery dark, with nothing but frost pearls for company…she would have.

It would have been better than standing there, in the great atrium of Thorn Manor, having to face the look on Aunt Luella's face. Since the war, Aunt Luella had never looked at her with kindness, or affection, the way she had before. Since her father's betrayal, Aunt Luella only looked at her with suspicion. And contempt.

But now, at Thorn Manor, Aunt Luella's eyes showed a rage that might burn Bernadine to cinders if she stood any closer. Bernadine held tighter to Marmoral, nestled and sleeping in her arms. If she did burn, what would happen to the little cub?

At her aunt's side stood another Luella Lourdes—taller and older, with darker eyes and more silver in her hair, but still the same. Leona, her aunt's infamous sister.

"I want her banished from this house," Aunt Luella seethed. Her sister patted her arm reassuringly, but said nothing.

Bernadine could feel the glares of the Herman Guards, hear the whispers of the Felisbrook Fern Guards, the murmurs of the gaggle of other soldiers clad in various armors from around the Highen. *The Minor. Minor Bram's daughter. Showing her face. Why now?*

She would have thought the answer was obvious enough.

As she and Cadewyn and Marmoral had ridden up to the castle, the scars of a Nightlock attack could still be seen on the turrets. And it could be seen, too, in the faces of the guards and nobles and servants who had witnessed the shadows falling upon them. But the Manor still stood. Bernadine was glad of that.

"This is all your doing," cried Aunt Luella. "This misery. Isn't it!"

Bernadine breathed in deep, mustering her courage. "I was invited."

Aunt Luella laughed, a dark and humorless noise. "By the Nightlocks, I'm sure."

"Hush now, Luella," urged Leona.

But Aunt Luella wasn't listening. She pointed a slender accusing finger at Bernadine. "I want her gone. I can't stand to look at her traitorous face. Tell your men to remove her from the grounds."

"I won't do that," said Leona.

"You must do that! If not for the love of your niece, then out of respect for your Major!"

"She is the Minor, Lu. Control yourself."

"Her corrupt family is *swathed* in evil. She is the reason this darkness has fallen on us! The reason my Aster is gone!"

Bernadine paled. "Gone?"

But no one could hear her squeak of a question over Aunt Luella's shouting. "She brought this on us! *She did this!*" She addressed the guards now, as if to rally them. "She called the creatures down on my Aster and now she's here to take the throne, just like her father!"

Bernadine held her breath. Suppose they cut her down right here? She held tight to Marmoral, who didn't resist. The little cub's breathing was fast. Too fast? But not even the shouting had roused her from her sleep.

"Mother."

Bernadine looked up from Marmoral to see her cousin Ursula entering the atrium with Dev—High Keeper Dev, she had to remember—the Hound lords, Arthur and Lorc Conri, trailing behind them. But no Aster.

"That's enough," Ursula said, firmly.

Dev looked tired, drained by whatever had happened here. He barely glanced at Bernadine, his eyes far away. He and Ursula stood deliberately between Bernadine and her aunt, however, and Bernadine was glad of that.

"Aster is gone?" Bernadine asked in disbelief.

Ursula nodded somberly. "The Nightlocks have taken her to the Drakkan Range."

"Not the Moon Door?" Bernadine asked, a little too quickly, and realized that it was a mistake. Ursula's left eyebrow rose just a little higher than her right. But from what Bernadine knew of Nightlocks—and she'd come to know a lot—the Moon Door was invariably where they took mortal souls.

"No," said Ursula.

"Not yet," said Dev, less confidently.

Yet. So Bernadine had come all this way for nothing.

She tightened her grip on the bear in her arms. She'd risked Marmoral on the road, and for what? She hadn't even managed to get here in time to warn them. And now Aster was gone.

But if not behind the Moon Door... why was she taken at all?

"What do they want with her?" she asked.

"They are holding her for ransom," said Ursula plainly, as though she wasn't the least bit concerned. But she was. Bernadine had lived with Ursula long enough to know when her cousin was distraught. The tightening of her fingers against her palms, the way she chewed the corner of her mouth. "They are looking for a girl. They want her in exchange."

"What girl?"

"We don't know yet," said Aunt Luella's sister—the Felisbrook woman, Leona.

Ursula glanced at her sideways. "We might know," she corrected. "We'll need more time to be sure."

"Bernadine, where is Keeper Gwyn?" asked Dev, his eyes on the bear in her arms. "You brought Marmoral without her Keeper?"

Marmoral was trembling.

"She wouldn't leave me," Bernadine explained. "There wasn't time to—to gather everyone for the journey. And the bear wouldn't let me go."

The little cub's breathing was faster now. Much too fast. Her mouth agape as she greedily took in air, as if she couldn't get enough. And her eyes still hadn't opened.

"May I see her?" said Dev, a crease between his brows that turned Bernadine's stomach.

She handed the cub to the bear boy. "Is she all right?"

He cradled Marmoral gently, opening one of her eyes, but the cub still didn't react. "You came from Whitlock?" he said. "That's a long way for such a tiny cub."

"But is she going to be all right?" Waves of cold dread and searing guilt washed over Bernadine, radiating from her scalp down to her toes.

"What do you need for her, Dev?" asked Ursula.

"Sap of the azure tree would be good," he said.

Ursula looked at Leona, who shook her head. "We have creeper larch, or twisted oak?"

"No," said Dev, sitting on the floor and holding the bear close to his body. "Warm water, then. And blankets and towels."

Ursula dismissed a group of Hermans to fetch the things, and Bernadette dropped beside Dev, tears pricking at her eyes. She pulled off her coat and Dev wrapped it around the sleeping bear. "But I kept her warm," she said. "I did! I kept her close and always wrapped."

"It's not only the cold, Bernie," said Dev. "Marmoral is still so young, and it's not an easy journey for a grown body, let alone such a tiny…" He trailed off, inspecting Marmoral's ears, focused on the patient.

Bernadine had risked too much. Marmoral depended on her, and Bernadine had failed her. How she wished the little bear had never chosen her at the Northern Crowning. She knew it was a mistake the moment it happened. *Oh, Marmoral.* Tears spilled down Bernadine's face. *You're all I have, Marmoral.*

Screaming erupted somewhere in the Manor, and guards unsheathed their weapons.

"Are the Nightlocks back?" shouted Ursula.

A roar, thunderous and earsplitting, shook the walls.

And through a pair of grand doors from the dining hall burst forth the mighty Hemoth Bear, Alcor, with Umbra the Shadow Dragon by his side. The massive beasts seemed even larger inside a castle not built for their immense size, and the guards cowered and trembled as they walked past.

They were following a girl.

A girl with silver hair.

At the girl's side, Bernadine recognized Argos the Starhound, and Sileria the Great Lynx of Felisbrook. As the beasts were nearly upon them, Bernadine saw Quintin Wyvern, trying uselessly to get Umbra to listen to him. And with him was another girl, a girl Bernadine knew from the Northern Crowning—Iris Goreman.

The girl with silver hair…The High Beasts trailed after her like ducklings behind a mother duck.

Bernadine shivered. What forces did this girl command to make High Beasts follow her?

The girl approached Dev—the dress she wore, Bernadine recognized it as Aster's. She knelt before him and peeked beneath Bernadine's coat, at the panting cub sleeping in his arms.

"Give the little one to me," the girl said.

Dev hesitated, but then he began to shift Marmoral.

"Dev!" cried Bernadine, reaching for the bear.

The girl with the silver hair met Bernadine's eyes then—the girl's eyes nearly as black as the night. Bernadine could see into infinity, they were so dark, so endless. Bernadine dropped her arms.

Dev placed Marmoral in the silver-haired girl's arms, and she rocked and hummed, stroking the sleeping cub's cheek. Bernadine watched, her heart racing as the little bear's breathing slowed, keeping time with the girl's stroking until the rhythm was back to normal.

The bear began to squirm, and her eyes blinked open, bright and inquisitive as ever. She climbed up the girl's front to lick at her nose, cooing and grumbling in the happy way she did whenever she greeted Bernadine.

Relief flooded Bernadine, and she laughed, reaching for the cub, who snuggled into her arms, warm and strong and just as she'd always been. "Oh, Marmoral, I'm so sorry, On-High forgive me!"

The silver-haired girl laughed, watching Bernadine and the cub, and when she did, Bernadine became aware of the silence around her. Everyone was staring, wide-eyed, mouths gaping, at the strange girl with silver hair.

Holding Marmoral close, Bernadine regarded the girl. Whoever she was, she had some kind of power within her. A power to influence High Beasts.

And a power like that…So this was the girl the Nightlocks were looking for.

*Creeper larch grows in the Drakkan Range—winding roots of strong black wood, resistant to the bite of the gargoyle and the flame of the Shadow Dragon. There is no plant on this earth as strong as the creeper larch.*

—THE WRITINGS OF THUBAN,
On the Flora and Fauna of Dracogart: The Star Majors, *Star Writ*

# TWENTY-FIVE

THE rocks that made up the Drakkan Range were slick. Smooth and gleaming, the obsidian mountainside was more ice than rock beneath Aster's feet. Slowly, carefully, she made her way down the slope from the Nightlocks' cave.

She much preferred to try her luck in the wild, rather than wait to be offered up like a prize in exchange for Seren.

At least…she'd thought she would. Now, inching her way down the perilously steep mountainside, she found the terrain much more difficult than expected. Indeed, she'd spent no time in the Drakkan Range. Quintin would have fared better.

She kept close to the mountainside, not venturing out onto ledges or into open spaces where she might be spotted from above. Malice and the Nightlocks could be soaring overhead. And in the dark, Aster knew they'd see her before she saw them.

Her thoughts lingered on Seren—Seren of Nowhere, who acted like she'd never seen a bed or worn a dress in all her life. Where had she come from? What was so important about her?

Aster's stomach growled. She couldn't remember the last time she'd eaten anything. But the ache in her belly did, at least, make her more certain of her actions. If she'd stayed in the Nightlocks' lair, she would have starved—she doubted very much that Malice or her sisters had plans to feed her. She was better off on the slopes, where she could at least try to find something to sate her hunger.

Aster picked her way down the rocks, eyes peeled for anything that might be food. But the world was so, so dark, with no sign of life anywhere. What she wouldn't give for one of Lorc's fire-roasted rabbits! A skilled hunter, he could flush out a hare almost as easily as Argos—there was no environment he couldn't make use of, couldn't survive. She wished he were here with her now. He would have found something for them both to eat. When they'd been alone in the Shiver Woods, he'd roasted a rabbit with a medley of earthy, meaty fungi. Aster salivated just thinking of it.

She didn't think she'd find a rabbit in the Drakkan Range. And even if she did, she had no weapons with her. She'd have to catch and kill it with her bare hands.

No. Plants would be her best bet. But from what she could see, there wasn't much growing in the glazed rock.

She stopped and tried to focus her thoughts. One of her best friends was the King of Dracogart. These slopes were his playground. Surely, in all their friendship together, he'd told her *something* about the mountains she could use now.

They were cold. He always spoke of that. The mountain peaks, the skies where he flew with Umbra—the higher you went, the colder it got. The cold was seeping into Aster's bones even now. She had only her gown from the ball for warmth. If only she had one of the scalecoats Quintin wore when he rode Umbra...And she would have liked a flame even as small and pitiful as the one Malice had made her.

But to descend the slopes was to find warmer temperatures. And she was already on her way down. She just needed to eat. She thought of the flaming, juicy shadow plum at the ball...What was it Quintin had said?

That Shadow Dragons dig for the plums under creeper larch.

Aster flipped the nearest loose rock, but there were only more rock, more dirt, more darkness. Not even the slightest wisp of a root. She flipped the next rock. And the next. And the next. But there was nothing. She wondered if there were no plants this high in the mountains at all.

She had to keep looking.

She continued climbing down the slopes, flipping every loose rock she came across, until finally she flipped a rock and found a pair of shiny black eyes staring back at her.

A tiny serpent weasel—no bigger than a mouse, with a body long and thin like a snake, but as fuzzy and black as the rock it called home. It blinked at her before scurrying away. Aster watched it go, slithering out across an open ledge and then across a rocky spar—a natural bridge—over a deep crevice to a plateau, until it disappeared beneath a pile of rubble that had fallen down the mountainside.

Her stomach raged and her heart leapt as she looked back across the natural bridge to the pile of rubble the weasel had disappeared into. Squinting, she could see the barest hint of roots peeking out beneath the rock—creeper larch.

And where the larch grew, so grew the plums.

Aster glanced up at the sky. Crossing the bridge would expose her to the night sky. There would be nothing to cover her from anything watching above. But her stomach howled.

She looked up at the great image of Tawn where her father's star burned in the heavens.

The bear's light was dim tonight. Fainter than Aster could ever remember seeing it. Unless—was it a trick of the clouds? The sky looked clear…but in the dark maybe her eyes were playing tricks on her. Father was there. His soul burning bright with Tawn.

She had to eat.

Steeling her nerve, Aster carefully stepped out onto the rocky bridge. As she inched her way along, she became aware of how fragile it was. Beneath her feet she could feel the density of the rock as she moved; the farther out, the thinner the stone—more like a thin wedge of ice than rock. The bridge creaked and groaned under her weight.

She glanced back the way she'd come. She was too far out to turn back now, but not close enough to the other side to jump if she had to.

Aster looked out over the edge and saw nothing but endless darkness below. Her heart seized in her chest, and she held her breath. With her arms spread out for balance, she felt the wind move over her limbs, pull her hair, cold and teasing in her ears.

And then the first crack sounded.

Aster looked down to see the fissure between her feet, spidering out in all directions. The bridge would shatter. There was no time to lose.

She ran.

She raced across the bridge as the thin rock splintered and fractured like ice in springtime. She jumped, hurling her body onto the hard ground of the mountainside, the bridge cracking and grinding behind her. It would not hold for long.

She laughed and rolled onto her back. She'd made it. Getting to her feet, she made her way over to the pile of rocks where the serpent weasel had disappeared and lifted the first stone.

"Tawn be praised," she breathed, staring down at a knobby, crooked finger of creeper larch, and growing from it, three fat shadow plums. She grabbed all three and huddled close to the mountainside, biting into the first plum greedily.

She cried out, her teeth nearly shattering. It was hard. Almost as hard as the rock it grew under. No wonder the Dracogartians soaked these plums in syrup for months; no wonder the Shadow Dragons roasted them with their flames.

But she had no fire and no syrup. So she gnawed at the flesh, shaving off the fruit bit by bit. The taste was sour. And bitter.

Nothing like the spicy, sweet delicacy she'd enjoyed at the Felisbrook ball. She ate it all the same: she would need her strength to get out of the mountains, every bit of it. And there was no telling when she'd find another meal.

She *would* get out. She knew that in her bones. No matter what Malice said. Aster was the daughter of Major Jasper Lourdes, the Death Chaser. His strength lived in her veins.

How proud he would have been, she thought, if he'd been alive to see Aster escape the Moon Demons. It was exactly the kind of story he loved to regale her with over dinner in the great hall back home at the Manor in Tawnshire. She wondered if, one day, this adventure in the mountains—however hard it was right now—would be a memory, her own tale to tell her children around the dinner table.

She looked to her father's star again, as though it would agree. But there was nothing. Just a faint light in the heavens. All the stars that made up the image of Tawn—they were dim. It wasn't a trick of the clouds. They were fainter than they should have been. But how? Not far away, the moon glowed its pale light—just a sliver— the door to death wide open.

It would close soon. And before it did, the Nightlocks would have to return. Everyone knew that the moon would call them back when the door closed: it ruled them, controlled their movements.

Aster just hoped that when it did, Malice and her sisters wouldn't be taking her or Seren with them.

Terror Maids. Not like the Nightlocks Aster had heard of in the *Star Writ*. Those were silly little gremlin things, speaking in riddles and made up of shadow. The Nightlocks she'd seen—the ones who'd come for Uncle Bram—they had been larger than what the *Star Writ* described, more human, but still mostly shadow. Malice and her sisters, though…they were solid things. Not shadow at all. What other horrors hid behind the Moon Door?

Malice, Aster had to admit, was not a fool. Why did she think fear of dying on the mountains would be enough to keep Aster from running? Then again, perhaps it would have been for most people. What would the Nightlock do when she returned to the cave to find that Aster had gone?

Probably try to find her.

Aster finished the plum and tossed the pit over the edge of the crevice. She listened, but there was no sound of the pit striking solid ground. It seemed to fall into forever. She swallowed, trying not to think what would have happened if the bridge hadn't held. She slipped the last two plums into her skirts and continued her descent.

Nightlocks, Aster had thought, were vicious, hungry, riddling things. Nonsense beings that delighted in confusing the minds of men. But Malice—her eyes burned with a fierce intelligence that could not be denied. A focus. Aster did not believe that Malice subscribed to any sort of nonsense whatsoever. Who had Malice been before she became a Moon Demon?

Aster shuddered.

She didn't want to think about that. Didn't want to think of that scaled, winged creature as having been mortal once upon a time. A girl. Maybe not much different from Aster at all. What had happened to change her into the terrible Nightlock she was? Change her sisters?

"Stop it," Aster growled at herself. These questions only led to terrible answers. And to still more questions—the worst one being: Could the same thing happen to Aster, if she failed to escape the mountains, and the Nightlocks took her behind the moon?

Aster picked her way down the mountainside, the feel of the rock and the slope of the mountain becoming more familiar and easier with each step. The plum in her stomach burned like fire, warming her. No wonder Shadow Dragons liked them so much.

Still, she was unsettled. Maybe it was the knowledge that Malice and her sisters could fall on her at any moment.

Or maybe it was the feeling on the back of her neck; or the prickling, tickling sensation of the tiny hairs on her arms rising to attention. A sense of being watched.

Something was following her.

Aster stopped. It was too dark to see much. The black of the sky and the rock nearly melted into one curtain of darkness. So she listened. Listened to the wind. And her own frightened breath.

And then a sound. Quiet and distant, but there all the same.

The shifting of rock.

She glanced up. And saw a glint in the dark above. Eyes. A hunter's eyes.

And they were watching her.

Aster stared back—equal parts frightened and angry that something might derail her progress out of the Range. The creature moved, shifting its weight, and what Aster could just make out was caught by the moonlight—massive horns, muscular arms. A giant toothy muzzle.

A gargoyle.

Her heart leapt into her throat, choking her.

Gargoyles were terrible indeed. Insatiable and impossibly strong, territorial and aggressive. What Aster had heard about gargoyles had given her nightmares as a little girl. It must have seen her when she stopped for the shadow plums.

She began to tremble, and she bit into her lip, trying to ease her racing heart. *Focus now,* she heard her father say inside her mind. *Panic will do no good.*

Slowly, she turned and headed back up the slope the way she'd come, disappearing out of the creature's sight. It was above her, that was a problem. She needed to take back the high ground. But then what? Hide? No. Hiding wouldn't be enough to shake the creature, which, with a snout like that, surely had ahold of her scent. She wished for Alcor, his heavy girth and epic strength. His thunderous roar. How she wanted him by her side for what came next! But Alcor, she knew, could not help her now.

Now, on the slopes of Mount Draccus, she would have to slay the monster herself. Somehow. With no weapons. No armor. Only her wits.

She climbed as fast as she could, her arms trembling with fear as she pulled herself back up the mountainside. She could hear the shuffling of the creature, somewhere above her on the far side of the slope. She needed to stop shaking. She would need all the speed she could muster for what she knew she had to do. The only thing she could do.

If her plan failed, the gargoyle would eat her. It would gorge itself until her bones were picked clean.

She pulled herself back on to the ledge with the shadow plums, her breath ragged and her heart hammering. And she heard a snarl. When she looked, she saw the gargoyle, perched on the far side of the shadow plum rubble. The creature stared at her, unblinking, and Aster paled at the sight of it: the curves of its bulging, veiny muscles; its gray, leathery skin; its long yellow claws. It stretched out its neck slowly.

Aster scrambled to her feet and ran, the creature screaming as it lunged for her.

She raced for the thin sheath of the rock bridge, the bridge she knew to be cracking. She prayed to the On-High, hoping they were with her now. And she ran across the bridge, placing her feet as lightly as she could.

The creature screamed again behind her—an awful raptor's cry—as it followed her out onto the bridge. There was a thunderous crack, and Aster felt the spar give way before she leapt for the safety of the opposite ledge. She landed with a thud as the bridge fell away and the gargoyle cried out, going down like solid stone.

Aster lay there on her back, staring up at the starry night. And laughing.

Or was she crying?

Even she didn't know.

But she'd done it.

The Death Chaser's daughter. She'd cheated death again.

At least she thought she had.

Snarling—

Snorting—

Growling—

And when Aster looked, she lost her breath as the thick, black claws of the gargoyle scratched at the ledge's edge. The beast pulled itself up, and Aster screamed, turning and running as fast as she could. But there was nowhere to go. Nowhere clever. Nowhere she could use.

Aster threw herself at the slope, sliding down jagged rock, her palms and elbows shredding on the sharp, glassy stone. The beast barrelled after her, impossibly fast, its feet and arms sure—the mountains were its home. Not Aster's.

Her unpracticed feet found a loose stone, and she slipped, tumbling head over heels and landing hard on her stomach so that all her breath left her. She lay there on the rock as the creature caught up, standing over her, chittering with glee. She felt its massive palm take hold of her head, and it screamed in triumph. Aster closed her eyes tight. Malice was right. The mountains would kill her after all.

But the creature released her. It vanished, thrown sideways by an assault from above.

Aster clambered away on her hands and knees and pressed herself against the mountainside. She saw the gargoyle, struggling to get up from where it had been hurtled, shaking its head. It roared and stared up at the sky as a black shadow swooped low and landed another blow to the gargoyle's face. Another shadow, too, flew at its side, knocking the gargoyle down.

Aster watched the shadows climb back into the sky, regrouping with a third—the biggest of the three.

The gargoyle screamed with rage and the shadows dove, grabbing the creature by the arms, the legs, and hurling it over the ledge. Aster squeezed her eyes shut and clamped her hands over her ears, trying to block out the gargoyle's fading screams as it fell, down and down and *down* into forever.

And then the world was silent.

Aster felt a presence standing before her. The shadows.

She opened her eyes to see the Nightlocks—Avarice and Despair—panting, faces twisted in irritation and disgust. Malice stood between them, looked down at Aster, nostrils flaring.

"I'll say this for you, Major Lourdes," said Malice. "I'm surprised you made it this far."

A tide of emotions overwhelmed Aster—fear and relief and shame and despair—and she collapsed, her body too exhausted and weak to stand any longer.

The Nightlock said nothing and scooped Aster into her arms, her powerful wings lifting them both into the night, Avarice and Despair taking wing on either side.

*The words of the Nightlocks are poison. Heed the words of Nightlocks, and seal the fate of your soul.*

—THE WRITINGS OF RIZLAN,
The First Coming: The Lunar Offensive, *Star Writ*

# TWENTY-SIX

 $\mathcal{D}$ EV burst into the Major's quarters, flipping cushions and dresses until he found his *Star Writ*, closed and lying comfortably at the end of Aster's four-poster bed. He lunged for it, flipping furiously through its pages.

The Fore—

The first book of the *Star Writ*—

Keeper Wip? No.

He could hear a commotion outside the apartments, voices arguing about who was doing what and why.

"The Keeper and the Minor have much to discuss now that Minor Lourdes has come to Felisbrook," he heard Ursula saying, her voice commanding as ever. "In Aster's absence it falls to them to keep the Highen safe. I will join them, so as to properly inform the Minor of what has occurred here. Everyone else, your voice is not needed at this time."

There were shouts of disagreement as Bernadine burst into the room, a squirming Marmoral in her arms. Beside her was Seren, pushed by Ursula, who slammed the door on all the dissenting voices.

Bern. It was Bern who wrote about the start of all things—

Bern who was obsessed with the first High Beasts—

"Dev, what is it?" asked Ursula, joining him beside the bed. "You're like a hound with a scent. What are you looking for?"

"You saw it," he said, eyes ever on his pages. "Saw how the High Beasts followed Seren into the Manor—" He looked up toward the door as if expecting to see the beasts inside the apartment. "Where is Alcor?"

"Still in the front hall," said Ursula. "Argos and Sileria are outside the door. Alcor and Umbra, I imagine, would be here too—if they could fit on the stairway."

"Is Quintin with them?"

"Yes," she said. "And Iris. I sent Arthur to help them keep people away."

"And Lorc?"

"Lorc is just outside the door."

Outside looking sour, no doubt. If Dev didn't get to the bottom of what was happening with the Nightlocks soon, he was sure Lorc would feed him to the Dust Dragons. Dev *harrumph*ed, going back to flipping through the *Star Writ*.

*Bern. Bern.* "The Arrival of High Beasts"? *No.* It was a different chapter.

"What are you trying to find?" asked Ursula.

"The High Beasts. They made me think of something I'd seen in the *Star Writ*."

"About Nightlocks?"

"No. About High Beasts. About the *first* High Beasts."

Bernadine set Marmoral down on the floor and the little bear hopped about, playing with a loose thread from the massive purple rug. Seren joined the bear, pulling at the thread.

Bernadine came to the other side of Dev. "But the Nightlocks," she said. "What is it they want with Aster? With this…girl?"

The answer was here, somewhere in the *Star Writ*. It was in his memory, gathering dust in the corners of his mind. Something about the Great Lady Berenice…"We don't know yet," said Ursula. "Apparently Keepers don't know much about Nightlocks, because there's not much written about them in the *Star Writ* at all. Which is why I can't say I understand why you are so furiously rifling through it now, Dev."

"That's why I had to come." Bernadine sat down on the bed, pulling a small black book from the pocket of her cloak. "I've been...reading about things that might be useful now." She kept her eyes on the volume in her hands, a blush in her cheeks, shame radiating from her like heat from a fire.

Dev glanced at the cover of the tiny book—*The Compiled Tales of Keeper Kalamity—Children's Stories and Folktales.*

"Keeper Kalamity?" he read. "I've never heard of any Keeper Kalamity."

"No, you wouldn't," agreed Bernadine. "He wasn't really a Keeper. He just called himself that. He was banished from the Highen hundreds of years ago for being heretical. All his books were destroyed. This is one of the last surviving copies left."

"Heretical how?"

"He had a keen interest in the ways of Nightlocks."

Dev and Ursula blinked at Bernadine. A man who was not a Keeper but called himself one—that was hard enough for Dev to comprehend. But a keen interest in Nightlocks? Dev instantly felt the hairs on his arms stand on end.

"Aster said you were dwelling on dark things," said Ursula, brow furrowed.

Not that Dev could blame Bernadine. After what had happened to her father—corrupted, damned, dragged behind the moon in front of her eyes. Dev wasn't surprised that she wanted to know what had become of him. He'd be a Moon Demon by now, she knew that as well as anyone. Of course she'd want to know more about Nightlocks, about what he might have become.

Dev had just never imagined there would be any information out there for her to find on the subject. If there were, the answers she found—Dev paled just thinking about it. What had she been tormenting herself with, up there all alone in the snow-covered lands of Whitlock?

But Bernadine was to the point. "What did the Nightlock tell you?" she asked, thumbing through the pages of her strange little book.

"It identified itself as a Terror Maid," said Ursula.

"Malice?" Bernadine asked without looking up.

Ursula's eyes went wide. "Yes!"

"You know it?" asked Dev, equally stunned.

"I know the story." Bernadine flipped to the page she was looking for and turned the book toward Dev. The title read "The Birth of the Terror Maids," and Dev grabbed the book.

"It's my favorite story of all of them," Bernadine admitted, casting her eyes down in shame. "Three sisters, divided by the love of one man. And Malice wanted to punish him for it. So she asked the powers behind the moon, the Nightlocks, to destroy him. And in exchange, she gave herself and her sisters to the Moon Door. Though I get the sense she didn't realize she was agreeing to becoming...what they all became."

"Nightlocks?" said Dev.

Bernadine nodded. "Not just any Nightlock. There are four categories of Nightlocks, four kinds. All of them wicked, but some more so than the others." She reached over Dev and flipped to the back of the book. A diagram of fanged faces, dragon wings, horns and spines, spiked tails, all coiling and slithering around the phases of the moon. Dev wanted to throw the book across the room. "See?" said Bernadine. "On the bottom are the Follies—the weakest and smallest of the Moon Demons. They're tiny things, no bigger than a child, and they are more ghost than matter. Intangible. Shadows. Speaking in riddles and delighting in confusing and tormenting the minds of mortals. This is the type of Nightlock that presented itself to me when my father...when the Minor took the Manor at Tawnshire."

Dev remembered it well. Remembered the shadow that fell over Bernadine back then, the way it weighed on her, frightened her.

"Then you have the Esurience," she went on. "Shadows still, but not so small. Not much different from humans in size, really. But ravenous ghosts that thirst for mortal souls. This is what..." She stopped, and Dev knew what she still could not say.

"What carried your father away," he finished.

She nodded.

Dev swallowed, staring at the demonic faces on the page. So much was compiled here. So much information and figures and writings. How had the Keepers not amassed such information for themselves?

"But what about this Malice creature?" asked Ursula. "She's no ghost."

"Well, that's the thing," said Bernadine. "The more powerful the Nightlock, the more tangible their form." She was almost excited, Dev noted. What frightened him, frightened most people, it was *interesting* to Bernadine. She seemed confident talking about these things, more confident than Dev had seen her about anything since she arrived. She must have studied this book a great deal. "So after the Esurience Nightlocks come the Cunning, and they are very solid beings, you can reach out and touch them. They hide among mortals waiting to strike and steal souls. They are very beguiling, and you wouldn't know the creature even if you were to meet it on the street and talk to it—until it was too late. Tricksters and swindlers, they're very good at hiding their activities. But they are very rare, thank the On-High."

The cold in Dev's skin sank into his bones. "How does Keeper Kalamity know all this? Who could possibly know all this?"

"He spent his lifetime collecting stories of Nightlocks," said

Bernadine, a little defensively. "Folktales and rumor. He chased them all down and found the commonalities between them."

Dev didn't like it. Didn't like the idea of someone masquerading as a Keeper and trading in such dark matters.

But more than that, he couldn't shake a rising anger at his mentor, Rizlan—at all the Keepers who had come before him. An anger that someone outside their rank had to compile this information alone, all because the true Keepers refused.

He knew *why* they didn't, of course. Moon Demons were attentive things—they watched the activities of mortals. Spending so much time writing and ruminating on their deceits would make a person vulnerable to their predation. What Keeper Kalamity had done was not safe, and because it was not safe, it was written off as heresy.

But heresy or not—Nightlocks were real, they were dangerous, and they were apparently quite complicated. With so little information in the *Star Writ*, Dev felt useless and vulnerable.

"I would certainly know Malice was a Nightlock if I were to meet her in the street," said Ursula impatiently. "Not well hidden at all, if you ask me."

"Yes," agreed Bernadine, "you would indeed. Because Malice and her sisters do not belong to the Cunning." She pointed to a shadowed figure on the right-hand page, a swirling mass of black ink with eyes glinting in gold leaf at its center. "After the Cunning come the Malevolencies. The most powerful and merciless class of Nightlock. Malevolencies are tied to their mortal selves—the people they were before they…changed. The Follies, the Esurience, and even the Cunning—they are the souls of the damned twisted beyond recognition. But the Malevolencies…they are different, because their mortal selves *asked* for the moon's powers to transform them. Like Malice does in the story….I believe the Malevolencies is the class Malice and her sisters belong to."

Dev swallowed, transfixed by the darkness on the page.

"So what do they want?" asked Ursula. "What could these…
Malevolency Nightlocks need from a mortal like Seren?"

Dev turned to look at Seren lying on the floor, staring at the
ceiling while little Marmoral nipped and pulled at her sparkling
hair. Mortal? Absolutely not.

He went back to the *Star Writ*, its familiar pages warm and
crisp beneath his fingers as he frantically flipped through them.

"I don't know," said Bernadine. "Perhaps she did something terrible that attracted them to her?"

Ursula and Bernadine were quiet, watching the girl lounging on
the floor with the little bear.

"Bern," said Dev, flipping back and forth. Why did the *Star Writ*
have to be so thick? "Keeper Bern wrote all about the Fore."

Ursula and Bernadine said nothing, and Dev could feel their
confused stares on him. But it was here. Somewhere. In the *Star
Writ*, he knew there was an answer. The answer that had been
picking at his mind since they found Seren in the Deadwood. The
answer he could feel but couldn't quite grasp hold of.

"There!" he exclaimed. "I was wrong, it wasn't in the Fore. Age
of Tawn, I should have known that."

The cousins leaned over Dev to see the double-page spread,
Bern's famous illuminated illustrations glinting with gold leaf and
lapis.

*The Coming of the Great Lady Berenice: The Age of Tawn. The
Writings of Bern.*

A line of High Beasts ran from the left side all the way to the
right, each sacred beast of the Highen following single file beneath
the gilded stars of the On-High—behind a young woman.

"The Great Lady Berenice," said Dev. "She was born of the
On-High. Born of the stars. When she came to the mortal realm

from the kingdom of the On-High, the High Beasts felt the power of the On-High within her. They followed her everywhere. Don't you see?"

Ursula and Bernadine blinked at him.

"The fallen star in Felisbrook!" he cried. "The Dust Dragons swirling around Seren! The way Alcor and the others follow her! The way she saved Marmoral!"

Ursula frowned, stepping back from the book. "What are you saying, Dev?"

"Seren!" he shouted. "She is not a mortal girl. She's a star! She's a *fallen* star!"

Seren sat up, suddenly interested now that the conversation was about her. "Yes."

The three looked at the silver-haired girl on the floor.

"Yes what?" asked Bernadine.

"Yes, I am a star. I am one of the Infinite."

Dev blinked. Infinite. That was what she'd told Iris. The stars were infinite.

So it was true. A fallen star. An On-High. She was real and she was there and she was looking up at them like it was the most normal thing in the world.

Dev felt a surge in his stomach. All this time. All this time she'd been one of the On-High. All this time, everything they'd been dealing with—

It was all so much bigger than Dev could have imagined.

He felt sick.

He bent over, hands on his knees, and tried to breathe, tried to keep the vomit from spewing out of his stomach.

*On-High save us.*

Should they be kneeling? Should they have been kneeling all this time?

Ursula approached the girl, slowly, cautiously, as though Seren were some kind of wild animal that might attack at any moment. "And the Nightlocks?" Ursula said. "What do they want from you?"

Seren shrugged, turning back to Marmoral. "I haven't the faintest idea." She forgot all of them completely, content to play with the bear cub on the floor, completely oblivious to the earth-shattering impact of who—of what—she really was.

"Dev," said Bernadine, her voice dry and small and trembling. "Dev…what do these Nightlocks want?"

"I keep telling you all, I don't know," he whispered.

He hadn't imagined anything could be worse than Aster being stolen by Nightlocks. But the Nightlocks were not just Nightlocks now. They were Malevolencies. The worst kind of Moon Demon. And Seren was a star. A real, true On-High in the flesh.

The problem was big. Bigger than thrones and crowns and Keepers. So much bigger than Dev could even comprehend. What did the Nightlocks want with a star?

"I think we can assume that whatever they want, it won't be good. For Seren. For Aster. Or for the Highen."

*Learn from life's mistakes and you will be the better for it.*

—TWIGATIAN PROVERB

# TWENTY-SEVEN

ASTER lay facing the wall at the back of the Nightlocks' cave, her sleep restless and fitful. Her body was sore, her stomach empty, and her fingers and toes stinging from the cold. The tiny flame that had been built for her offered only a faint glimmer of warmth at her back.

A sudden thump woke her. When she turned, she saw the limp, lifeless body of some kind of rodent—a mountain hare, perhaps. And Malice, stoking the tiny flames into a larger fire.

"You will eat," the Nightlock said. "Restore your strength."

Aster sat up, her head pounding from exhaustion and the lingering effects of the gargoyle holding her down. Despair and Avarice sat near the mouth of the cave—Despair preening her scaly wings, watching with longing as Malice stripped the skin from the meat. Avarice's gaze narrowed, however, and her lip curled, revealing her fanged disgust. This was how the smaller sisters always looked, Aster had come to understand. She didn't want Aster around any more than Aster wanted to be around. And she wanted her to know it.

Aster's presence was Malice's doing, and the other sisters had had no say in the matter at all.

As the meat spat and crackled in the flames, its sweet smell made Aster's mouth water. Her stomach screamed, and it was all she could do to keep from reaching into the fire.

When the meat was roasted through, Malice set it before Aster. Avarice hissed. Aster hissed back, claiming the hare for her own. She bit into the meat, hot and greasy and warming as it slid down her throat.

Malice sat opposite her, the fire between them. The Nightlock's wings were folded primly behind her back. "You are still thinking you can escape?" she asked.

"I will escape," said Aster through stuffed cheeks.

"You failed once already."

"I won't fail again."

"Why?"

Aster stopped chewing and glared at the Nightlock. Malice blinked, the question more genuine and less challenging than Aster would have liked. "Why what?"

"Why wouldn't you fail again?"

Aster sat back, setting the meat down. Avarice moved closer, lips smacking, but Malice didn't so much as glance at Aster's meal. "You are the same as you were the last time you tried. Except you are hungry."

"I'm eating."

"But when will you eat again?"

Aster wiped the grease from her lips on her wrist. She didn't know. She didn't even know if Malice would ever feed her again after she finished this meager meal.

"You are hungry," continued Malice. "And tired. So you are weaker. You will fail, and you will do it faster."

"You don't know me," rejoined Aster.

"Yet I know all that just by looking at you, and you don't seem to know any of it?"

Aster swallowed. Something inside her began to falter, like a flame against a strong wind. Because Malice was right. Aster was tired. She didn't feel strong.

And more than that, she was frightened. If Malice and her sisters hadn't intervened, Aster would have been eaten by that gargoyle—and how many more gargoyles lived out there in the Drakkan Range? Her courage, the courage of the Death Chaser, flickered inside her, nearly blown out. And Aster hated Malice for blowing the wind that could do such a thing.

"You think you know me?" Aster shot back. "Well, I know *you*, Nightlock. I know what you are. You're a monster because you did something terrible when you were mortal. Something hideous and vile."

But Malice only grinned—as much as she could, with her enormous incisors. "No," she said. "The moon changed me because I asked it to."

At that, Avarice and Despair hissed and screeched, and Aster flinched. The sisters clawed at the ground and their heads, Despair sobbing and Avarice snarling.

Aster's courage dimmed again, her stomach clenching. *Asked it to?* What sort of person would *ask* to be made into a Moon Demon? Her voice came out as nearly a whisper. "Why would you do that?"

Malice watched her sisters, clawing and screeching in torment. "For the love of my family."

"Your sisters?"

"Aye."

Avarice turned, snarling at Malice. Malice did not respond, but she looked…ashamed? That couldn't be. Malice was a Nightlock. Avarice and Despair, too. They were monsters. "Once, maybe. But not now. Nightlocks don't feel love."

Malice turned back to Aster, frowning. "Who told you that?"

Aster lifted her chin, defiant. "My father."

"He was wrong."

Aster's courage, dim as it was, was instantly replaced by anger. How dare this demonic creature speak of her father? "My father was the Major Jasper Lourdes. My father was the Death Chaser."

"And he was wrong."

"Why?" snapped Aster. "Because you say so?"

"Aye. Because I say so. Did your father ever speak to a Nightlock?"

No. In all her father's many adventures, both the ones he told her and the ones in the *Star Writ*, he never did speak to a Nightlock—not at length, anyway. If he exchanged words with them during the Lunar Offensive, they would have been brief and angry. Aster went quiet.

"No. But you have," said Malice.

Yes. Aster had.

She'd spoken to one more than any mortal she'd ever known or heard of.

And she hated the truth of that more than anything. How could she know what to do here, alone in the mountains with Moon Demons? How could she survive this? There were no lessons. No readings. No legends to give her any idea. No guidance. No hope. Her eyes burned, and she wiped at the tears, determined to hide them from Malice, but it was no use. The Nightlock had seen them.

Malice leaned across the fire, caring nothing for the flames grazing her chest. "Your people don't know everything," she said. Aster shrank back. The Nightlock hadn't spoken with coldness or cruelty. She had only spoken plainly. And it filled Aster with terrible dread.

"There are truths in this world, Aster Lourdes," Malice said, "that you must discover for yourself."

"What would you know about it?" asked Aster.

The Nightlock sat, stoking the fire. "I chased down a truth once."

Aster waited, but the Nightlock offered nothing more. Aster watched the creature, her yellow eyes ever on the flames, and tried to fight the urge to ask the question burning in her heart. But it couldn't be helped. Alone, out here in the mountains, with nothing but Nightlocks for company, Aster had to know. "What truth was that?" she asked.

"It was a mistake," Malice said, looking back at her sisters, their eyes reflecting the fire in the dark. "And with you, Aster Lourdes, I shall rectify it."

*The fruit of the blushing tree blushes for all the lovers that meet beneath her branches.*

—ROARSH SAYING

# TWENTY-EIGHT

THE earthly realm was a noisy place. Nothing here was still. From the dragons to the insects in the grass; from the howling wind to the groaning rock. Everything insisted on being heard by Seren's mortal ears.

The star girl sat in the branches of a massive tree—it smelled sweet and smoky, like the Infinite, but with a flowery perfume all its own, a spice that warmed her insides and helped to distract her from the infernal noise. The tree grew out of the cobbled courtyard of the Manor, a place of man-laid stone where no plants could grow without their permission. This tree had been permitted. Why, Seren couldn't begin to guess. Why prefer one tree over another? Were they not all lovely things? The calmest of earthly creatures. The rest of them—beasts and men and wheeled contraptions—thundered below Seren, hurrying to and fro on the Manor's grounds. People: pulling carts and shouting orders, leading horses and talking loudly, all of them rushing and buzzing and clanking with noise.

Only the lynx girl and her dragon friend, sitting at the base of the tree, approximated quiet. They sat together, still and hushed, apart from the chaos, appreciating the tree's shade. The tree liked that; Seren could feel its delight at being noticed. It had been so long, it told her, since anyone had paid it any mind. The inhabitants of the Manor were too busy and loud to care for something as quiet as the marvelous tree.

The noise.

It overwhelmed Seren.

And so did the change.

She could feel herself changing. Feel her celestial strength building in the pit of her belly. Volatile, her sisters in the heavens called her. She was always too volatile for the quiet, for the other stars. She had felt and tolerated their disapproval since her beginning, for millennia, eons. Since the time before time. Seren's presence upset the quiet and delicate balance of the Infinite, and they were forever wondering—silently—if she would ever cool her burning center, stabilize her raging core. If she would ever shine as the Infinite were expected to do. No, was the answer Seren had come to long ago. She never could and never would live up to their expectations. So she'd stopped trying. She didn't mean to be difficult—didn't mean to upset the peace. She was just too different. Too discordant to maintain her position in the skies.

But soon, she wouldn't have to worry about that.

Soon, Seren wouldn't need the Infinite's approval.

Soon, she would be something altogether different from the Infinite.

Soon, she would be more.

Quintin glanced up at Seren, sprawled on a branch of the blushing tree, for what must have been the hundredth time. He was nervous, Iris understood—the whole of the Manor was. When High Keeper Dev identified Seren as the fallen star, everyone was sent into a tailspin of anxiety and fear. Not that Iris wasn't nervous—of course she was. Suppose they offended the On-High somehow? Suppose they failed to protect Seren and lost the On-High's blessing forever? To Iris, the questions were too big and too spiritual. But Seren was here, that much couldn't be helped. And *lonely*—so it seemed to

Iris. She'd watched her enough, and listened enough, to know loneliness when she saw it. The least Iris could do was try to ease that loneliness.

And give her a break from the High Beasts. The Hemoth and Shadow Dragon slept curled up at the base of the tree, the Starhound Pack lazing about between them. Even Sileria, so focused and aware of her surroundings, was distracted. The Great Lynx lay beside Iris, attentive and alert, all her attention on the silver-haired girl in the tree. All the beasts glanced up every so often to watch the star girl, just like Dev. All of them waiting for Seren to come back down to earth.

Seren had wanted to venture out into the Deadwood again, but High Keeper Dev and the rest of the nobles had forbidden it. So Iris had brought the star girl to the only green thing on the Manor grounds. The blushing tree—a gift from Roarque over two centuries old. Its shade was Iris's favorite place in all of Thorn Manor, and it seemed to bring Seren a bit of peace.

"We should probably go back," said Quintin.

"Let her stay longer, please," said Iris. "If anyone knows what it is to seek peace from the Manor, it's me."

"Do you think it's safe for her to be up there?"

Iris snorted. "She's used to being much higher. Would have thought you'd be quite comfortable with heights, Quintin Wyvern of the House of the Shadow Dragons."

He frowned. "I *am* comfortable with heights."

Iris regarded him a moment. She'd meant it to be funny. She supposed that was a mistake—she hadn't much practice with humor.

These last few days with Quintin Wyvern had been the most time she'd spent in anyone's company besides Leona's. She liked his company and his easy disposition. It was nice to have someone to talk to about something other than Felisbrook for once.

"What's it like to fly?" she asked, hugging her knees to her chest.

He thought a moment, his brow furrowed as he looked for the words. He settled on only one. "Cold."

Iris frowned. "That's all you can think to say about it?"

He laughed. "Well, what do you want to know?"

"What do the clouds feel like?"

"Also cold."

Iris scoffed. "Then tell me what it's like to be so high above the world? What does it all look like from up there?"

He winced, looking guilty before he said, "Small."

Iris glanced away, trying to hide her disappointment. Perhaps it was rude of her to ask these questions. After all, Quintin only flew because of Umbra. And if Quintin felt as protective of his High Beast as Iris felt of Sileria, she couldn't blame him if he didn't want to share with her the experience he shared with Umbra.

But still, she wanted to know.

"Shall I take you with me someday?" he asked suddenly.

Iris felt a thrill in her stomach. "On Umbra?"

"Yes, why not? You'd like that, wouldn't you, Umbra?"

The Shadow Dragon opened one yellow eye and *harrumph*ed, a spurt of black smoke escaping her nostrils before she closed her eyes again.

Iris saw Quintin's smile fade as he watched the dragon sleeping beneath the star girl.

"It's painful, isn't it," said Iris, "how quickly they seem to have forgotten us?"

"Heartbreaking," he agreed. "That dragon's all the family I've got."

Iris nodded. She felt the same way about Sileria.

"Who needs family?" said a voice from above. When they looked, Seren was straining to reach for one of the blushing citrons growing from the tree's branches. Had she been listening all this time? From all the way up there? Iris suppressed a shudder. How much did the On-High hear? "You are lucky not to have one."

Quintin's nose scrunched, the loss of his parents still fresh.

"That's not nice to say, Seren," said Iris.

The star girl forgot the fruit, looking down at them, curious. "Is it not? I forget how sensitive you mortals are to words. Your lynx was right."

"Sileria?"

Seren nodded, turning back to her efforts to reach the pink fruit.

"You can speak to Sileria?" Iris asked, her heart quickening.

"No, not as I speak to you," said Seren. "But I can see inside her head."

Iris swallowed. Could she see inside all their minds?

"What about Umbra?" asked Quintin. "Have you spoken to her?"

"Ugh, yes," said Seren. She inched farther along, the branch groaning under her weight. Umbra raised her head. "She says the foulest, most profane things about the Hemoth, but then he is rather annoying."

Umbra snorted, as if in confirmation, and Alcor, for his part, sniffed at the shadow dragon, *bope bope bope*.

Quintin laughed, but Iris was less amused. If Seren could see inside the minds of the High Beasts, then surely she could see inside the mind of anyone. Could she see into the secret corners of men's hearts? How much did Seren know, she wondered, about how Iris hated her crown—the crown bestowed upon her by the On-High?

Seren lunged for the fruit and toppled forward, screeching as she fell, pulling leaves and blushing citron down with her.

"Seren!" shouted Quintin, and all the High Beasts rose, Alcor groaning as the Starhounds howled frantically. Only the dragon stayed where she was, her massive scaly back catching Seren on her way down.

"Are you all right?" asked Iris.

The silver-haired girl scrambled off the dragon's back and held up her fruit triumphantly. "I got it!"

"Queen Iris." Keeper Von stood just outside the shade of the blushing tree, his face grave, calling Iris back to the anxieties of the Manor. "High Keeper Dev has asked me to fetch the sacred On-High. The Oracles will be arriving soon."

Seren didn't need to be told twice, pushing back the sniffing muzzles of the High Beasts, which had begun to crowd her. "Yes, yes," she said, clutching her blushing citron. "To the Manor. Back to Dev."

With that, Seren headed to the Manor with Von, the High Beasts trailing behind, leaving Iris and Quintin alone beneath the blushing tree.

"The Oracles are coming," said Quintin. "Wonder how they'll feel about Seren reading their minds without permission."

"Don't you feel strange about it?" asked Iris.

He shrugged. "What the On-High can do, the On-High can do. Here on earth or in the sky, I don't imagine there's much difference."

No. She supposed not. There was wisdom in that. Still. The idea was unsettling.

"She's not what I imagined."

"No," Quintin agreed. "But I imagine that's part of why she's... well, down here. And not up there."

Iris considered that.

"Shall we go back?" he asked her.

"No," said Iris. "I'd rather stay and sit a little while longer. Just for a minute. If that's all right with you."

Quintin made no argument and sat down again with Iris, the two of them resting with their backs against the trunk of the blushing tree. Iris breathed the citrusy, sweet smell deep into her lungs and let the stillness wash over her. For now, beside the Dragon king, she felt peace and calm. For however long it lasted.

*No two stars shine the same*
*and no one star outshines another.*

—THE WRITINGS OF THE GREAT LADY BERENICE:

The Age of Tawn, *Star Writ*

# TWENTY-NINE

DEV stood on the balcony of Aster's rooms, watching as the gates to Thorn Manor were opened for the Oracles arriving from across the Highen. He swallowed, gathering his strength. They'd call for him soon.

Alcor paced at the base of the tower, the Starhounds of Hundford circling with him, howling. Umbra circled the skies, swooping past Dev, who was straining to get a glimpse inside the castle.

He glanced back inside the rooms, where Seren was carefully dissecting a fruit—a blushing citron from Roarque—lost in the study of its pulp and sections.

When Dev and Bernadine and Ursula had uncovered the truth about Seren, Ursula had been quick to summon the very highest of Oracles to provide counsel. A slither of unease worked through Dev's insides as he turned back to watch the Oracles' rickety old wagons pull into the courtyard—what Oracle, wise as they were, had ever had experience with an On-High in the flesh? The answer, Dev knew, was none. What if the Oracles could tell them no more about what the Nightlocks wanted of Seren than he could?

What would happen to Aster then?

Aster.

The sound of her voice—crying out for him in this very spot, calling for him in the dark as the creatures descended—it echoed in his ears day and night. It tortured him. And what tortured him more was wondering what was happening to her now. What the creatures were doing to her. Did she call for him still?

"The Oracles are here," a voice said.

Dev looked back to see Lorc Conri frowning at him, Argos the Starhound panting happily at his side. Lorc was always frowning at him.

"I can see that," said Dev.

The Hound prince joined Dev at the balustrade. The Starhound followed, licking Dev's hand in greeting. At least Argos was still his friend. As soon as he'd greeted Dev, the High Beast headed back inside, settling on the floor at Seren's feet.

"So can we go yet?" asked Lorc impatiently.

"Go?"

"Yes. Go," said Lorc. "Ursula has her sacred ears. They can handle Seren. But who will handle the situation with Aster?"

"The Oracles are here because they are trying to help get Aster back."

"Dragon spit. The Oracles are here because Seren is a star."

Dev felt that familiar wriggle of unease in his guts. The Highen would move mountains for the sake of their Major—unless mountains had to be moved for the On-High themselves. Dev knew in his heart that all allegiance in the Highen would shift from Aster to Seren. All resources, all interests, all care.

But without Seren—what would they offer the Nightlocks for Aster?

Nothing. Six days had already passed of the time Malice had allotted. The Nightlocks would be back tomorrow for their prize. Back with Aster to exchange. Dev and the rest had to be here when they did. "We can't leave."

"I don't care that she's a Tawn-forsaken star, Dev."

"Careful, Lorc." Not only were Lorc's words heresy, his tone was grating on Dev's last nerve. His patience, his understanding were about spent.

"Careful? Or what?" said Lorc. "Tawn himself will rise from his grave and tear me apart? Let him. I don't care about any of it. I care about Aster."

"I care too," snapped Dev.

"Good! Then let's go."

Dev's grip on the railing had tightened so much that his knuckles ached. It was all he could do to keep from throwing a fist in Lorc's face and silencing his ill-considered heroics. "Where exactly would you have us go, Lorc?"

"The mountains!"

"Where in the mountains? Have you any idea how many peaks, how many caves and caverns and animals there are in the Drakkan Range?"

"I'm not afraid."

"Not afraid." Dev paced. As if fear had anything to do with what made Lorc's plan impossible.

"Don't worry about it, High Keeper," said Lorc abruptly. "This isn't your place. You're a scholar. A religious man. I can't blame you for not wanting to go after her. I don't know why I came here."

Dev stared, blinking at Lorc, not quite believing what he'd heard. Had he forgotten how Dev had stood with him against the Minor Bram Lourdes? But believe it or not, Lorc *had* said it.

And Dev's rage bubbled over, anger and fear and despair overwhelming him.

"Speak plainly, Lorc Conri," Dev hissed through gritted teeth. He had listened to the Hound prince dance around his true feelings long enough. And he would be damned by Tawn if he listened for a moment longer.

Lorc stepped to Dev, welcoming his anger. "I release you, Honorable High Keeper," he said. "Release you from any shame at being too afraid to go after your Major."

There was nothing for it, then.

Dev's fist flew on its own, striking Lorc across the face. The Hound prince staggered back, blinking through the shock. Dev was shocked, too. He'd never thrown a fist in his life. But he'd done it now. Connected with the jaw of a Highen royal.

And it felt good.

Lorc dabbed at the blood dripping from his lip, and when he saw the crimson staining his fingers, hot fire surged in his eyes. He roared and launched himself at Dev—

—and the two went down, rolling on the balcony, fists flying. Argos raced out, barking, frantic and confused. Dev landed two more punches before the Hound prince had him pinned. Lorc Conri was a warrior. A trained fighter. And one of five brothers. Dev didn't stand a chance.

Lorc's fists hammered Dev's ear, his gut, his side, his eye. Every inch of Dev screamed in pain, but still he fought back. Fought with everything he had. Not just against Lorc Conri, but against the fears and the anger that had been trying to pull him under ever since he had visited his mother. His fists flew at the thought of the Keepers before him, at Rizlan and everyone since the Age of Tawn who'd never thought it meet to write about Nightlocks. Who'd never thought it a sin to take babies from their mothers.

And before Dev knew what he was doing, he'd managed to get out from under Lorc, to rain down his rage on the prince, who whaled back. Both of them were bloodied and bruised, and still they brawled.

Hands grabbed Dev below the arms and pulled him off. "Dev, turds of Tawn!"

Quintin Wyvern dragged him back as Lorc scrambled to his feet. The Hound prince rounded on him, but Quintin leapt between the two. "*Lorc!* Enough of this! What in the name of the On-High?!"

Dev stood there, panting, barely on the edge of control as Lorc glared back at him, Argos licking nervously at the Hound prince's balled fist, Quintin's hand pressed against Dev's chest. "Have you both lost your *minds*?"

Iris Goreman and Sileria stood in the doorway, both of them staring in that curious way they had. Evaluating. Judging. What did those eyes make of Dev now?

Even Dev didn't know what to make of what he'd done. Lorc's lip was split, his eye swelling. And Dev could feel his own bruises—many of them—feel them purpling and stinging as his blood began to slow.

*Had* he lost his mind? Maybe Quintin was right. Maybe he'd lost his mind the moment Aster was taken from them all. Maybe Lorc had too.

"They fight over the girl." Seren was still at her table, prodding at the blushing citron. "The Major girl. They fight to prove their love."

Everyone was silent.

And Dev laughed. "What!" Of all the absurd—

Lorc stiffened. "Who asked you, Seren?"

Seren shrugged. "No one. But I find your mortal conflict interesting all the same."

Dev felt heat rush to his cheeks. She was wrong, of course. This star. This On-High. She was new to the subtleties of mortal behavior. Whatever she thought she understood about this fight, she was wrong.

"Seren, that's not—" Dev began, but she waved a dismissive hand.

"I grow bored here," she said, dropping the blushing citron and pouting. "You mortals talk too much but never say what you mean." And then there was a flicker—it flashed across her skin like a spark beneath a blanket.

Dev frowned. But no one else seemed to have noticed.

"Well, then," said Lorc, rolling his eyes. "Forgive us for boring you."

"Whatever this is about," said Quintin, "you two have been at each other's throats for days. And I'm tired of it. If you care about Aster at all, you'll know that what she needs is for us to come together—not tear each other apart. You are not the only two feeling the strain of our circumstances."

Dev looked away, ashamed. Quintin was right. What was happening to him? To all of them? He had once counted Lorc Conri among his closest friends.

"Quintin?" said Iris from the doorway. "They're waiting."

The Dragon prince nodded and turned back to Dev. "They sent us to fetch you. You and Seren. The Oracles are ready for you both."

Dev doubted that. No one could be ready for Seren. Even Dev, who'd been with her for days, wasn't sure he was ready for whatever came next.

*How the Starhound stays unfailingly loyal to one king? Love. That's the secret of it.*

—THE WRITINGS OF RIZLAN,
Queen Conri of the House of Hounds on Her Coronation:
The Lunar Offensive, *Star Writ*

 THIRTY

LORC Conri was not a Keeper like Dev. He was not a king like Arthur. No one expected him to command an army; no one expected him to negotiate or lend counsel or participate in diplomatic discussions. No one expected him to understand the will of the stars. He was—for all intents and purposes when the Highen found itself in crisis—nothing at all. So going unnoticed for Lorc Conri was really very easy.

"Lorc!"

If not for Quintin Wyvern.

Lorc made his way down the back hall through the Manor's kitchens, where the servants were preparing acorn bread and twisted-fig jam for the Oracles. He moved quickly. The discussions would be starting anytime now, and Lorc didn't intend to miss a moment.

As long as Quintin didn't slow him down.

"Lorc Conri!" Quintin shouted, running to catch up, Iris Goreman and Sileria trailing behind. "As King of Dracogart I order you to stop!"

Lorc snorted. "You didn't really think that would work, did you?" He pushed open the door into the sunlight of another day. The sixth day. Time was running out.

The courtyard was bursting with wagons and carriages—the many Highen guests for the Shooting Star Parade were all still in

Felisbrook, and the Oracles' wagons barely fit in the spaces of cobble that were left. Lorc moved through the narrow openings, making his way around the west side of the Manor to the north-facing edge where the great hall stood.

Alcor and Umbra lay in the Manor's shadow, Umbra's nostrils smoking and Alcor moaning. The Starhounds barked at the wall, as if it might give way to let them in. They paced the Manor all day, trying to get a glimpse of Seren.

Lorc looked up at the massive rose windows, the image of the Great Lynx in purple and blue stained glass looking down on him with disapproval. They were in there. The Oracles. Seren. And Dev.

Lorc's lip still throbbed. The taste of blood stung his tongue.

"Lorc!" Quintin appeared, out of breath and eyes full of concern, Iris and Sileria standing just behind him. "Where are you going? Don't you think we should get someone to look at your lip?"

"My lip's fine."

"It's pretty swollen."

"I won't die!" Lorc snapped. Of course he knew Quintin was right: he probably *should* have a surgeon see it, given all the blood that had come out of his mouth. Who knew the Keeper had such a good left hook?

"What are you doing?" asked Quintin, staring up at the manor.

"It's the great hall."

"I see that."

"I want to get in."

"Lorc, the Oracles are sitting in council with Dev and the Minor right now—"

"Yes, thank you, O observant King Wyvern," said Lorc. What else did Quintin think he wanted to go in there for? The architecture?

For the first time in a long while, Lorc resented his position in the Hundford court. Because he was a prince, one of five, the attention he was paid was limited. He was respected, of course—a hero, many said; the boy who should have been king, others whispered. But he was *not* king. And that had always been the way he liked it.

But now—the people with power got to stand in the room where the decisions were being made.

And he was not there.

No matter how much he wanted to be. Needed to be. No one had any interest in what he thought at all.

"Lorc," said Quintin. "We *can't* go in there. Even *I* can't go in there. This is a religious conference of the highest sensitivity!" He looked at him closely. "Even if you were king, you'd be here—outside. Aren't I outside?"

"Well," said Lorc with false easiness. "We can't go waltzing in the front door, naturally. I'm looking for something a bit more…subtle."

"You're trying to sneak in?"

The masonry of the Manor was heavy, chunky brick and stone. There were many notches for climbing. But climb to where? He cursed himself for not paying more attention during the ball. Drop a son of the House of Hounds into any forest in all the Highen and he'd figure out where the best tubers grew and which game path led where. But indoors, Conris were lost. "Is there a gallery in the great hall?" Lorc asked. "Quintin, do you remember?"

Iris stepped closer. "There's a triforium," she offered. "At the clerestory windows."

Lorc grinned. If anyone knew the secret places of Thorn Manor, of course it would be the reclusive Queen of Felisbrook. He looked where she pointed, at the blush-rose glass of the clerestory windows grouped in threes beneath ornate arches that lined the wall beneath the Lynx. "And do those windows open?"

"Some do."

"Iris!" said Quintin.

She shrugged. "I'm curious too."

"Right." Lorc began to climb, ignoring Quintin's protests. He was King Wyvern now, after all. Such mischief was hardly becoming a king. Iris Goreman, on the other hand, seemed less concerned with her queenly reputation. She climbed after Lorc, her practiced feet making her ascend faster. He heard a groan from below and looked down to see Quintin reluctantly begin the climb.

"Loyal to a fault, Wyvern," Lorc laughed.

"I know I am," Quintin grumbled. "You'd better hope Umbra doesn't fly up and make a scene." The Shadow Dragon shrieked in disapproval below.

"Doesn't like heights?"

"She doesn't like *me* at heights," said Quintin. "Without her."

Lorc couldn't help feeling a twinge of jealousy at that—at Umbra's love. He looked down to see Sileria, sitting dutifully, neck craned upward to watch her queen climb. Argos, too, would die for Lorc's brother Arthur, the King of Hundford; once, Lorc had been his choice, but Lorc had not stood at the Northern Crowning, and the starhound's love went to his brother. And Alcor—how Alcor must be panicking with Aster gone.

If the beast could ever stop mooning over Seren.

The bear cried quietly—*bope bope bope*—as the children climbed. The dogs, too, began to whine, wanting to follow.

Seren.

The reason everything had gone wrong. And the reason for the sick feeling in Lorc's guts. A star, Dev had said.

Iris cracked open one of the blush-colored windows, the pane tilting up just enough to squeeze under. She held it, and Lorc wedged his way inside, spilling out onto the stone floor of the triforium, the second-floor gallery that looked out on the hall below. He peeked over the stone railing and saw a red sea of Oracles—there had to be every sacred ear from Felisbrook to Tawnshire. Dozens of them. They stood together at the head of the room, shifting, wringing their hands nervously. Seren sat on a chair before them, disinterested and annoyed in the center of the floor. Ursula Lourdes and the Minor, Bernadine Lourdes, stood off to the side, their faces grave with concern.

And Dev, the Honorable High Keeper, stood opposite them, the *Star Writ* clutched in his arms.

"I don't understand," the Keeper was saying. "Seren is a star. An On-High. You said so yourself. How can that be anything but a blessing upon the Highen?"

The sick feeling in Lorc's guts swelled.

The smallest of the Oracles, an ancient and withered thing, back hunched and body frail, spoke for the group. "This star is an unhappy thing."

"What does that matter?"

The old Oracle approached the silver-haired girl. "You are changing, aren't you, blessed star?"

Seren shrugged. "Everything changes."

"But the On-High," said the Oracle. "Your blessed family, they must miss you terribly, bright one."

"The Infinite do not notice me," said Seren. "They are endless. They endure. Forever lighting the dark. They will go on as they always have."

"But what will become of you, O bright On-High?"

"Something more exciting," said the girl, and something happened to her hair. Iris gasped quietly beside Lorc as silver threads fanned out from Seren's head, weightless, and a spark lit the ends before her hair fell around her shoulders once more. "Something *else*."

There was more movement among the Oracles, heads turning to one another with an anxiousness that made Lorc uneasy.

The Oracle bowed, lower than Lorc could have thought such an old body could bend, and turned back to Dev. "This On-High has begun a Great Lumina. A supernova."

Dev flipped frantically through the *Star Writ*. "I know that," he said. "I've heard of that. I just can't—"

"An On-High that undergoes the Great Lumina is a dangerous thing," said the Oracle. Seren barely looked up from whatever had interested her on her toes. Lorc felt the hairs on his neck rise, his skin tingling. "A Lumina is the raw, unrestrained power of the On-High. If she undergoes this change here, in the mortal realm…she will destroy us all."

The rest of the Oracles nodded their agreement, and Lorc swallowed. Destroy the Highen?

"It falls to us, then," said the old Oracle, "to prevent this change from occurring."

There were murmurs among the other Oracles, heads shaking their disagreement.

The old Oracle raised her hands for quiet. "We must call upon our brothers and sisters in red across all the Highen. We must work as one to speak with the On-High. The On-High will want their lost daughter back. The On-High will know how to help her."

"So what happens now?" asked Dev. "Six days have already passed since the Nightlocks took Major Lourdes. They will be upon us tomorrow."

"Which is why the star's safety is of the utmost importance." The old Oracle raised a hand to the Fern Guards standing by the door, and they opened it, a garrison of guards from around the Highen spilling in and surrounding Seren.

"Wait," said Dev. "Wait, where are you taking her?"

"To keep her safe, High Keeper," said the Oracle, "while we confer with the On-High on how to prevent this calamity."

Seren shouted, "Unhand me!"—indignant as any Highen queen. They dragged her out the doors, the Oracles filing out behind her one by one, Seren roaring at them all to let her go.

Iris looked to Quintin and Lorc. "They can't just take her, can they?"

Quintin gaped, unbelieving, but Lorc was not so surprised. Utmost importance—feh. He knew it all along. Seren of the On-High was no queen. She had no army. No allies. For all the reverence she was paid, reverence did not equal power.

"But what about the Major?" asked Dev of the old Oracle. Lorc inched closer to the railing.

"The Major is the daughter of Jasper Lourdes," said the Oracle. "She is strong. She will defeat the Nightlocks."

Lorc's fists clenched at his sides, his palms slick with sweat.

The Oracle followed after the others, to wherever they were taking the star, leaving Dev standing there, fumbling with his blasted *Star Writ*, Ursula and Bernadine gaping with disbelief.

Lorc stormed across the floor, heading down the stairs and making no secret of his presence. So he wasn't supposed to be at the meeting with the Oracles. As if they could do anything about it now.

He landed on the final step with an assertive thud, Dev and the others' heads all turning at once. Dev's face was pale, his eyes wide with fear and disbelief. That was just how Dev looked these days, it seemed.

"Destroy the Highen?" said Quintin, he and Iris sheepishly making their way down the stairs behind Lorc. "What does this mean?"

Dev looked at the window, the Lynx staring down at the group with a pity that only made Lorc angrier. The Keeper said nothing, his knuckles whitening as he clutched the *Star Writ*.

If Dev didn't have the answers now, then Lorc would supply them.

"It means," he said, loudly, "they aren't going to save Aster." Ursula clutched her necklace and Bernadine frowned. "It means," he continued, "we have to save her ourselves."

*Dragon thistle—A highly aggressive and carnivorous thistle native to Dracogart, dragon thistle feeds off the blood of any creature that wanders too close. It is named for its three distinct leaves, which resemble the wings of the Shadow Dragon.*

—THE WRITINGS OF THUBAN,
On the Flora and Fauna of Dracogart: The Star Majors, *Star Writ*

# THIRTY-ONE

THE sky over Tawnshire in autumn was bluer than lapis, with clouds as soft as jackrabbits racing past on cool and changing winds. The grass turned gold, and the trees began to burn with color. Aster loved fall in Tawnshire. Because it also meant her father would come home.

Every fall, the kingdoms of the Highen became preoccupied with preparations for the Festival of Tawn, and no matter where her father had journeyed in the Highen for his responsibilities as Major, he would return for the Festival. And in the weeks leading up to the celebrations, he had nothing to do but spend time with Aster.

They spent the day on the green, now a sea of bright yellow grasses, near the Starlight Pond beside the Shiver Woods. Aster was seven. She and Ursula picked wildflowers while Bernadine read on a tree stump, not willing to dirty her dress by getting too close to the water's edge. The Major Jasper Lourdes dozed in the warm autumn light, reclined on the belly of the sleeping Mizar, the great Hemoth Bear.

Until Ursula screamed.

When Aster looked up from her tiny bouquet of pink-and-purple pincushion blossoms, Ursula was standing in the pond, clutching at her ear. "Something stung me!"

Bernadine barely looked away from her book.

The Major sat up, Mizar barely lifting her head to follow his gaze. "Are you all right, my ferocious girl?"

Ursula sniffled, trying to hide her tears as she pulled her hand away from her ear and blood stained her fingers. Her father helped her climb out of the reeds onto the shore and inspected her ear, Ursula sobbing quietly. Aster wandered over, curious as to what sort of bug could have drawn blood this close to the frosts.

When she was beside her sister, inspecting the blood at her ear, Aster saw a flower in her hair. "Isn't that dragon thistle?" she asked. She'd seen it many times in books and embroidered on her mother's dresses. Aster had always liked it because of the blue leaves that fanned out from its spiky head, like dragon wings. And because of its wickedness—dragon thistle was a very carnivorous plant indeed. "That's why you're bleeding."

Ursula's sobs grew louder, but her father only laughed. "Dragon thistle? That doesn't grow in Tawnshire, silly bear."

"But that's what it looks like."

"Oh, nonsense," her father chuckled, plucking the little plant from behind Ursula's ear. "It's nothing but a common mud thistle."

"No, Father," Aster insisted. "It's dragon thistle. It bit her ear!"

"Did I ever tell you about the time I found myself stuck in a thicket of dragon thistle?" her father asked.

Ursula sniffed and shook her head.

"Well, the first thing you should know about dragon thistle is that it grows in the mountains, and it grows big. Massive, it was! Huge, thorny stalks growing in a dark canyon of jagged rock, the stems taller than the Manor. The spiny blooms as big as Mizar—bigger, even! And ten times as hungry!" Ursula giggled as he tickled her side, but Aster only frowned. "I was thrown into the canyon by a band of killers escaped from Dracogart's Highest Keep. And I hit every spiky branch on the way down. Bruised and battered like a tumbled pear, I was. But there was no time to tend my leg, which was surely broken. Because my screams had roused the sleeping plants from their slumber. And they smelled my blood as surely as they smelled my fear."

Father lifted Ursula, cradling her like a babe, and carried her back to the Manor, his booming voice rising and falling with the action of his heroic tale in the distance.

Aster picked through the grass and found the little thistle. Blue. With leaves just like dragon wings. It was tiny, though.

She held it in her hand, but the little plant didn't move. And it didn't seem terribly dangerous. Then again, its stem was severed. Perhaps…Aster picked her way through the reeds, her feet numb in the frigid pond's waters. And found a patch of more thistles. Blue and winged.

"They're not mud thistles." Bernadine stood on the shore, holding her book open, her finger on the page. "Says here mud thistles are brown and orange. And they don't have those leaves."

"What is it, then?"

Bernadine shrugged.

A flash of orange on one of the bulrushes caught Aster's eye—an amber beetle.

Curious, she plucked the little bug from its perch and dropped it onto the bloom of one of the blue thistles.

And instantly, the spiny bulb split open, its fanged mouth clamping shut on the little beetle, before it fell still and silent again. Aster grinned and looked at her cousin.

Bernadine nodded. "Sure looks like a dragon thistle to me."

Aster sat at the mouth of the Nightlocks' cave, feet dangling over the rocky ledge, staring at a dragon thistle poking out of the rock. He had been wrong, all those years ago. Wrong about the thistle. It was a small thing. Barely worth remembering. But still.

Aster tossed a rock over the ledge. *There are truths in this world you must discover for yourself.* There were no truths in these mountains. Other than one: Nightlocks were cruel things.

Of course, she had known that *before* she was dragged here. How long ago was that? Four nights? Five? An eternity, whatever it was. And she still had no sense of when or if she'd see home again. Malice was not the most forthright of creatures.

Still, Aster couldn't help but be curious about her. About who she was before she became a Moon Demon. About what mistakes she had made in her life. Nightlocks were supposed to speak in riddles—nonsense beings, bent on confusing the minds of mortals. Why, then, did Aster see a sort of sense in the things the creature said to her?

Perhaps that was the *real* danger of Nightlocks—when their nonsense stopped seeming like nonsense. If Aster wasn't careful, she could lose herself.

"Are you cold?" Aster turned to see Malice standing at the mouth of the cave, her yellow eyes glinting in the moonlight.

"I am fine."

A breath—a bull-like snort—escaped the Nightlock. "I have restored the fire for you. You mortals are vulnerable to chills, as I recall."

When Aster said nothing, the Nightlock left her, returning to the cave.

"She recalls nothing of what it is to be mortal." Aster jumped at the snakelike whisper to her left. Slinking from the shadows at the ledge was Avarice. "My sister," she said, "was cold as stone even when red blood moved through her veins."

"What happened to her?"

Avarice snarled, glancing nervously toward where Malice stoked the fire. Satisfied that her sister was not watching, the smaller Nightlock skulked closer. "What she asked for. It's her fault we became these…monstrosities."

Aster's heart began to race. "But why, though? Chasing a truth?"

"The truth of my love," hissed Avarice. "He wanted to wed me and only me. And she was jealous. They both were. So to spite me, she begged the moon to make us this."

Aster winced. "*She* did this to you?"

"But it will be undone," said Avarice, straightening. "Once we have the star in hand."

"The fallen star?" asked Aster. "I thought you were after a girl?" Seren.

Avarice grinned, her fanged teeth flashing. "We've waited many lifetimes for a star to come to the mortal realm. A star volatile enough to break the Moon Door open forever."

A star? Break the Moon Door open? Nonsense and riddles. That was the Nightlock way.

But still a chill worked through her.

Seren.

Was Seren a star?

"You...you want this girl," Aster said, her throat suddenly dry, "to break open the door to death?"

"When there is no door," said Avarice, "there is no prison. We will be free."

Aster's mind raced. No door to the netherworld. The Nightlocks, all of them, would spill out into the Highen. There would be nothing to contain them. Nothing to confine them. Without the restrictions of the moon's power, there would be no holy rules governing them.

"And we will be mortal," hissed Avarice. "My sister will give my life back to me."

"Avarice." Malice loomed over them, glaring down at Avarice, who cowered, slinking back into the shadows.

Aster looked up at Malice. "You would destroy the Moon Door? Have you any idea what darkness you will unleash on the Highen?"

The Nightlock said nothing, turning her back on Aster and flying off into the darkness.

*Do you hear me, Dog, said the Hemoth to the Hound,*
*I know the way to the On-High, I know where they'll be found.*
*I'll follow you where you will, said the Starhound to the Bear.*
*I'll follow you to world's end,*
*I'll follow you anywhere.*

—HUNDFORDIAN NURSERY RHYME

# THIRTY-TWO

THE Oracles had taken Seren to Thorn Keep, the best-fortified structure in the castle complex, surrounded by a collected infantry of the best spearmen from each of the Highen's kingdoms. In the courtyard, soldiers ran to and fro, shouting orders and readying for whatever was to happen when the Nightlocks arrived. Alcor and Umbra and the Starhounds had already sniffed out where Seren had gone, and the High Beasts made their displeasure known, howling and roaring and screeching at the keep's base. Dev watched, head pounding, as a dozen crossbowmen rushed past him, heading to the keep's uppermost battlements. The Oracles intended to keep the Nightlocks out, but, it was increasingly clear, they also meant to keep Seren in.

Lorc Conri stood beside Dev in the chaos, the entirety of the Highen's gathered forces mobilized around them. But for all the frenzy, Dev and Lorc were still. Quintin, Bernadine, Iris, and Ursula stood with them, frozen too. All of them at a loss. All of them stunned by what the Oracles had decided.

They would not save Aster. The Major. They would leave her to the Nightlocks.

There was no real choice, perhaps. But what was to happen now?

Dev shuddered. How would the creature Malice react when she arrived to find nothing for her?

Finally, Lorc broke the silence between them. "The Nightlocks come tomorrow. We are the only hope Aster has."

Hope. Dev desperately clung to it. Held on to any shred of it he could find.

She would be here, that much was true. Tomorrow, the Nightlocks would bring Aster home.

"This power of Seren's," Dev said slowly, "whatever she's becoming. It jeopardizes the whole of the Highen to let the Nightlocks have it. We need to keep her safe."

"I'm not suggesting we hand her over!" Lorc snapped. "But how about a feint? Quintin and Umbra could create a distraction—lots of dragonflame. Then you and I could free Seren and use her like a carrot. We wouldn't let them *take* her. We'd have to be clever—clever enough to rescue Aster."

Bernadine hushed the Hound prince, glancing around to see if anyone was listening. But the soldiers called to defend the keep had no interest in them.

Dev glared at Lorc, his familiar frustration with the Hound prince rising. Lorcan Conri was an *act now, think later* person. He was rash and he was impetuous. Dev was a *think first* person.

And think. And think. And think. He was so tired of thinking. His brain thundered with the pain of all the thinking he'd been doing.

And still he had no solutions. Aster herself, Dev knew, would not want to pursue any course where the Nightlocks would win what they most wanted. But if the Nightlocks weren't getting Seren, that left nothing to bargain with for Aster.

Terror Maids.

What did they have that a Malevolency Nightlock could possibly want?

"Bernadine," said Dev, the wheels in his head turning. "What did the sisters Faith, Hope, and Mercy tell the fisherman?"

"What?" said Lorc.

"In the story," said Dev, "Keeper Kalamity. What did it say?"

"They—they offered to be his bride," stammered Bernadine.

"And that was what upset Mercy—er, Malice. Right? That the fisherman took each sister's offer?"

Bernadine nodded. "Her sisters offered themself up to the fisherman, to escape their island home. And when he agreed to both their offers, it tore the sisters apart."

A bright glimmer of hope swelled in Dev's chest. "Too much to choose from."

"Dev?" asked Ursula. "You've got that look again...."

"What if we give Malice too much to choose from?"

"What are you on about?" said Lorc. "Choose what?"

"What she wants," said Dev. "She's looking for a star. Let's give her a few." He looked at Ursula, then at Bernadine.

"Do you mean us?" said Ursula.

"We can re-create what happened," explained Dev. "The star is a girl. The Nightlocks won't know what girl. If we present the Nightlocks with multiple potential stars, maybe, *just maybe*, it will be enough of a distraction to get Aster back. I mean, they'll bring her for the trade, won't they?"

"I don't know, Dev," said Quintin. "Surely the Nightlock will know they're not stars?"

"Then why does the Nightlock charge us with finding the star, if it knows a star when it sees one?"

No one said anything for the longest moment. Dev watched the doubt and uncertainty move across their faces.

"It will enrage Malice," said Bernadine.

It would indeed. But rage didn't matter. All that mattered was creating an opportunity.

Lorc grinned, clearly warming to the plan. "I think you might have gone a bit mad, High Keeper. I like it."

Bernadine straightened. "Aster is my family," she said. "I will be a star."

"As will I," said Ursula.

Iris stepped forward. "I will be a star."

Three stars. Three Terror Maids. So it was agreed.

But the Dragon king seemed less convinced. "Our elders will never entertain this," he said. "Lady Luella? Lady Leona? Arthur Conri?"

"I don't know," said Ursula. "They're worried about the state of the Highen without Aster, make no mistake. As Major, she is the pillar on which everything stands. She is very, very popular among the people. She has proved herself in battle. She has made the strongest alliances seen in generations—with you, her friends. Without her, they fear the collapse of the whole kingdom—maybe even another war. We *need* her."

"But girls masquerading as stars?" asked Quintin.

Ursula shrugged. "It's not really up to them, is it? Bernadine is the Minor. She is the Major's proxy in Aster's absence."

They all looked at Bernadine, who chewed the inside of her cheek nervously. She breathed deep, eyes closed. "I will speak to the Heads of Houses. I will tell them the Major will not be forgotten. We will stand together against the Nightlocks, and we will try this gambit."

*The chill of winter is in the White Bear's bones. There is no cold they cannot weather.*

—THE WRITINGS OF BERN,
On White Bears: The Fore, *Star Writ*

# THIRTY-THREE

BERNADINE'S stomach felt as if a flock of snow owls had taken wing inside her. She stood at the head of Thorn Manor's great hall, beneath the face of the Lynx, while the Heads of Houses and other Highen leaders stared at her, speechless. Standing there, Bernadine wished she hadn't come to Felisbrook. She knew she had to. Knew that if the Highen was going to face a threat of Nightlocks, it would be wrong to stay away and keep her considerable knowledge to herself. But she'd spent so long avoiding the judging eyes of the Highen, and now here she was—standing before them all, asking them to follow her.

*For Aster*, she reminded herself. *For the Highen.*

Ursula smiled encouragingly, but the silence was deafening. Bernadine breathed deep, willing her nerves to settle.

Lady Luella was the first to break the quiet. She rose from her seat, one skeptical eyebrow perked. "We are supposed to trust you now?"

Bernadine flinched. No, she supposed they weren't. Bernadine had given the Highen no reason to trust her. She'd been a ghost in Whitlock for so long. And after what she'd let almost happen to Marmoral—Bernadine could barely trust herself. She had no right to ask anything of the Highen at all.

But she wasn't asking for herself. For her cousin, for the Highen itself, she would face the judgment of the realm.

"I trust her," said Ursula, rising.

"So do I," echoed Lorc Conri, who also stood, determined.

His brother, the King of Hundford, stood with him. "Hundford is with you."

"Dracogart will stand with Bernadine Lourdes," announced Quintin Wyvern.

Bernadine exhaled. Their voices gave her strength. But still, she had to wonder if it would be enough to convince the others.

Lady Leona clucked her tongue disapprovingly. "The foolishness of youth." The Lynx woman stepped out into the center of the room, in front of Bernadine. "The royal cubs of our Highen may have forgotten about the blood that runs in our Minor's veins." Bernadine caught Aunt Luella nodding vigorously. "It is a great thing you ask of us," Leona went on, "trusting *you* to save the Major. When indeed, in her absence, you rule the Highen."

Bernadine's throat went dry.

It was true, Bernadine ruled. The very thing Aunt Luella had so long suspected her of wanting. The very thing her father had wanted for her—had killed to get for her. How Bernadine detested crowns and thrones!

"No one has seen you since you took the post at Whitlock," said Leona. "And here you stand, when the Major is gone. How convenient."

The Lynx woman's words were barbs to Bernadine's heart. They were wrong about her. She was not the same as her father. But how could they expect anything different, after what he'd done to the Major Jasper Lourdes? If the father could kill his brother, why could not the daughter wish her cousin dead?

"I—I am the Minor," Bernadine stammered. "This is my command."

"No," Leona said, finally. "Felisbrook will not support this plan."

Dev stood up, commanding the attention of the room as High Keeper of the Highen. "She is chosen by the White Bear Marmoral," he said to Leona. "You would question the will of a High Beast?"

"Forgive me, Honorable High Keeper," Leona said. "But White Bears have been known to make questionable choices."

Father again. Would Bernadine never be rid of his shadow?

Bernadine looked into the crowd for Iris—she was a part of this plan. If Felisbrook did not support them, Roarque and Twigate might object as well. And they were going to need every blade they could get.

Iris Goreman stood suddenly, her chin held high. "Felisbrook," she said, "will stand with you, Minor Lourdes."

"Iris!" Leona shouted.

"I have already volunteered myself for the role of one of the stars," said Iris, indignant. An icy tension flared between the two Lynx women, and Bernadine wondered how long Iris had longed to stand up to her advisor like that. She was glad for her, glad she had finally been moved to.

"Iris," said Leona, "you can't possibly—"

"As Queen of Felisbrook," said Iris, "I declare Felisbrook's support of the Minor Bernadine Lourdes."

"Iris—"

"Be seated," snapped Iris, "Lady Leona."

Chin quivering, Leona dropped back into her seat, and Bernadine was relieved. But still, her aunt did not look convinced. Aunt Luella. Her hatred for Bernadine ran so deep, the young Minor didn't think she could ever have the woman's love again.

"Lady Leona is right," admitted Bernadine. "I've no right to ask you to trust me after all the time I've spent away. But the hour does grow late. Felisbrook is divided, the kingdom in a state of unrest. If we lose the Major, the stability of our beloved Highen will only be further weakened. It is not just important to get my cousin back from the Nightlocks—it is imperative. And Aunt Luella, trust me or not, this plan—our plan—is the only option to save Aster."

Aunt Luella kept her eyes on her hands, folded primly in her lap.

Bernadine could see her chewing her lip—she'd grown up watching Aunt Luella chew her lip when she was unsure of something.

Finally, Lady Lourdes looked up, and Bernadine could see tears of frustration welling in her eyes.

"Save her, then, Minor Lourdes," she said. "I pray to the On-High I am proven wrong about you."

Bernadine nodded, grateful that her aunt would grant her that much.

She would prove Luella Lourdes wrong. And that would be the first step. So that maybe someday, they could be family again.

The ambassador from Roarque rose. "Roarque fought with Hundford against the Minor. Roarque would be honored to fight again."

The Ox King of Härkädia stood. "Härkädia will fight for the Major's safe return."

The Duchess of Sapphire from Twigate joined him. "Twigate stands with you."

Bernadine released her frozen breath. It was done, then. The whole of the Highen would face the Nightlocks. Together.

And get Aster back.

*The greatest indication of the sensibilities in a person's head is revealed by what they wear on their feet.*

—Etiquette for Majors and Courtly Persons: A Guidebook

# THIRTY-FOUR

THE fire had long since died, and Aster's toes were nothing but pins and needles inside her formal slippers. The slippers themselves were scuffed and filthy, the right torn at the big toe from her scramble through the mountains. She kicked them off. They were useless against the elements. She massaged her feet, trying to rub feeling back into them, but it only hurt all the more.

Malice and her sisters had been gone since the night before, leaving Aster alone from sunup through the whole of the day.

From her seat by the dead fire inside the Nightlock cave, she could see the daylight fading to pink in the world outside. Night would be upon her again soon. And when it came, would it bring the Nightlocks back?

Aster hugged her middle and walked to the mouth of the cave, stepping into the waning evening light, hoping to absorb the last of the sun's warmth. She was so hungry. She hoped when Malice returned she would have another rabbit.

*If* Malice returned.

Aster searched the sky—was the moon visible yet?

If the Moon Door closed, it would call the Nightlocks home. If the Moon Door closed, Malice would miss her opportunity to break it using Seren. And the Highen would be safe.

But if the Moon Door closed and called the Terror Maids back before Malice returned Aster to the Highen—Aster would be stranded in the mountains.

With the gargoyles.

She swallowed. How she hoped Malice would return. A perverse hope.

Aster curled up on her side and watched the world change from pink to purple to a deep inky blue. She watched stars blink to life, the On-High looking down with pity as her empty stomach raged. The image of Tawn—it was even dimmer tonight. How long before it faded into nothing at all? What hope was there then? Father's star...she could barely make it out.

"It was dragon thistle, Father," she whispered. "It was."

The tiny light flickered just the slightest. Did he know he had been wrong?

And there was the Moon Door—still a sliver in the heavens. Open. A time for mischief and trouble. So the Terror Maids had not been called home yet.

What she wouldn't give to see Umbra, the mighty Shadow Dragon, blot out the sky with her massive wings, Quintin riding on her back. Tears welled in Aster's eyes. She did not have the strength to go back on the slopes of the Drakkan Range. She was tired and she was hungry and she was *afraid*—of gargoyles and dragons and all the hundreds of other hungry beasts that lived in these altitudes.

Most of all, she was afraid of Tawn's fading light.

Was it Malice and her sisters? Was their presence in the Highen dimming the lights of the On-High somehow? *Break the Moon Door.* Even if Malice succeeded, how could the On-High allow her to get away with it? What reckoning would come for her and her sisters if she did this evil thing? Malice didn't seem concerned with that at all.

Aster looked to her father's star. Her guiding light. If it went out, how would she know where to turn?

As soon as she'd thought it, her father's star was blotted out by massive bat wings—the Terror Maids, sailing through the night, black shadows in the dark. Aster sat up, as if to greet them when they landed, but she said nothing when they dropped onto the landing, one after another, Avarice and Despair snarling and chattering before disappearing inside.

Malice stood there, her back to Aster, but Aster could see the creature's clawed hands hanging tensely at her sides. The fingers clenched and unclenched, the thumb pressing the knuckles anxiously.

"What?" asked Aster. "What is it?"

"Tonight, Aster Lourdes," said Malice, "you go home."

Aster's heart swelled with relief, but only for a moment. "And then you destroy the Moon Door?"

Malice nodded. "And then I destroy the Moon Door."

With Seren. A star. An On-High. The exact antithesis of the darkness behind the moon. It didn't make sense. "Why do you think Seren can do such a thing?"

Malice's head twisted around, like an owl's, yellow eyes flashing, and Aster jumped. "Seren...," the Nightlock hissed, fangs flashing, looking more monstrous than Aster could have believed possible. "You know its name...."

Aster's stomach turned. She should not have spoken.

Malice smiled, her smile a hard and pitiless thing, and Aster felt the cold sink deeper into her bones. What *had* she come back as? Malice was a Nightlock, yes. Aster had never lost sight of that. But this creature, whatever she'd returned as, was something...something even *more* malevolent. "Did your father ever hold the name of a star on his tongue, young Aster?"

No. He hadn't. That would have been a story he'd have loved to tell most of all. "I thought about what you said," said Aster. "About my father being wrong. He was wrong. You were right."

Malice turned to face her, a smug look of triumph on her face.

"But how do *you* know *you're* not wrong?" Aster asked. "In this thing you are doing? How do you know that the On-High won't punish you for breaking what they put in place?"

Malice blinked at her, as if she couldn't comprehend the question. Finally, she shrugged. "I don't."

Aster didn't understand. "Then how can you do this?"

The Nightlock sighed. "My path is my own, Aster Lourdes," she said. "I choose it. I walk it. And I accept the consequences."

The consequences of this choice, Aster knew, would be terrible indeed. For all of them.

"Malice," Despair whimpered from the mouth of the cave. "What if the mortals won't deliver the star?"

Malice snapped without turning, "They will."

Despair cowered, but Avarice looked less convinced. The Nightlock slunk onto the ledge. "What if, Malice," she hissed, "the Moon Door has already begun to close!"

"Then we call upon the three tiers. The Follies, the Essurience, and the Cunning."

Aster's heart froze. More Nightlocks? "You can't do that."

Malice laughed, hollow and humorless. "What do you know of Nightlocks, child? Of the power we have?"

Aster knew nothing. Nothing about the Terror Maids; nothing about what further secrets the Moon Door held.

"We are no ordinary Nightlocks, girl," hissed Avarice.

Despair cackled, delighting in Aster's surging fear.

"We are the Malevolencies, Aster Lourdes," said Malice, rising to her full and terrible height. "We are the commanders of the armies of the moon."

Aster shrank back. The armies of the moon. They appeared in the *Star Writ*—she knew it well, the chapter where her father became the Death Chaser—"The Lunar Offensive."

"We will call upon the moon's armies," said Malice to her sisters, her wings lifting her up so that her feet rose from the ground.

"And they will fight until we have what we came for. Until our mortality is restored."

Aster looked up to the stars—Tawn, the Great Bear. She couldn't find his image at all now. The lights had faded to nothing. And her father's star. It was gone.

Despair kept laughing, cruel and wild, but Avarice hissed, not satisfied. "And if the people of the Bear Highen fight back?" she demanded.

Malice dropped to the ground, nostrils flaring, fangs bared. "Then you can eat them…and their Major."

Look up high,
  The On-High's light,
    It burns for you and me,
      The On-High's light above the world
        How lucky we are to see.

—*A Children's Guide to the On-High*

# THIRTY-FIVE

ᗞECKED out in his battle armor, Arthur Conri, King of the House of Hounds, looked like a king of Hundford legend. He hardly looked like Lorc's big brother at all. Pauldroned shoulders and a chest plate molded with the crest of Hundford—he was huge, thick, and broad. A man. Lorc tugged at the collar of his armored doublet—it chafed the base of his neck, but it was the practical choice for him, slight as he was in comparison. Full armor was heavy and not well fitted to his frame. The doublet gave him more mobility. Still…he couldn't help feeling small and childlike next to his brother.

The Conris made their way through the basement corridor to the keep, to where the Oracles were holding Seren. Ursula had asked them to inform the Oracles that they were about to get into position for the "exchange"—the Terror Maids would be on them any moment.

Ursula, Iris, and Bernadine were together in the Major's chambers, readying themselves to play the role of star. Lorc and Arthur had spent the better part of the afternoon with Dev, Quintin, and a dozen grooms and soldiers, sequestering the High Beasts in the stables. It was a greater struggle than any of them had expected. Their need to be near Seren was intensifying by the hour. No amount of treats or pleading made them budge—not until Iris ordered her chefs to prepare a full trough of trout did the High Beasts cooperate.

How long the stables would hold them, Lorc couldn't guess at. He hoped long enough.

"I don't like this, Lorc," said Arthur.

"Ursula will be fine." Arthur had been anxious all day about Ursula masquerading as a star. The idea of losing his bride to a flock of Nightlocks was not something that sat well with him, and he'd been vocal about it. "She volunteered for this, Arthur," Lorc reminded him. "She told you herself. She's brave."

"I know it, but it's not only that," Arthur said. "If this goes poorly, as it most surely will, we are facing a trio of Nightlocks without the High Beasts. Have you ever known a king to go to battle without a beast?"

No.

The *Star Writ* was bursting with tales of Majors and kings and queens, all of their victories fought and won with their High Beast at their side. But what choice did they have?

"You know why we have to lock them away, Arthur."

"I know. Because they will lead the Nightlocks to Seren." Arthur sighed, rubbing the bridge of his nose. "I want you to promise to stay by my side. Right with me. At all times. You understand?"

Lorc rolled his eyes. He did not need his brother playing nursemaid, as if Lorc had never seen battle before. "Need me to protect you, do you?"

"I'd feel much safer." Arthur grinned.

They'd come to the armored door of the keep, and Arthur nodded at the Fern Guard who knocked twice—a pause—and knocked again. The door was opened from inside and Arthur and Lorc made their way up the damp stone stairs to the great chamber—where the Oracles were working to stop Seren's transformation.

When they entered, it didn't seem to Lorc that things were going well.

Seren sat on a chair in the middle of the room. The Oracles stood with their massive brass ear trumpets, listening for the voices of the On-High. They were humming hymns around the girl—droning, bone-chilling dirges that reminded Lorc of his mother's funeral. But that wasn't what sent goose bumps racing up his plated arms.

It was Seren.

Sitting there.

Eyes blank, staring at nothing.

And glowing.

All of her glowed and blinked, silver like her hair, like a fish moving through sunlight, like a terrible white-hot forge, like the Dust Dragons. Lorc looked at his brother, and Arthur's eyes were wide, unbelieving. There was no denying what she was now. An On-High. Real and here and frightening.

When the head Oracle saw them, the singing faltered, and Seren's light dimmed.

"What do you want?" she said shortly.

Arthur checked his expression, and Lorc marveled at how composed he seemed. "The Lady Ursula sent me to inform you that the hour is upon us. The Terror Maids will be arriving any moment. We have stationed extra forces here for protection."

"We don't need extra forces," snapped the Oracle. "We don't want to call attention to our position."

"They have been positioned strategically about the Manor. They will not call attention to the keep unless necessary."

"And the High Beasts?"

"Sequestered."

The Oracle nodded, satisfied.

Seren stood, her eyes narrowed and full of rage. She looked directly at Lorc, and he felt his knees turn to jelly. "I wish to be released from this nonsense," she said darkly.

The Oracle shooed them. "Begone from here! You are distracting her."

"I am not distracted," seethed Seren. "I am done here. I wish to be freed."

"Blessed On-High," said the old Oracle, "the heavens need your light."

Seren screamed, loud and furious, and her light rushed back, flowing out from her heart to the ends of her silver hair.

"Sing!" shouted the Oracle. "So that the skies can hear you, all of you, sing now!"

The gathered Oracles held their trumpets to their ears and began their monotonous humming, while Seren's scream grew louder and more furious, her light growing brighter, hotter, like the very center of a hearth. She rose from the ground, as if the very force of her scream was lifting her up, and Arthur threw a protective hand in front of Lorc.

"On-High, we beg you!" shouted the old Oracle. "Call your daughter home to her place in the sky!"

Seren stopped screaming, but her light remained, her body aloft like a phantom. "You don't want me here, Oracle," she whispered. "The Infinite do not want me there. You cannot stop me from becoming what is next."

The light at the core of Seren, emanating from her chest, swelled.

Lorc cried out, and Arthur covered him as the light exploded around them and there was a rushing in his ears. Lorc closed his eyes, and he could see the red of his lids illuminated by Seren's light.

And he fell, he and Arthur both, thrown with the growing sound of rushing air, a hot breeze.

And then the world was dark.

And there was a ringing in Lorc's ears.

When Arthur let him go and the Conri brothers stood, the Oracles were all on the floor, dazed and groggily struggling to rise.

On the floor at the center of the room lay a pile of ash where the chair had been, scorch marks radiating across the stone.

And Seren.

The star girl.

She was gone.

*The Malevolencies: The largest, most powerful, and most tangible of the Moon Demons. The Malevolencies are unique among Nightlocks in that their former mortal lives were not necessarily wicked. Their mortal selves were not taken by Nightlocks for their terrible deeds in life and changed behind the moon. The Malevolencies asked for the moon's dark blessing. The Malevolencies pledged themselves to darkness. And so the Malevolencies are the commanders of the moon's dark forces.*

*And the Malevolencies are the worst evil beneath the On-High's skies.*

—KEEPER KALAMITY,
*A Compendium of Nightlocks*

# THIRTY-SIX

THE fire had been burning for ages. The Hermans had lit the massive pyre as the sun set over Felisbrook, and now, in the dark of night, it was as tall as a building, its tips licking at the top branches of the twisted oaks that lined the edge of the Deadwood.

It was decided among the commanders that it would be best to meet the Terror Maids beyond the walls of the Manor, away from the city. A massive fire was set to direct the creatures' attention to the spot they had chosen, but as the night grew deeper, Dev had to wonder if the Terror Maids would know to come to the flames.

The soldiers of the Highen surrounded the fire in concentric circles, fifty men deep, grouped by kingdom. They were, all of them, tense with uncertainty.

At the center of the soldiers, the "stars" stood on all sides of the fire: Quintin with Iris, Arthur Conri with Bernadine, and Lorc behind Dev and Ursula. Ursula had insisted on being beside Dev, wanting his Star Writ knowledge readily accessible. Lorc stood behind them, ready to lend aid should anything go wrong. Arthur Conri, the best warrior in the Highen, was chosen to stand by the Minor, the Highen's highest ruler in Aster's absence. Quintin stood with Iris, the royal team a formidable pair in the face of the Nightlock threat.

Ursula Lourdes stood rubbing her neck. She'd been watching the skies for too long. She wore a purple velvet cloak, the color of

Felisbrook, and her hair was powdered so that in the dark it looked as silver as Seren's.

"She wouldn't come here, would she?" Ursula asked. "Seren, I mean?"

Dev couldn't say. Who could? Where Seren had gone after escaping the keep was anyone's guess. "I hope not."

They'd sent a separate unit of men into the Deadwood to look for her, but they had yet to return. Every moment they didn't was a moment Seren brought herself closer to her Great Lumina. Every moment the Terror Maids did not descend from the sky, Dev had to wonder if it was because they had found Seren themselves.

He looked to the sky. The image of Tawn had all but disappeared from view. What did that mean for the battle to come? He couldn't imagine it was a good sign.

His vision flashed across his memory again, the Great Lord Tawn swallowing the moon. Did it foretell victory for the Bear Highen?

Or was the starry bear just Seren, destroying the moon and all the Highen with it? His throat felt dry.

Ursula took his hand in hers. "Whatever happens, Dev," she said, "Aster is lucky to have you as her Keeper."

Dev looked at the ground, unable to meet Ursula's gaze. She didn't know how he'd spoken to Aster before she was taken. Didn't know the things he'd said. *I'm stuck with you.* The shame of it…the hurt he'd seen in her eyes…

If this plan of theirs didn't work…he'd see those eyes in his tortured sleep for the rest of his days.

A murmur rippled through the soldiers behind them, all of them looking skyward.

"They're here," said Lorc Conri, looking to the northeast.

Dev's heart thundered behind his ribs as the shadows in the sky drew near. Three winged creatures. The Terror Maids. They descended into the circle, landing softly, the two smaller ones hissing and screeching at the soldiers, who readied their weapons, shifting nervously on their feet.

The biggest of the Nightlocks, Malice, spread her wings to their full width. Cradled in her arms—Dev held his breath—was Aster.

The creature placed her gently on the ground and Aster stood before them, her face pale, her fine clothes from the ball tattered and filthy, her shoulders covered in dried blood. Her chin was scraped, her shoes were gone. Dev wanted to run to her, to throw his arms around her and hurry her into the fold of the gathered forces waiting to protect her.

But he stayed rooted to the spot.

He could hear his pulse pounding in his ears, counting the seconds. They would have only this one chance.

Aster searched the gathered forces, and he knew what she was looking for—Alcor. When she didn't find him, she looked to Dev.

"Well?" Malice boomed. The soldiers quaked at her commanding voice, and the Nightlock sneered at their spears, rattling and knocking each other as they tried not to cower. "Where is she? Where is the star?"

Dev heard Ursula breath deep. And then she stepped toward the Nightlock. "You seek a star," she said. "I will be your star, Nightlock. Take me as your own." Her words echoed those of Keeper Kalamity.

"What?" snarled Malice, stepping back.

The other two Nightlocks hissed, slinking toward Aster with hungry gazes.

"Stop!" Malice shouted, and the two Nightlocks were still. "You are Ursula Lourdes," she snapped at Aster, "daughter of the Death Chaser."

"I am the star you seek," Ursula said. "Take me as your own."

"No," said Bernadine from the other side of the fire, removing the hood from her head, revealing her curly, powdered locks. "I am younger and more radiant than she. I am the star you seek."

The smaller Nightlocks chirruped, heads tilting in confusion. "Malice?" one of them snarled. "What is this? Which is the star?"

Malice's glare narrowed on Bernadine, and she slunk toward her.

And Iris stepped into the light, her hair powdered and her lynx absent from her side. "I am the star you seek, Nightlock," she said. "I am younger and more radiant than my sister."

One of the smaller Nightlocks screamed, a terrible, bottomless wail, her clawed hands gripping at her head. "I was young and radiant!" she screeched. "I was mortal!"

"Shut up, Despair!" roared Malice. She spun on Ursula. "What nonsense is this? Who is the star?"

"I am the star," said Ursula, defiant and strong and as unintimidated as if she were speaking to a petulant child.

The Nightlock advanced on her. "You are a liar," she growled.

The other Nightlock, the nameless one, slunk closer to Iris. "It is this one, Malice," she said. "See the silver in her hair."

Malice roared in anger. "It is a trick, Avarice!"

The little one called Despair was sobbing. "I was mortal!" She lunged at the one called Avarice. "*You* stole that from me!"

Avarice lifted one muscular leg and connected with her sister's gut. "It was *Malice* who took that from you!" she snarled.

Despair recovered from the blow and launched herself at her sister again, the two fighting savagely as Malice hissed at them both. When Malice stepped toward the brawl—moving only a few feet from Aster—Aster ran.

She ran to Ursula, and the sisters raced for the safety of the soldiers, Iris and Bernadine retreating too. Malice screamed, thundering after the Lourdes sisters. Lorc sprinted to the girls, pulling them behind the pointed spears of the soldiers, and Dev ran as hard as he could, ran for Aster and threw his arms around her.

Dev clung to her, and she clung to him, and he could hardly believe she was there, *with him*, that she was really and solidly there.

But it wasn't over. Dev and Aster stood together with Lorc Conri who unsheathed his blade, and Ursula, the four of them behind the safety of the spears, facing Malice who screamed to the sky, furious at having lost her prize.

The sound was booming, rattling Dev's brain, and the other two Nightlocks stopped fighting to cover their ears, cowering at Malice's rage.

When the Nightlock was done, she glared at the four children standing together behind the soldier's wall of spears, then moved to Iris and Bernadine, safe behind their own barricade of weapons. She looked to the faces standing protectively beside the girls—Arthur, Quintin.

And she grinned a fanged smile that sent terror searing through Dev's core.

"Where are all your High Beasts?" the Nightlock purred.

Dev's breath caught on his ribs, and Ursula looked to him, eyes wide with fear. Aster frowned, not understanding.

But Malice knew.

The Nightlock threw back her head and cackled, a hideous crackling sound, like lightning splitting a tree trunk. "Your High Beasts have forsaken you!" Dev tried to keep his composure. Tried to not let anything show on his face for the Nightlock to read. But Malice *knew*. "For the star," she breathed, her massive wings unfurling. "I will find her. She is here. She is with them. If I have to level the Highen to the ground to find her, I will." She lifted herself skyward, and her sisters joined her, the three Terror Maids hovering above them in all their nightmarish glory. "I call forth the armies of the moon: the Follies!"

"The Esurience!" said Despair.

"The Cunning!" added Avarice.

"And all the Malevolencies," finished Malice, and as soon as she did, the moon in the sky began to bleed darkness like a wound—a torrent of black shadows spilling out into the night, faster than a waterfall.

"Dev…," said Lorc, the same terror Dev felt filling his voice.

The Terror Maids screamed with laughter, soaring into the night. The soldiers began scrambling to prepare for the onslaught that was coming for Felisbrook. Just like the Lunar Offensive in the *Star Writ*.

"Ursula!" Arthur Conri rushed to her, Bernadine keeping close to his side. "You'll need these." From his boot he pulled her sharps, and Ursula strapped them to her hands.

"What have we done here, Keeper?" Arthur asked, looking to Dev.

Truly, he didn't know.

They all watched the moon, paralyzed by the horror that continued to spill out. All except Aster.

"Dev!" she said, grabbing his face in her hands, calling him back from the bleeding moon. "Dev, where is Alcor?"

"We had to lock him away," said Dev. "With the others, or else he'd have given away where we hid Seren."

And only then did he realize how foolish they'd been for doing it. Alcor's job was to defend the Highen. Alcor's entire reason for *being* was to stand against darkness like Nightlocks. That was true of all the High Beasts.

"Where is Seren?" asked Aster.

"Gone," said Lorc. "She ran off just before you arrived."

"Gone *where*?"

"We don't know."

"Dev," Aster pressed, "where are you keeping Alcor?"

So many Nightlocks. The havoc they wreaked during the Lunar Offensive. The stories in the *Star Writ*—they were horrors.

Aster grabbed his face tighter. "Dev! Where?"

"The stables," he said, focusing on the flecks of gold in her eyes. "Aster, your father in the Lunar Offensive…"

"My father is not here." She released him. "It is only me."

Lorc Conri grinned. "True enough. What are your orders, Major Lourdes?"

"We release the High Beasts." And with that, she ran, racing for Thorn Manor as the moon's armies descended on Felisbrook and sounds of screams and clanging steel filled the night.

# THIRTY-SEVEN

THE streets of Felisbrook were overrun. People spilled out from their little houses, screaming and running and stumbling as the Nightlocks fell upon the city. Aster ran too, her bare feet throbbing from the cobblestones.

Malice had done the unthinkable.

She had called down the armies of the moon.

Even now—ducking and dodging shadowy, hungry little demons—Aster could hardly believe it was true. They were everywhere, massing on common folk and soldiers alike, biting, tearing, drawing blood, taking fingers, taunting, piling on—

"Aster, this way!" shouted Iris, leading them to the gates of the Manor. Dev, Quintin, Lorc, and Bernadine: they were all together. The High Beasts would need them all. Ursula had stayed with Arthur Conri, the two of them fighting the onslaught of Nightlocks, defending the city with his men.

But the Highen's armies would not be enough to stop Malice now. They needed Seren.

And the High Beasts would find her.

"Oh, little Major!" taunted the snakelike voice of Avarice. The Nightlock flew overhead, a sickly grin upon her face. "Didn't my sister say I could devour you?"

Avarice dove, and Aster ducked—just as Lorc lashed out with his blade. He missed, and the Nightlock climbed, cackling as she rose into the night. Aster's pulse quickened. The Nightlock had wanted this since that first night—she would not give up so easily.

"Aster, hurry!" shouted Dev, taking her by the hand. They ran together, Iris, Quintin, and Bernadine pushing ahead into the courtyard of Thorn Manor, Lorc Conri guarding their backs.

Aster could hear Avarice's laughter growing louder and louder, and she readied herself for another attack. She spun and saw Lorc, blade ready, and Avarice—talons outstretched, fanged mouth set in a bloodthirsty grimace, speeding toward him from the sky. She would take him, Aster knew.

She released Dev's hand and lunged for Lorc, pushing him to the ground. The two of them landed hard on the cobbles as Avarice, passing overhead, screeched in frustration.

"Lorc, your knife!" Aster shouted at him, scrambling to her feet. Lorc handed her one of his hunting knives and she gripped it by the hilt, eyes trained on the Nightlock.

"*Come for me, Avarice!*" she screamed, tired and furious and sick to death of the creature's cackling and screeching.

The Nightlock laughed and banked, and as she did, Aster hurled the knife. It missed its mark, but it sunk deep into her arm, and the creature screamed, a new rage taking hold.

"Right," said Lorc Conri, the Nightlock banking hard again and diving toward them. "Time for Alcor, then!"

Aster, Dev, and Lorc raced after the other three, who waved them into the tightly packed stables at the end of the courtyard. Aster could hear the High Beasts: Alcor's unmistakable earth-shaking roar, the screeches of a furious Umbra, the howls of the Starhounds. She plunged after them into the dim stables, Dev and Lorc pushing her along.

Shingles rained down from above as Avarice slammed onto the roof, her wings too wide for her to fit into the hole she'd made. Aster ducked as one of her massive clawed hands lashed out.

"Where are they!" Aster shrieked.

"Further in!" Quintin Wyvern called from the next block of stalls. "Just through here!"

With a shattering of tile, Avarice dropped from above, blocking their path.

Aster could see the Nightlock's arm—she was bleeding an oozy black substance that made Aster sick to look at, thick as glue. The creature's teeth were bared, and she moved so fast—there was no time to react before—

Avarice leapt, her taloned feet grabbing hold of Aster's shoulder and slamming her to the floor.

"I haven't drunk a soul in such a very long time," the creature hissed, crawling on top of Aster like a snake over rock. Aster screamed, and the Nightlock made a terrible rattling sound as her jaws opened wide, impossibly wide—

But then the earthquake—

The ground shook with the might of the Hemoth's bellow—

And Avarice was tossed like a rag doll, hurled into the stable wall with such force she wailed as her right wing was snapped.

Alcor stood over Aster, his massive, towering frame and glorious orange coat shielding her. He roared again, the sound of it enough to shatter worlds. Avarice screamed, launching herself into the sky, her flight low and unsteady with her broken wing.

Aster crawled out from beneath the Hemoth as Umbra the Shadow Dragon took to the sky, chasing after the flagging Nightlock. Umbra closed the distance between them easily enough, and the last Aster saw of Avarice was her diving to escape—just as Umbra released a burst of flame that engulfed the Terror Maid.

# THIRTY-EIGHT

THE city flew by in a blur as Alcor barreled through the streets of Felisbrook, Aster atop his back. The High Beast tore Nightlocks down from the air, crushing them beneath his mighty paws as they made for the Deadwood.

There was a cry overhead, and Aster saw Umbra sail past, Quintin riding her to wherever the High Beasts were leading them—to Seren.

Flanking Alcor, Dev and Lorc rode on horseback, the Starhounds beside them with Argos at the head of the Pack. And Iris Goreman rode a white gelding, firing arrows from horseback to strike down Moon Demons, Sileria racing beside her. She looked every inch the queen now. Marmoral was left with Bernadine back at the keep, the little cub too small to take up arms against the Nightlocks.

A voice, like the sound of wind through the mountains, howled overhead. "*The Major Assssster Lourdes*." Aster looked to the sky and saw the winged shadow sail overhead. Despair.

Aster crouched low on Alcor as the creature dove at her, swooping by in a rush of warm, rotten wind.

Iris Goreman suddenly stood in the saddle, then leapt for the nearest gable of one of the houses that lined the street.

"Iris!" Aster screamed, bringing Alcor to a halt. She fumbled for the sword she'd strapped to her hip—she'd taken it in the castle courtyard from the hand of a dead Herman.

"What's she doing?" shouted Lorc.

Aster had no idea. The Lynx queen pulled herself up onto the rooftop, and she ran, pulling her bow.

"Where's Sileria?" asked Dev.

The Great Lynx was gone.

"Tricks and deceit, little Major!" screeched the Nightlock, and dove again. This time her claws came so close that Aster had to roll off Alcor, hitting the cobbles with a hard thud. "Perhaps you do belong with us behind the Moon Door!" The creature cackled, rising higher into the sky.

And then the arrow.

It struck Despair's side, and the beast let out a shriek, tumbling to earth, landing hard on the roof before Iris in a spray of tile. Aster could hear the creature's ragged breath, a wet growl rumbling somewhere deep inside her.

"Iris!" Aster screamed. "Iris, get out of there!"

Iris didn't move. She stood square against the beast, holding her bow. Despair crawled for her, muscular arms propelling the Nightlock impossibly fast along the gable. The creature lunged, but at the last moment Iris stepped aside, and Sileria—

The Great Lynx—

She flew in from nowhere—

A ghost in the dark—

And sank her fangs and claws into Despair.

The Nightlock's screams ripped through the streets—so shrill and earsplitting, Aster doubled over, covering her ears against the sound. Dev and Lorc cried out, pressing their own hands to their heads.

And Iris—the true Lynx queen—Aster watched as she nocked another arrow.

Calm. Steady.

She took aim at the writhing mass of Despair and Sileria. And she loosed the bolt.

The screaming stopped, and the Nightlock went still, the shaft protruding from her horned head. Sileria stepped back, yellow eyes glinting in the dark.

Cheers rose up from the soldiers and the people of Felisbrook in the street around them, all of them fighting bravely against the moon's armies—with swords, with poles, with brooms, with fire irons, with anything they had.

"*The Lynx queen!*" they bellowed, and Iris raised her bow.

"*Felisbrook!*" she roared back, her courage giving them new strength as they fought for their lives.

Iris nocked another arrow, firing at a Nightlock skittering along the street. "Aster!" she called, pulling yet another arrow from her quiver. "Go! Find Seren!"

The Lynx queen would not go with them, Aster realized—her people needed her by their side. But Felisbrook could not fight forever. And the battle would only end when Seren was claimed by them—or by the Nightlocks.

Aster scrambled back on top of Alcor, urging him onward. They had to find Seren, as fast as they could.

Alcor plunged into the Deadwood, splintering branch and tree as he went. Aster stayed low, doing her best to hang on.

"Look!" Dev called behind her, and when she looked, he was pointing to a trail of light through the trees—the familiar glittering trail of Dust Dragons. Aster knew where Alcor was leading them. To the place where the star had fallen.

Umbra screeched somewhere above, and Aster looked up through the branches to see the Shadow Dragon spiraling downward.

"Quintin!" screamed Lorc.

The Shadow Dragon righted herself, but only just, as dark shadows dove at her and sent her spiraling again. She collapsed in an explosion of wood and dirt on the forest floor.

A chorus of hideous laughter rose up around them, and

through the trees seeped the Nightlock armies. They slithered through the trunks like tendrils of smoke, eyes in the dark laughing and glinting.

"*We smell the souls of men,*" they whispered. "*Stinking wretched fear...We feast.*"

Lorc leapt down from his horse, pulling his blade, the Starhounds and Argos growling in front of him. "Aster, go!" he said. "Get Seren! I have to defend Quintin and Umbra!"

Aster slid down off Alcor—

"Aster, no!" cried Dev. "We can't stop!"

She stood with Lorc, drawing her blade. The Nightlocks rushed in, surrounding them completely, but they'd faced the impossible before.

"We're together in this, Conri."

Alcor roared, furious and deep, swiping at the creatures as they moved toward Dev.

"You have to go!" Lorc shouted at Aster, striking at the first of the advancing demons. The creature dispersed like steam from a kettle, its vapors billowing into nothing. "This doesn't end unless you find Seren!"

"Aster, there's no time!" Dev shouted.

"But—"

Another demon drew near, and both the Major and the Hound prince struck out with their blades. The *smell*, acrid and bitter—burning iron and the stink of sulfur!

"Go!" Lorc barked. "We'll be fine. You and Dev have to leave! Now!"

How could he know that? How could he possibly believe he'd be fine alone against the onslaught?

Because he was Lorc Conri.

Arrogant. Bullheaded. Reckless Lorc Conri.

He pulled his blade free of another demon, and before Aster

could think, she grabbed his face and kissed him—kissed Lorc Conri of the House of Hounds. Even with her lips pressed to his, she could hardly believe she'd done it, hardly believed she'd thought to do it at all. When she let him go, Lorc's eyes were wide—more stunned now than at any of the nightmares they'd seen that night.

But then he grinned. "End it for us, Major Lourdes."

The Nightlocks moved in, and Lorc struck at each one, moving brilliantly like the warrior he was. But he was right. There was only one way to end it. Behind him, Umbra lifted her head and shot a jet of flame into the demons; Quintin, alive, slipped down off her back, his blade held in the wrong hand, his sword-arm hanging uselessly at his side. He was injured. They were running out of time.

Growling, Aster hurled herself back onto Alcor and kicked his side, plunging into the forest, Dev doing his best to keep up on his mare. Alcor led the way, the High Beast driven to find where Seren had run to—to the end of the trail of the Dust Dragons. To the spot where the star had fallen from the sky.

Aster looked up through the trees and could see Malice turning on the wing—she, too, was, following the trail of the Dust Dragons, circling like a vulture. Aster leaned into Alcor. "Hurry, Alcor!"

When they came upon the clearing where the star had fallen, the Dust Dragons were coiled around the light, just as they had been before. Only now, Aster could see, the light at the center of their gathering dust was Seren.

The girl stood, motionless, eyes faraway and unfocused.

And she glowed.

And flickered.

Her hair floating around her as if underwater.

Aster slid off Alcor's back, one hand ever on his fur, steadying herself. Seren *was* a star. An On-High in the flesh. Aster swallowed. How did one speak to the On-High?

She looked at Dev, who gaped from the back of his mare. "What do we do?" she asked him.

"I'll try to talk to her," he said, dismounting.

Aster gripped her blade, and the two of them stepped into the clearing, Alcor following behind. Aster kept her eyes on the sky, where Malice still circled. What was she waiting for? Could she not tell Seren was down here?

As they approached, Seren made no sign that she was aware of them at all. She just stood there, staring at nothing, glowing so bright Aster had to shield her eyes.

"Seren?" Dev asked.

As soon as he did, he was grabbed by Despair, the Nightlock still smoking and charred from Umbra's dragon flame. She screamed into the night, flying off with him in her grip, her efforts labored, her broken wing barely able to keep them aloft.

"*Dev!*" Aster screamed, Alcor roaring as Dev thrashed in the Nightlock's talons. Despair laughed, dropping him from the tree-tops, and he fell, crashing through the branches of a twisted oak. Alcor ran to his Keeper, groaning, and Aster hurried after them.

And then a boom shook the ground as Malice dropped out of the sky.

The Nightlock stood before Seren, teeth bared. She slunk toward the star.

Dev dangled, slung across a lower limb, his feet scrabbling for purchase. Alcor stretched himself against the tree, trying to reach him. Aster couldn't leave them.

"Aster!" Dev shouted, pointing at the Nightlock. "Help her!"

Malice was reaching for Seren.

Aster pulled a dagger from her boot—another find at the Manor—and hurled it at Malice, the blade sailing through her wing with a burst of blood. Malice spun on Aster, hissing.

Alcor roared at Malice, and Despair dropped on Dev again,

shaking him loose from his branch onto the next. Alcor moved beneath him, trying to position himself to catch the dangling Keeper.

"Malice, you have to stop this!" Aster shouted, sword clutched in her hands. "You asked to be this! You *asked* to be a Nightlock!"

"I made a mistake!" Malice screamed.

"I know," said Aster. "You did it for your sisters, but you did it wrong. You were *wrong*, Malice!"

The creature bared her teeth, squaring herself against Aster. "I will set it right," she said, reaching for Seren.

"What did you tell me, Malice?" Aster shouted, inching closer to the Nightlock. "You walk your path. You get it wrong. You accept the consequences!"

"I accept the consequences, little Major," snarled Malice. "Whether we all die tonight from this volatile star's power or not, I accept what comes next."

The Nightlock's claw snatched Seren by the throat, and the star's eyes flared, focusing on Malice.

Alcor roared again. And the Dust Dragons swelled, their plumes billowing as they swarmed the pair in a storm of glittering dust, the whirling wind of it nearly knocking Aster down. But Malice was not moved by their assault; her grip held firm.

Aster steeled herself, held tight to her sword, screamed, and ran forward. She plunged the steel into Malice's back.

The Nightlock didn't falter; it kept its hold on Seren, attempting to rise into the air with her against the Dust Dragons' river of wind.

Aster tried to pull her blade free, but it was no use: it was too deep, and Malice didn't seem affected at all. With her free arm, Malice struck Aster in the side, and Aster fell, coughing and bruised, her rib cracked. The Terror Maid laughed, finally lifting Seren off the ground.

The star's light flickered, and Aster held her breath.

"*I will show you what comes next,*" whispered Seren.

Her light swelled, and Aster heard a screaming of wind in her ears. She covered herself as Malice roared, the light growing so bright that her retinas burned, and more screams rose up—first Despair, and then a chorus of screeching Nightlocks. Aster shut her eyes as tightly as she could as the voices reached an agonizing crescendo.

And then the night was dark.

Malice was gone, and so were the Dust Dragons. Seren sat on the ground where the Nightlock had dropped her. The star's light was so dim, it fluttered in her chest in time with her heartbeat.

Aster looked up at the moon.

Full. The door was shut.

"Is it over?" Aster asked Seren. "Are the moon armies gone?"

"I put them back," said Seren quietly. "Back where they belong."

Aster exhaled, staggered up, stumbled forward, and then dropped to the ground beside Seren. Malice was trapped behind the Moon Door again—trapped with a broken Despair, and her third sister dead. Would she ever attempt to escape again?

But Felisbrook was safe tonight. That was all that mattered. There would always be demons, just as there would always be the On-High.

"And you?" asked Aster. "Where do you belong?"

"I don't know," said Seren.

Aster glanced up at the sky, to where the image of Tawn used to be. "You're the last star in the image of Tawn, aren't you? That's why it doesn't shine when you are gone."

Seren looked up to the sky, staring at the empty space in the heavens. "I don't shine like they do."

"But you shine all the same," said Aster.

The two girls stared at each other.

"Shine for what?" Seren asked.

"Us, I hope," said Aster. "We look to your light. Always."

Seren nodded. "You mortals are fragile things. Delicate. Like flower petals."

"You On-High give us strength."

"As we must," Seren agreed. "As we always have. As we always will."

"That's where you belong, Seren," said Aster. "I think you know that."

Seren closed her eyes, breathing deep, her face tilted up to the heavens. Her silver hair shimmered in the dark, the pulsing light at her chest growing—but warm this time, not cold, not overwhelming. She stood, and when she did, the stars in the image of Tawn began to wink to life. They pulsed in time with Seren's beating heart. And then, like the Dust Dragons, she began to shimmer, glittering dust pulling away from her, up into the night.

"And you?" asked the star, her image fading as she returned to the sky. "Where do you belong?"

"On my throne," said Aster. "As the Major Aster Lourdes."

And just like that, Seren was gone.

She left the Deadwood dark and quiet save for the *bope bope bope* of Alcor, and Dev's grunting as he tried to climb down from the tree.

Aster watched the image of Tawn, watched the last star complete the constellation. Seren's star. And her father's not far away. Aster was grateful to see it back. Alcor nuzzled her hand with his massive nose.

Dev appeared beside her. "Seren's gone, then?"

Aster nodded.

"And the Nightlocks?"

"Yes," Aster said. Gone. She couldn't help but feel a bit of pity in her heart for Malice. She was loathsome, she was cruel, she was their enemy, but still...some part of the woman she had been was still there, inside her. Her strength. Her stubborness. Her courage.

Part of Aster had wanted Malice to be become human again, just as she had wanted.

What did that say about Aster? How different were they? How hard would it be to make a mistake as terrible as Malice's?

Aster swallowed. Perhaps not very hard at all.

"So everything is as it was?" Dev asked, looking up at the image of Tawn.

"No," said Aster. "Nothing will be as it was."

*And so it was that the Major had looked upon the darkest shadows of the moon. So it was that she had spoken to the stars. So it was that the Major was returned to her Highen—*

*with moon dust beneath her feet,*

*and stardust in her eyes.*

—THE WRITINGS OF DEV,
The Falling of an On-High: The New Rule, *Star Writ*

# THIRTY-NINE

THE ink was set with Aster's signature, and with just a few lines of her quill, centuries of Highen tradition were crossed out of existence, making way for something new. She handed the parchment to Queen Iris Goreman of Felisbrook, who bowed, the Great Lynx Sileria purring with satisfaction at her side.

Sunlight spilled in through the balcony, a bright and beautiful day; a crisp day in the Lynx kingdom promised a pleasant road home to Tawnshire. The parties from Härkädia, Twigate, and Roarque had already left that morning, returning to their homes after the Highen victory in the Second Lunar Offensive.

Dev would be writing in the *Star Writ* for days, Aster was sure. Meticulously recording everything that had transpired over the last week in the Kingdom of the Lynx.

"The acting Keeper will arrive in Felisbrook within the week," said Aster, rising from the desk. "High Keeper Dev will see that the best possible Keeper is sent to serve your new lynx until her true Keeper comes of age."

Dev nodded in agreement. The secret child identified as the new lynx's Keeper would remain with their family until they turned thirteen. A thousand years of custom, gone...for something better.

"Felisbrook thanks you, Major Lourdes," said Queen Iris.

"And the Highen thanks you for your courage, Lady Warden,"

said Aster. The new title had been Aster's idea. With Keeper of Crowns promised to Quintin, and the resurrection of the defunct title of Oath Guard ready to be gifted to Arthur Conri on his wedding day, Aster had come up with something new for Iris on her council—something to suit her stewardship of the forests of Felisbrook. Lady Warden of Wood and Mountain. Iris Goreman would now guard all the natural treasures of the Highen, advising on the uses of forests, coasts, rivers, and slopes.

Behind Iris stood Aunt Leona, beaming with pride at her charge's newfound poise. When Aster had announced that she would change Highen law, Leona and Keeper Von had protested. But Iris, as their queen, supported the change, and their arguments were silenced. Aunt Leona, for her part, actually seemed relieved that Iris was taking charge of her rule, and that her people were celebrating her reign after her courage in the battle against the Nightlocks. There was no more talk of Pan Leander now.

Aster, Iris, and Dev headed down the main stairwell and out into the courtyard, where Aster's carriage was waiting, her mother seeing to the loading of their things. Ursula was by the carriage, standing close by Arthur Conri, the Hound king holding her hand in his as they spoke in whispers. The plans for the wedding would need to begin as soon as they got home. It would be nice to have something to celebrate after all they'd been through.

Farther down the row, Alcor rolled in the sun, scratching his back along the cobbles. Things were back to normal between the Heads of Houses and their beasts: inseparable, devoted, united. She was very glad for that. She supposed she could forgive Alcor his devotion to a star.

"Aster!" Bernadine appeared on the stairwell, Marmoral bounding along beside her. "You're leaving, then?"

"I am," said Aster. "It's good to see you out of the snows, cousin. The sunshine suits you."

Bernadine shrugged. "I like my snows. But you were right. It's not good to hide from warmth for too long."

"You will visit me in Tawnshire, then?"

Bernadine bit her lip and glanced over Aster's shoulder at her mother, who watched them from the bottom of the Manor steps. Bernadine was still afraid of Lady Lourdes.

That would not do.

"What do you think, Mother?" called Aster. "Shall we invite Bernadine for the Berry Teas at next month's harvest?"

Her mother smiled. "Bernadine, dear, you know the bogberry juices are good for your skin. I insist you come for the Berry Teas."

Bernadine smiled, then reached for Aster and hugged her tightly. "I will be there," she promised.

"I'll hold you to that," Aster said, squeezing her cousin hard. "I've missed you."

"I've missed you, too," said Bernie, drawing back and smiling.

"Farewell again, is it?" Quintin Wyvern appeared on the steps, his arm in a sling. His fall from the skies had left it broken and Umbra's wing bent. They would have to stay in Felisbrook until the High Beast had recovered.

"You'll be all right if we leave you here, King Wyvern?" asked Aster.

Quintin laughed. "I have Dust Dragon studies to occupy myself."

"But the Dust Dragons are gone, aren't they?" asked Dev. "Back into the earth?"

"Sileria and I will take the Dragon king into the Deadwood," said Iris. "He wishes to record what he can of whatever the Dust Dragons left behind—for Dracogart."

"Besides," said Quintin, "I promised Iris a flight on Umbra before I go. I can't leave before I can make good on that."

Aster exchanged a look with Bernadine, who turned to leave.

The Dragon king and Lynx queen had become as thick as thieves, and Aster had no doubt Quintin would not want to leave Felisbrook *too* soon.

Aster, though—she couldn't wait to get home to Tawnshire.

But she still had one more goodbye to offer.

Lorc Conri sat on the bottommost step of Thorn Manor, tapping his sheathed sword's pommel impatiently. A flutter rose in her stomach. Aster excused herself to the others and took a seat beside him. He was watching Arthur and Ursula with a wrinkled nose.

"Pathetic, aren't they?" he said.

Aster watched as Ursula laughed, Arthur smiling, the two oblivious to all the world but each other. "They seem happy enough to me."

Lorc *harrumph*ed and kept tapping his sword. Ages passed between them, an awkward silence opening up into forever. Her mind replayed the moment—brief and eternal as it was—when she'd kissed him in the Deadwood. She thought about mentioning it, but stopped herself. The moment was just that—a moment. It was brief but it was theirs. And if he wasn't going to mention it, Aster resolved, then neither was she.

He raised a brow at her. "You know they'll never let you marry me now."

Aster laughed. "Thank the On-High for that."

Lorc grinned. "Glad you're back, Bloomnut."

"Glad to be back, Lorc."

His eye fell on the scab on her chin and Aster covered it, suddenly aware of how gruesome it must look. He moved her hand away and brushed it lightly with his thumb.

Aster swallowed.

Another moment passed between them, and Aster felt as if she'd dropped into an abyss, a place where time didn't exist, the same place where their kiss lived. She held her breath.

Finally, and suddenly, Lorc's hand dropped. He glanced behind them, to where Dev was standing at the top of the steps, watching. "Take care of the old Keeper, will you?"

Aster nodded. "I always do."

Lorc stood and turned back to Dev. "Farewell, Honorable High Keeper Dev."

Dev nodded, smiling warmly at the feigned formality. "Prince Lorcan."

"Better get writing. I expect a couple of new chapters on Nightlocks to be added to the *Star Writ* right away."

Dev rolled his eyes. "I know what the *Star Writ* needs, thank you."

Lorc grinned, delighting in Dev's obvious irritation.

"Lorc?" Arthur had moved away from Ursula, their lengthy farewells over at last. "It's time to go."

Lorc nodded. "See you at the wedding, Aster," he told her, and joined his brother, the pair headed for the stables where the Starhounds and horses were ready for the journey back to Hundford.

The wedding. That wouldn't be for months. Maybe years. Was that how long it would be before she crossed paths with the Hound prince again?

Dev came to sit with Aster on the bottom step. They sat in stillness, watching the Hermans readying the carriages and wagons, Luella Lourdes barking orders.

A screaming silence filled the space between them. Aster could feel it as sure as dragon flame.

"Do you fancy him?" Dev asked suddenly.

Aster looked at her shoes. Did she?

Yes. She supposed she always had.

But telling Dev that—

She shrugged.

Another raging silence. Why should it matter to Dev who Aster fancied? Why should it make things so…complicated.

Dev cleared his throat, breaking the quiet at last. "Thank you, Aster. For the Felisbrook Keeper."

"Don't thank me," she said. "You were right. About all of it."

"I wasn't," said Dev. "I was wrong when I said I was stuck with you. You're a great Major, Aster."

She shrugged. "You weren't wrong. You *are* stuck with me. Major and Keeper: they are bound to each other for life." She smiled at him.

He laughed. "Forever and always," he agreed.

She took his hand and gave it a squeeze.

"Well…" Aster's mother dusted off her hands, as though she'd done all the heavy lifting herself and not the Herman Guards. "Now that's all settled, time we get ourselves home, don't you think?"

"Yes," agreed Aster, jumping up from the step. She could have run home, she was so eager to see the skies of Tawnshire again. She practically leapt into the carriage, relishing the feel of the soft cushions, the soft velvet. After so long in the rock of the mountains, it warmed her soul to feel cushion beneath her.

"Good," said her mother. "Now we'll have plenty of time together to sort out the right suitors for you. Surely there's *some* suitable options in the Highen."

Aster leapt up, leaning out the window. "Dev, would you ride with us?"

He waved her off. "Nope!" And he left her, heading to the back of the caravan where Alcor was waiting for him.

Aster sighed and collapsed in her seat. The journey to Tawnshire would be long after all.

# ACKNOWLEDGMENTS

FIRST and foremost, I want to thank editor extraordinaire Mora Couch - this was a whirlwind process through major life and world changes and through it all I had so much fun geeking out over love triangles and medieval architecture with you! You are a word wizard and I am so grateful Aster and the Highen have your magic on their side.

To copy editor Pam Glauber and everyone at Holiday House who help bring Aster's world to print and are so supportive while they do it! And special thank you to the incredibly talented Fiona Hsieh for yet another stunning cover, and the incredibly talented Virginia Allyn for the epic map that always blows my mind.

And finally thanks to my family - especially my husband, Ian, who, even while we were all down with COVID as the deadline approached, helped me make sure the work got done. You're my hero.